BURNED BY MAGIC

JASMINE WALT

DYNAMO PRESS

Cover illustration by Judah Dobin

Cover typography by Rebecca Frank

Edited by Mary Burnett

Electronic edition, 2015. If you want to be notified when Jasmine's next novel is released and get access to exclusive contests, giveaways, and other awesomeness, sign up for her mailing list here. Your email address will never be shared and you can unsubscribe at any time.

1

—————

"Hey, shifter girl!" a human with sandy hair shouted as he leaned over the bar counter. He waved his hand as though I were a cab he was trying to flag down. "Can I get another whiskey over here?"

"Coming right up." Fighting the urge to roll my eyes, I grabbed a glass from beneath the counter and the requisite bottle of liquor. Strobe lights bounced off the dark walls of the club as I splashed a generous amount into the shot glass and slid it across the glossy countertop. The place was in full swing tonight, shifters, humans and mages all clamoring for their shot of liquid courage so they could go rub their bodies all over each other on the dance floor and hopefully take someone home with them tonight.

"Thanks." The human threw back his shot in one go. His pale cheeks turned bright red, and his wheezing cough told me taking shots was a new pastime.

"Another," he gasped, slamming his glass down on the counter.

I arched a brow. "Don't you think you should take it easy?"

The human grimaced. "I need it if I'm going to ask that girl over there for a kiss."

He jerked a thumb over his shoulder, where a brunette in a skin-tight red dress leaned against the wall, her dark orange gaze scanning the crowd. The lack of whites in her eyes combined with the dark orange color of her irises told me she was a tiger shifter, likely here searching for a male to help her get through heat.

"Why her?" I glanced back at the human, taking in his white polo shirt and short, neatly trimmed hair, which was so different from the loud clothing and hairstyles the residents of Rowanville boasted. This boy was from Maintown, the section of Solantha reserved specifically for humans, and I doubted he'd ever set foot into the melting pot of Rowanville in his life.

The boy bit his lip. "I lost a bet, and now I have to get a shifter girl to kiss me. Unless you'd rather do the honors?"

"Ugh. No thanks." The kid looked all of nineteen years old; at twenty-four I had *some* pride.

"Aww, c'mon." The kid leaned forward, desperation in his eyes. "The guys are watching me from across the room right now. If I did it right now I could get out of here."

"Save it, kid." I curled my lip, exposing the fangs sliding out behind my gum line. The kid blanched. "I'm not getting involved. My advice, you hightail it outta here and go tell your mother. That girl over in the corner is looking for a lot more than just a kiss. She'll tear you apart if you lead her on and then try to ditch her later."

"Fine." The boy slumped back down into his barstool and gave me a sullen glare. "Just give me the shot."

Why did I even bother?

"Suit yourself." I poured him another and watched him down it. He wasn't the first to come in here on a bet. Most of the human customers were regulars who knew the deal – so long as you were within these walls you treated everyone with the same amount of respect regardless if they were shifter, human or mage. That's how it was supposed to be in Rowanville – the only neighborhood in Solantha where shifters, humans and mages lived together. But every once in a while someone from one of the segregated neighborhoods wandered in to cause trouble. Usually they got more than they bargained for.

"Thanks." The kid slapped a coin down on the bar. "Wish me luck."

Yeah, right. I shook my head as he disappeared into the crowd, then turned back to my work. Tempted as I was to watch the tigress wipe the floor with him, I had a bar to tend, and it was nearly as packed as the dance floor.

I reached for the coin the kid had left for me on the counter, intending to pocket it. But as soon as I touched it, searing pain shot straight through my fingers.

"Oww!" I dropped the coin like it was a hot coal, and shook my smoking hand. Fucking Maintowner. Didn't he know shifters were allergic to silver? The little bastard had probably left it there on purpose. I had half a mind to drag him back out of the crowd so I could beat on him myself.

"I'll trade that for you." Cray, the other bartender, offered. He pocketed the coin, then handed me a pandanum coin of the same value. He was a black-skinned human, and didn't have any issue handling the silver.

"Thanks." I smiled at him and tucked the coin into one of my pouches. Most of the humans around here were pretty decent.

"Hey. Can I get a glass of *teca* with a twist of lime?" a woman with ice-blue shifter eyes asked. My nose told me she was a wolf.

"Coming right up." I ducked beneath the bar to grab the bottle of liquor. I could use a little *teca* myself – it was one of the few substances that could actually get shifters drunk. On another night, I could have been that wolf shifter, standing at the bar asking for a drink after a long day chasing bounties. Instead I was here serving them up.

As I reached for the liquor bottle, the inside of my forearm brushed against the crescent knives strapped to my leather-clad thigh. A familiar longing seared the inside of my chest, and I sighed.

All it would take is one blowjob, and you'd be out of here and back to your real job.

I fought the urge to shove my hands into my mass of curly hair and yank on it until I'd come to my senses again. There was no way I was wrapping my lips around that dick's... well, dick. I'd much rather stay here at The Twilight, even if that did mean dealing with snotty little shits like that Maintowner.

Still, being stuck behind the counter like this sucked. Yeah, I could mix a decent drink, but I wasn't meant to be a bartender. As a black panther shifter I was a natural hunter, much better suited to chasing down criminals and turning them in like every other licensed Enforcer in the city. That's what we do – we clean the riffraff off the streets so the mages don't have to get off their entitled asses and do it themselves. And since we get paid per head, most of us are pretty motivated about the whole affair.

Unfortunately for me, Garius Talcon, the Deputy Captain of the Enforcer's Guild, was in charge of distributing all the mission dockets. And ever since he found out that I was only half-shifter, he'd been treating me like a lesser being. Recently he'd decided that if I wanted to continue getting jobs I needed to get down on my knees and suck him off.

I'd told him that if I ever got down on my knees in front of him he'd better run like hell because it meant I was going to rip his balls off and feed them to him. And ever since then we'd been at an impasse.

I'd tried going to Captain Galling, but my word was useless against Talcon's, and there was no one to corroborate my story.

Truthfully, it was better not to draw attention, because as far as Talcon and Galling knew I was a shifter-human hybrid. If I gave them a reason to dig deeper, they would find out about my real heritage, and money would be the *least* of my problems.

Until I figured out a way around Talcon, the only Enforcer jobs I was getting paid for were the ones I brought in by answering the emergency response calls broadcasted by my Enforcer bracelet. As much as I hated to admit it, right now bartending paid the bills.

Turning my attention back to work, I served up the *teca* with a big, fat smile on my face, and was rewarded with a big, fat coin for my trouble. I nodded my thanks at the she-wolf before she disappeared into the crowd – the shifters here were always my best tippers.

"Sunaya!"

I nearly jumped out of my skin at the sound of my mentor's voice in my head, calling my name. Heart pounding, I scanned the crowded bar for him, though part of me wanted to simply shrink behind the counter and pretend I didn't exist. Even though Roanas Tillmore knew about my bartending job, I didn't like it when he saw me here – after all the time and effort he put into training me it was shameful that I was tending bar for a living. But I caught no sight of him, and weeding through the hundreds of clashing smells, I didn't catch his scent either.

Shaking my head, I picked up another glass to get started on the next order. Must've imagined it. Mindspeech didn't work well from more than a couple hundred yards away, so if I couldn't smell him then he wasn't here.

"Sunaya! Co... quick... need..."

The glass slipped from my fingers as Roanas's garbled voice echoed inside my ears. It hit the ground and shattered, tiny pieces shooting across the floor, but I hardly noticed as acid-sharp panic filled my lungs – panic I realized wasn't from me at all, but from Roanas.

As the Shiftertown Inspector, Roanas rarely ran into a situation he couldn't handle. If he was able to reach me with a mental call from afar, he was in big trouble.

"Hey!" Cray snapped as he tapped me on the shoulder. "What the hell are you doing, standing around with all this broken glass everywhere!"

I whirled on him, baring my fangs. "I have to go," I growled. He took a step backward, his eyes wide – Cray was a big guy, but as an unarmed human he was no match for me.

Turning away, I slapped my palm on the counter and launched myself over the bar. Patrons yelped as I sailed over their heads, and Cray cursed me, but I hardly heard them over the blood pounding in my ears. I landed in a crouch halfway from the bar to the door, then sprinted outside to where my steambike was parked on the curb. I was going to lose my job over this, but I didn't care – nothing mattered more to me than Roanas.

With that thought taking up all available real estate in my mind, I hopped onto my bike and shot into the street, leaving a white-hot cloud of steam in my wake.

TWENTY MINUTES LATER, I skidded to a halt in front of Roanas's house in Shiftertown. The lights spilling out from the windows and into the darkness of the street told me he was home. I charged up the steps of the two-story brick townhouse, my veins full of fire as I prepared to face an army of enemies. I fully expected to open the door and find the place wrecked, the furniture splintered and the floor splattered with blood, because nothing short of a fucking army would be able to take down Roanas.

Instead, I found him lying on the red and gold carpet in the living room, his big body splayed next to the coffee table.

"Roanas!" I was at his side in an instant, an icy fist of fear squeezing my heart. He was lying on his back, his skin pale beneath his dark complexion as he shook. Foam spurted from his blue lips, and his tawny lion-shifter eyes rolled.

"Fuck, fuck, fuck," I chanted as I scrambled for the vial of antidote I kept in one of the pouches strapped around my torso. I knew the signs he was exhibiting all too well. This was silver poisoning.

I carefully positioned Roanas's head in my lap, then pried open his mouth and poured in some of the antidote. The pale amber liquid trickled right out of his icy lips, but I tried again, doing my best to get it into his mouth despite the tremors. Still nothing. I bit my lip as his cheek came into contact with my hand – his skin was frigid – and then tried a third time. Finally, his throat bobbed and the liquid stayed down.

Instantly the tremors receded to slight vibrations, and his breath came a little easier. A huge wave of relief rushed through me, and I wanted to sag against the couch. Instead, I fed him the rest of the antidote, drop by drop until the entire vial was gone. Even so, the symptoms did not completely subside – his lips were still blue, his skin ice-cold.

"Sunaya," Roanas croaked in a voice like crushed gravel. He shifted his head in my lap, his black mane of tiny braids sliding against my legs.

"Shhh," I soothed, sliding my arms beneath him so I could lift him onto the couch. His dark cotton shirt was soaked in sweat. "Don't speak. You need to conserve your energy."

"No... point..." he said with a weak chuckle. My leg muscles flexed as I rose to my feet with Roanas cradled in my arms. I carefully deposited him atop the couch, then sat down next to him and pulled his head into my lap again. "I'm dying."

"No," I said firmly. I ran my hand through his braids, pushing them back from his clammy forehead. "You just feel like you're dying. Which is perfectly understandable since you just experienced silver poisoning, but –"

"The antidote... wasn't enough." He wrapped his long fingers around mine, and a tremor went through me – his grip, normally so strong, was as weak as a newborn babe's. "Too much silver... too fast. Not... going to... make it."

"What the fuck is that supposed to mean?" I snarled, tightening my grip on his hand. This wasn't real. This wasn't happening. Roanas was only eighty years old – not even close to middle-aged for a shifter. He had a long, full life ahead of him, at least another two hundred years or so. Fuck, he was supposed to meet me tomorrow afternoon for a sparring match. Dying was *not* on the agenda.

"How could this happen to you?" I choked out as the tears spilled down my cheeks. "You... I... you'd never be so stupid as to accidentally poison yourself with silver!"

Shifters are hypersensitive to silver, so if it's within fifty yards of us we'll catch a whiff of it. The only reason I'd been burned by the coin earlier was because I'd been distracted. There was no way Roanas, who could hit a moving target with a chakram a hundred yards away – thirty more than my personal best – would miss such a thing.

But the empty glass lying on its side on the carpet told me that Roanas had done exactly that, and I couldn't understand why. Leaning over, I picked up the glass and sniffed it, certain I would catch the scent of silver.

But I scented absolutely nothing except the burning stench of liquor and a hint of saliva.

"What... how?" I gaped down at the glass as if it were a

foreign species clutched in my palm, and to me, it might as well have been. "Why don't I smell anything?"

"The silver was mixed... with some kind of chemical... that masked the taste and scent." Roanas panted the last word, his voice edged with pain. My heart ached at the sight of his pale skin and strained expression. "That's why none of the others... detected it either."

"There are others?" My throat tightened. "As if it isn't bad enough you're dying." My voice broke on the last word.

"Please, Sunaya." Roanas's fingers curled around my jacket collar, pulling me closer. Even though he was sinking fast, his tawny eyes burned with a ferocious intensity. They cut through the fog of tears and pain in my brain, demanding my attention. "You must find out... who did this. There are other shifters... being targeted. Not just... about me."

"Targeted?" My eyes narrowed as my brain tried to catch up with the implications of that. "Targeted how? And why?"

"The facts... are in my case file..." Blood spilled over Roanas's lower lip, and I blinked back tears. "The Enforcers have been slow... to put the different cases together... but they are related." His voice strengthened. "I was investigating... and so they've taken me out. You must connect the dots, Sunaya. Find out who did this. Stop the killings, avenge me, and... and..."

"And what?" Shards of ice scraped along the walls of my insides, the fear inside me painfully sharp. I gripped Roanas's hand hard enough to grind the bones against each other, holding on for dear life. I never wanted to let him go.

"And... be careful."

His face went slack then, the life gone from his eyes. And as he slid from this world to the next as silently as the hot tears rolling down my cheeks, I vowed not to rest until I caught the bastard who did this.

2

By the time I left Roanas's house at seven in the morning, every last tear in my body had been burned away by the seething fury in my heart. I'd called the Enforcer's Guild using the telephone in Roanas's kitchen to report the murder, only to have two Enforcers show up at the doorstep – several hours later, the lazy fucks – and start interrogating *me*.

Yeah, okay, I get it. I was with him when he died, so I couldn't be ruled out as a suspect. Even though I've only worked on homicide cases a handful of times, I'd done enough to know that this was part of procedure. But what really pissed me off was that they'd brushed me off, when I'd asked about similar cases.

"Oh, come on Baine," Nila, a blond Enforcer, had scoffed as the coroner and the crime scene technicians filed out of the house with Roanas's body and what pertinent items they'd found in tow. I studiously ignored the covered stretcher as it went past us, but my heart clenched all the same. "You should know better than to believe in conspiracy theory crap like that. We'll find out who did this to your old man, but don't be surprised if we drag some rat out of a hole who happened to have a bone to pick with him, rather than a serial murderer."

"He *told* me someone was targeting shifters before he died," I'd said between gritted teeth. "And don't try to tell me he was just hallucinating or paranoid, because I don't believe it. Roanas doesn't make mistakes like that."

"Didn't," Nila corrected me.

"Look," Brin, the other Enforcer, had interjected before I ripped Nila's face off. "I'm not going to deny there have been other silver poisonings in Shiftertown recently." He'd given me a stern glare, as if I were a whelp that needed to be put in her place rather than a fellow Enforcer. But then, Brin and Nila were part of the Main Crew, many of whose members routinely treated the other Enforcers like we were beneath them. "But we don't have enough evidence to determine whether or not the murders were related. We'll work to find your friend's killer, but in the meantime you need to back off and stay out of our way." He stepped forward and shoved his nose into my face, menace bleeding from every pore in his hulking body. "Have I made myself clear?"

I'd responded by flipping him off, and then I walked out with the case file Roanas had mentioned tucked beneath my leather jacket, which I'd torn the house apart to find while I was waiting for the Enforcer's Guild to arrive. No way was I turning it over to them. Brin and Nila weren't exactly known for being thorough – their work was half-assed at best, and more than likely they would end up pinning this on the wrong person just so they could collect their bounty and go home. Besides, they were both humans and didn't give a rat's ass about Roanas.

Roanas deserves better than them, I thought as I swung my leg over the seat of my steambike. A few people passing through the streets on foot glanced nervously at my bike and then scurried to the sidewalks as I turned the engine on – steam-powered vehicles were a rather new invention, less than fifty years old, and steambikes in particular were considered dangerous. It didn't help that mages abhorred technology as a whole, sticking to either magical methods of transportation or the horse-drawn variety.

I took my rage out on the streets of Solantha, whipping around corners at breakneck speeds and leaning the bike so close to the ground my leather jacket scraped against the asphalt. I raced the bike up and down the hilly roads reserved specifically for steam-powered vehicles, zipping past clusters of townhouses huddled together and groupings of small shops where you could get anything from takeout to bridal gowns. My helmet shielded me from most of the scents, but I still caught a few of them – the briny air drifting in from Solantha Bay, freshly baked goods wafting from an open shop window, and the unique burnt-sugar smell that I recognized as magic.

Magic and I have a complicated relationship. I can't survive without it, but it's bound and determined to be the death of me. The mages in this country have a monopoly on magic, and use it to beat us into submission. Since they're the most powerful race in this country, they rule us by default, which really sucks because they don't care about anyone outside their own ranks.

However, magic isn't all bad. It's what gives us shifters the power to change forms and communicate via mindspeech – all useful talents to have, even if they were given to us by the mages experimenting on our human ancestors. And the various charms, amulets and spells for sale on both the black market and the regular one have their uses. Lots of people rely on them, convinced they can't live without the mages who provide them.

I'm not one of those people. I may use the amulets, but I hate mages more than anyone else. My father was a mage, and he left me before I was even born with a talent I've had to hide for years in order to avoid execution. A talent that's failed me more often than not, and has never worked when I needed it.

The crush of buildings began to thin out as I reached the bay, giving way to wider streets, fancier shops, and luxurious apartment complexes Solanthans paid a premium for so they could sit in their living rooms and enjoy the waterfront view. The scent of brine grew significantly stronger as I approached the shoreline, where the sun had broken over the horizon, painting the stone boathouses at each pier a pale pink and gold. The line of piers stretched in either direction as far as the eye could see, covering the coastline along the bay from end to end.

This section of town was known simply as the Port – but a lot more happened around here, than just ships coming and going to pick up and drop off cargo and passengers. While most of the piers lining the south end of the shore were exclusively devoted to shipping, the ones up north each had their own hubs of activity. I stopped at a corner to allow traffic from the perpendicular street to pass, glancing to the pier on my right that was known as The Fish Market. Even if you didn't catch the stench from a mile away, you could spot it by the cawing seagulls constantly trying to swoop down and snatch bass or mussels from the vendors. I watched a particularly haggard-looking man waving his wide-brimmed straw hat at a gull who was circling his stall, only to get blindsided as another one swooped in from behind and snatched a silvery-looking fish right from the cart. It made me wonder whether the feathery bastards worked in tag-teams.

The traffic cleared and I sped off, blowing straight past a black steamcar as I headed towards Pier Eighteen – also known as Witches' End. Here mages and other magic users set up shop, selling charms, amulets, potions and other magical bric-a-brac.

I parked my bike in a nearby lot, stuffed my hands in my pockets and walked briskly down the boardwalk. A bitter sense of irony filled me as I passed by most of the shops, which were owned by witches, seers, healers, psions and more. Very few mages actually operated shops out of the Port, as most of them preferred to work out of The Mages Quarter. The very existence of Witches' End was proof the rules only exist for us humans and shifters to follow – they don't apply to the magic wielders who consider themselves above us.

In Solantha, as well as the rest of the country, anyone who is born with the power to wield magic, aside from a mage's acknowledged offspring, either has their magic stripped from them or is executed. It's a brutal method of control that's existed for hundreds of years to ensure the current regime stays firmly in place, and most citizens give in rather than try to circumvent the law because the older you are when you're found out, the greater risk of mental damage when the mages strip the magic from you.

The law that hung above my neck like a guillotine, however, doesn't apply to the magic users who run Witches' End. The residents of Witches End are allowed to practice their craft because they are foreigners who paid a hefty fee in order to obtain a special license to come over here. And because they aren't actually the local mages we all love to hate, and charge quite a bit less than the ones in the Mage's Quarter offering the same services, they do a brisk business here at the Port.

My boot-clad feet finally took me near the end of the pier, where my friend's shop, *Over the Hedge*, sat nestled in between an apothecary and a fortuneteller's shack. It was a small brick building with a glass storefront, the company name frosted on the large glass window in simple but charming letters. A small bell tinkled as I opened the door and stepped inside, and some-thing inside me relaxed as I inhaled the scent of herbs, wax, and burnt-sugar magic.

Every piece of furniture and decoration in the place was crafted out of natural materials – from the white cotton curtains hanging in the windows, to the driftwood tables and shelves scattered throughout the shop and laden with merchandise, to the hand-woven and colorfully dyed rugs covering the wooden floorboards. The only machinery in the entire shop was the clock on the wall and the register on the counter.

Behind said register stood my friend Comenius, the shop owner, muttering under his breath and tapping at the keys. At his shoulder was Noria Melcott, a human redhead dressed in denim overalls, a loud t-shirt, and an aviator's cap. An annoyed scowl was stamped all over her freckled face as she watched Comenius try to ring up a purchase for the customer standing in front of the counter. She was the younger sister of an Enforcer friend of mine named Annia, and a college student who paid her way between a scholarship and the wages she made working at Comenius's shop.

"Com," Noria huffed as she rolled her eyes. "Would you *please* just let me do it?"

"No," Comenius said, his crisp, throaty Pernian accent tinged with annoyance. He impatiently brushed back his ash-blond bangs with one long-fingered hand that was stained with herb residue, drawing attention to the strong bones of his face. "I've been operating this register long before I hired you. I am perfectly capable of ringing up a sale."

"Not when the machine's broken, you're not."

"Look, can I just come back later and pay for this?" the customer whined. "I'm going to be late for my shift."

Amused despite my dire mood, I leaned up against the counter and tapped the table to get Comenius's attention. "Com, let the geeky girl have a go at it. You don't want to lose a paying customer, do you?"

Comenius's pale eyebrows shot up as he glanced over at me. "Naya? What are you doing here?" He took a step toward me, and Noria used the opportunity to dart in front of the register and open up the back end to unstick whatever little gears had jammed inside it. He hardly noticed though – his cornflower blue eyes were firmly fixed on mine. "You're usually asleep this time of day... or did you get the night off?"

"Not exactly," I muttered. All the dark emotion, which I'd pushed down somewhere behind my lower intestines, came bubbling up into my chest again. "It's more like I took off."

"Why would you do that?" Noria asked. The bell jingled as the customer left the shop with his purchase in hand. It had taken her about two seconds to fix the machine and ring him up – which was not surprising, as she had a real bent for machinery. Narrowing her coffee-colored eyes, she hopped up on the counter, placing herself directly between Comenius and me so she couldn't be ignored – a tactic that was both endearing and annoying. "I can't imagine that they'd be able to forgive you leaving in the middle of a Friday night crowd."

"Yeah, well they're just going to have to deal." I shoved my hands into my hair, promptly tangling my fingers into the black ringlets. "Roanas was murdered."

"What?" Comenius and Noria both gasped at the same time, their eyes huge.

"When?" Comenius asked.

"How?" Noria demanded.

I sighed, exhaustion dragging at the edges of my brain. I hadn't slept in over twenty-four hours – it had been nearly midnight when I'd gotten Roanas's cry for help – and on top of that, I was emotionally exhausted. Comenius, sensing my fatigue, had Noria lock the front door and flip the 'OPEN' sign around to 'CLOSED', then brought out a pot of his soothing tea and had us all settle into the small sitting area in a corner of the shop so I could tell them the story.

I told them everything between sips of tea, silently thanking Magorah, the All-Creator, as the herbal concoction soothed my ragged nerves and bolstered my flagging energy levels. Comenius was a hedge-witch; all of his spells, amulets, concoctions and devices were created using nature magic, and he made some of the most killer herbal remedies around, amongst other things. Hence why everything in the shop was made out of natural materials, and also the reason Comenius couldn't operate the cash register to save his life. It was like he had an allergy to anything remotely made of machinery.

"By the Ur-God," Noria whispered. Her dark eyes shimmered with tears. "I'm so sorry, Naya. That's terrible."

"Silver poisoning?" Comenius's eyes were narrowed as he pondered the issue. "And you say he told you the silver was some kind of solution that was undetectable by scent or taste?"

I nodded. "Do you know any herbs that might be able to do that?" I asked, leaning forward in my chair. I'd hoped his vast knowledge of plant lore might point me in the right direction. And since I was currently an outcast at all my usual haunts, he was the only person I could turn to for help.

Comenius tapped his square chin as he thought. "I might," he muttered, his gaze scanning a shelf filled with jars of dried leaves and roots. "But most of them wouldn't meld with silver." He paused, turning his narrowed gaze back to me. "Are you investigating this in an official capacity?"

"No." My cheeks flushed, but I stubbornly held his gaze. "The Guild sent two goons from the Main Crew to handle it. You know they wouldn't let me investigate my own mentor's murder."

"Shouldn't you –"

"Com," Noria interjected, her brows drawing together as she cut him off. "You don't really expect Naya to sit back and let those half-assed jerks investigate Roanas's death, do you?"

"Well, no." Comenius hesitated, uncertainty flickering in his eyes. "But I can't say I'm entirely comfortable putting my shop on the line by aiding Naya in an unauthorized investigation either." He leaned forward to pin me with a gimlet stare. "Haven't you considered that this might be the reason your mentor was killed? Because he was sticking his nose where someone thought it didn't belong?"

"Yes," I said evenly before Noria exploded. While the kid's outrage on my behalf was admirable, I didn't need her losing her job over it. "But that isn't going to stop me from flushing out the bastard who killed him, and bringing them to justice. Brin and Nila care more about getting their bounty than getting actual justice for Roanas, which means that whoever murdered him is going to keep on knocking off other shifters unchecked. This is a lot bigger than a revenge kick, Com. It's about the safety of the shifter community in general."

Comenius sighed, running a hand through his pale hair. "I wish that you could go to the Shifter Council about this. That would be much more appropriate, and possibly more effective too."

I scowled. "You know why I can't do that." As a half-shifter, my word was worth significantly less than that of a full-blooded shifter, and on top of that my aunt Mafiela, the head of the Jaguar Clan, was on the Council. Normally that would be an advantage, except that she regarded the shit stains on her under-wear more highly than she did me, especially after my mother passed away. There was no way the Council would allow me to participate in an investigation if I initiated one with them, not if she had anything to say about it.

"I know. And that's why I'll look into it." He rose, and the loose fabric of his dark green tunic rippled with the motion. "I'll be right back."

"Thank you." I sighed a little as Comenius disappeared into the back of the shop. This reticence to take action, this stickler attitude about following the rules was the reason Comenius and

I hadn't worked out as a couple a few years back when we'd tried dating. Sure, he had a pretty hot bod beneath those conservative clothes of his, and those long fingers were good for more than enchanting amulets and grinding herbs. But I preferred to live on the edge, whereas Comenius tended toward camping behind the lines. Sometimes it amazed me that a man who made his living by working with the forces of nature could be so rigid... but then again, it took all kinds.

"You know," Noria interrupted my inner monologue. She leaned back in her wicker chair, a thoughtful expression on her elfin face. "I might have some ideas myself about how the silver could have been masked."

"Oh yeah?" I leaned forward, hope sparking in my chest. Part of me knew that it was wrong for me to involve Annia's little sister – she was a smart kid, not yet eighteen years old, with a bright future ahead of her, and I didn't need to mess it up by dragging her into my bullshit. But I was also desperate and without leads, and I needed all the help I could get. "You think you might be able to track down who did it?"

Noria shrugged. "Sure, if I can figure out how it was done. I'll jump on investigating how the silver could have been diluted. A couple of my friends at the Academy have done experiments with metals and electricity. It's very likely that whoever did this was human."

I nodded. "That makes sense. I couldn't imagine it being one of our own." Shifters didn't use silver to kill other shifters – we preferred to settle things with our fangs and claws.

Comenius came back from around the counter, a bracelet clutched in his fist. "I couldn't find anything in the books I have here," he said. "But I'll check the Mage Guild's library and see what else I can find. In the meantime, you should wear this." He held up the hemp bracelet to reveal a small, circular amulet dangling from the center. "It will help quiet the spirits around you and sharpen your focus, so you can concentrate on the investigation."

"Thanks." I smiled, touched by his concern, and held out my arm so he could fasten the bracelet around my wrist. Electricity buzzed up the nerve endings in my arm as his long fingers brushed against my skin, and from the way Comenius's pupils dilated, I could tell the same thing had happened to him. Which wasn't exactly strange, since we'd tumbled together in the sack before, but it was pretty awkward with Noria sitting right there watching us, so I settled quickly back into my chair, breaking the contact as soon as he was done.

"So," Noria said. "What now?"

"Now we look at this." I unzipped my jacket and pulled out the file. Com and Noria's eyes widened, and they both leaned forward.

"Is... is this a *case* file?" Comenius said.

"Yep. From Roanas's house." It had taken me quite a while to find it, so I hadn't had a chance to do more than stuff it down the front of my jacket before Brin and Nila arrived. "He told me to get it before he died."

Comenius looked like he wanted to say something about stealing evidence, but he wisely kept his mouth shut. I flipped open the file, scanning the notes and various newspaper clippings. My eyes smarted at the sight of Roanas's handwriting – it was a painful reminder that he would never write another word again. But I blinked away the tears, knowing I couldn't afford them now – there would be time enough to grieve after the killer was caught.

"Naya? Isn't this about one of your own?"

I glanced down at the article Noria was pointing at. My eyes widened as I took in the photo of the beautiful woman depicted at the top of the article, dressed in leathers and armed with a short sword. It was Sillara, one of the more competent Enforcers, and one I'd been quite fond of.

"I had no idea she'd died of silver poisoning," I murmured, tracing the outline of her face with the tip of my finger. She'd been part of a crew, whereas I was a solo mercenary, so our paths didn't really cross. But she'd always struck me as frank and dedicated, one of the true diamonds amongst a sea full of rhinestones. And now she was gone.

Comenius said nothing, simply laying a hand on my shoulder as I read the article. It said that she'd been found in her apartment on a Friday night, dead on her living room floor. The Mage's Guild was conducting an autopsy, but there was no conclusive evidence pointing to a cause of death, murder weapon or killer, for that matter.

"They wrote her off," I muttered, my fingers curling so tightly around the edges of the paper that it started to shred. "I remember now. The Guild said she'd died from some kind of fucking heart failure." Which was incredibly rare amongst shifters, especially one who was as healthy and in shape as Sillara had been. Magorah, why hadn't I seen it? I should have questioned it, should have suspected something... but of course, I'd been too wrapped up in my own problems, and I hadn't.

"I'm sorry," Comenius said gently, rubbing his thumb along the edge of my shoulder. I wanted to lean into him, to sink into the comfort he offered, but I couldn't – someone was killing off shifters, and I needed to find out who.

"Do you think the mages might be in on this?"

I glanced up at Noria, who'd spoken. "You think the Mage's Guild is responsible for the murders?"

Noria shrugged, lines bracketing her mouth as she scanned another one of the articles. "I can't say for sure, but it seems like someone's definitely trying to keep all of these hush-hush. I mean, usually the papers are quick to connect cases like this, and yet we have six issues here, spread across three months, and not a single peep from the media. What gives?"

"But this is the *Shifter Courier*," I argued. "These stories aren't published by the Mage's Guild."

Noria shrugged. "Race doesn't seem to matter when someone shoves a pouch full of gold in your face. They probably bribed the editor or something."

Even though as a hybrid I wasn't fully part of the shifter community, my gut still twisted at the idea one of us was a sell-out. Sure, I'd had to take down my fair share of shifter bounties, but it was still tough to admit we were just as susceptible to the same weaknesses as any other race.

A gloomy silence descended as we all pondered the possibilities. So far, the beginnings of our theory suggested human involvement with mage cover-up, which didn't make a whole lot of sense because there was no reason I could think of that the mages would want to cover up for humans. I'd searched Roanas's house for clues while I'd been waiting for the Enforcers to show up and hadn't found anything helpful, but that didn't mean nothing was going on. I had a feeling that even if we were on the right trail, we were only scratching the surface, and things were going to get a whole lot messier the deeper we went.

"What about your cousin Rylan?" Comenius asked. "He might have heard some rumors about this underground."

"Huh." I hadn't thought of that. "I haven't heard from him in a long while, but I should ask." Rylan was a member of the Resistance, a ragtag band of humans and shifters who lived on the outskirts of civilization and worked tirelessly to overthrow the mages. He was the only one of my cousins I was close to, which was ironic considering that I worked for law enforcement. Unfortunately, his way of life meant I didn't get to see him much.

"I think that's a good idea." Comenius paused. "Are you

going to be alright?" he asked, his voice gentling. "I mean, if you lose your job at The Twilight –"

"I'll be fine," I cut him off, not wanting him to worry. For all of his self-preservation instincts and tendencies towards conservatism, Comenius could become a freaking mother hen when it came to keeping his friends safe. "I'll figure out a way to make ends meet."

"You haven't come to me for amulets in a long time," he said quietly. "Which means that you haven't been going after any new bounties. That Talcon fellow has been giving most of them to the Main Crew, hasn't he?" His brow darkened.

"Com, stop." I rose to my feet, agitated now. Most of the Enforcers Guild was made up of small crews – eight to ten people, usually – but there was always a Main Crew of at least forty people who got the best bounties. Unfortunately, since the Main Crew didn't have to work so hard to get their bounties, they were also pretty half-assed when it came to their job – and Brin and Nila were part of them. "There's no need to worry about this, because I'm going to change it."

Comenius sat back, skepticism written all over his face as he crossed his arms and looked up at me. "And just how are you going to do that?"

"By solving these poison murders," I declared, jabbing my fist in the air like a torch. "If I can show up the current Main Crew by catching this murderer, Galling will add me to the Main Crew roster and I'll get access to better bounties. Then Talcon will *have* to show me some respect." The thought of pressing a proverbial boot to Talcon's neck brought a fierce grin to my face. He wouldn't dare mess with me if I was on the Main Crew.

"Hmm." Comenius appeared to give the matter serious thought. "The idea definitely has merit."

I was about to roll my eyes when a loud buzzing sound filled the room as my Enforcer bracelet, a tiny bronze shield charm threaded through a brown cord, vibrated against my wrist. *"All nearby Enforcers to 228 Garden Street,"* a tinny voice blared, projected by the bracelet. *"Rogue shifter out of control."*

"Well, shit." I patted my legs down to make sure my weapons were still strapped on me – chakram pouch on the right leg and crescent knives on the left. "Sounds like there's trouble in Rowanville. Gotta go!"

I sprinted out the door and down the pier toward my bike, the thrill of the hunt racing through my veins. Emergency calls paid high, and were first come, first served, so if I took down this guy there was no way Talcon could skimp on paying me the bounty. Jumping on my bike, I started up the steam engine and raced out of the pier. My wheels screeched as I skidded onto the main street and blew past two mages coming out of a shop. I laughed as their robes flew up around their ankles and flipped them the bird as they shouted after me.

I didn't care about them, didn't care about any of my other troubles right now. All I knew was that I had a bounty to catch, and I was going to cash in on it even if it killed me.

3

I heard the screams long before I skidded to a stop in front of 288 Garden Street, a nice little one-story family house in one of the suburban Rowanville neighborhoods. The high-pitched wails of children curdled my gut, but I sucked in a breath and steeled myself for whatever nightmare I was about to face. I got off my bike and approached the woman sobbing hysterically in the front yard. Her dark hair was a wreck, the once-nice dress she wore shredded in places, and her leg was bent at an odd angle. Inside the house, I could hear loud thumping and crashing; the rogue shifter must be wreaking havoc in there.

Anger bubbled up inside me as I touched the woman's shoulder to get her attention. Why the fuck was nobody helping her? It had taken me nearly ten minutes to get here from the Port. There had to be an Enforcer in the area who could have gotten here faster.

"Ma'am," I said as Noria's bike pulled up behind me – she'd grabbed a protesting Comenius and insisted on following me here. "My name is Sunaya Baine, registered member of the Enforcer's Guild. Can you tell me what's going on?"

"Please!" the woman shrieked, grabbing my arm with bruising force. Her powder blue shifter eyes were crazed with fear, and my nose told me she was a rabbit shifter. "My babies are still in there! You have to get them out!" Tears poured down her raw cheeks as her body trembled.

"Can you tell me what's in there with them?" I asked, my heart pounding. "What kind of beast?"

"It's a rhino shifter," she sobbed as the house shook behind her. "He charged in, all wild and crazy, and went for me and the children. I couldn't get to them, so I came out here for help... but..."

"Naya." Comenius dropped to his knees beside me, his voice urgent. Compassion flickered in his eyes as he took in the sight of the woman. "What's going on?"

"There's a rampaging rhino shifter inside the house, and there are children in danger." I rose to my feet slowly, dread weighing down my movements. I wasn't equipped to handle a rhino shifter by myself, especially not one who was crazed with anger. But there was no one else around to back me up. "I have to go and get them."

"Are you crazy?" Noria snapped. "He'll kill you!"

"There are children in there," I said firmly, my gaze fixed on the house. "Com, you heal the mother. I'm going in to rescue her cubs."

"Like hell," Comenius snapped, rising impatiently to his feet. "You'll never make it out of there. I'm going in with you."

"You should help the woman –"

"I have some spells that could calm the rhino down." I shut my mouth at that. "If you can distract him long enough, I'll cast a sleeping spell on him that should stop him in his tracks so you can get the children to safety."

"Fine." Much as I didn't want to involve my friends with this, I knew I couldn't do it alone. I needed magic, and I couldn't use my own. But there wasn't any time to dwell on the irony – I needed to rescue the children.

I charged through the door first, my crescent knives clutched in my fists in case the rhino was on the other side. No, they wouldn't do much good, but I was a little more confident with the weapons in my hands. I brandished them like talismans as I followed the scent of the baby rabbits, creeping through the war-torn living room and down the hallway. The walls had been reduced to little more than rubble, so there wasn't much cover, and I had a clear sight of the rhino hard at work demolishing what had once been a very nice dining room.

Creeping across the tile floor as silently as I could in my boots, I followed the scent across the room and beneath the remains of a dining room table, where two baby bunnies were huddled together in beast form. They were absolutely adorable, little black fuzz balls the size of sugar melons, their eyes wide with panic above their little chins and pink noses. "Shhh," I whispered soothingly, reaching for them with outstretched arms. "I'm here to save you."

I reached for the bunnies, and the rhino shifter chose that moment to swing his head around. I froze in utter terror as his crazed eyes made direct contact with mine – blood was flowing freely from his flared nostrils. What the fuck was going on with this guy?

"Time to go!" I shouted, more to distract the rhino than to tell the bunnies. Thinking fast, I flipped the table in the rhino's direction, then grabbed both the bunnies by the scruffs of their necks and tossed them out the window and into the backyard.

The rhino bayed so loudly the sound shook the remaining walls of the house and made my eardrums throb. He charged me, his huge horn splintering the glossy dining table I'd thrown up as a makeshift battlement, and I dodged out of the way and raced down the hall, past Comenius who was frantically putting together a spell in the living room. I couldn't run outside, not while the mother and babies were still on the lawn, but I could lead the bastard on a chase until Comenius finished concocting his sleep spell.

"Any minute now, Com!" I shouted over the deafening sound of the rhino's crashing footfalls. The sound of crumbling drywall told me that he wasn't far behind, his huge body knocking down the walls, and I ducked inside the nearest bedroom, hoping that his momentum would carry him straight past me.

I was wrong. Somehow, the hulking bastard managed to make the turn along with me, and his huge snout crashed into the middle of my back. I went flying across a little girl's room, with lacy curtains at the windows and dolls covering the shelves, and slammed face-first into the pink wall.

Stars burst across my vision as I slid to the floor, flopping onto my back. The whole world felt like it was shaking apart around me, though really it was just the floor rumbling as the rhino charged me again. Fear choked me in its cold, vice-like grip as the beast reared up on his hind legs to trample me, having no other way to attack me in the small space. I threw out my hands instinctively, as if my comparatively twig-like arms had a chance of stopping the rhino's tree trunk legs.

But just before the rhino's legs came down on me, a surge of energy ballooned in my chest, rippled down my arms and blasted out of my hands in the form of a huge ball of blue-green fire. It crashed into the rhino, who bayed so loudly that my teeth rattled inside my throbbing head. There was a sizzling sound, like meat cooking, and then the rhino disappeared in a flash.

I lay there as flecks of ash rained down on my face, the edges of my vision darkening. Shouts and footfalls echoed in the hall-way, and a horde of people came crashing in through the door-way, Comenius in the lead and Noria close behind.

"Naya!" He skidded to his knees beside me, his eyes wild. "Are you alright?"

"Fine," I wheezed.

"Where's the rhino?" My fuzzy vision managed to pick out Brin, the Enforcer who'd responded to my call at Roanas's house, as the source of the question. He stood just inside the door, his burly arms crossed over his chest, a suspicious scowl on his face.

Curling my lips back in a sardonic grin, I slid my hand through some of the ash coating the ground, then lifted a fistful of it into the air. "Right here."

"Oh Naya," Comenius whispered miserably, taking my filthy hand in his. "This is so very, very bad."

He was right, of course. I had just used my magic to kill a shifter. While responding to a distress call. In front of a *whole* lot of witnesses. I was royally fucked no matter which way you looked at it, and the silver murders didn't have a chance in hell of being solved if I was executed. But as they all stood over me, arguing about whether I should be jailed, sent to the hospital, or crowned Queen for a Day – Noria's idea – the last bit of energy that might have allowed me to care left my body, and without it to anchor me there I sank into a blissful sea of darkness.

4

The next time I woke up, I found myself lying on a cot that must've been made of concrete, it was so damn uncomfortable. And that wasn't even counting the aches and pains running through my face and body from being smashed into a wall by a four-ton rhinoceros.

Was I in the hospital? Where was my damned nurse?

Opening my eyes, I twisted my head around and catalogued the iron bars surrounding my little room on three sides and the concrete wall behind me. Fear sprang to life in my gut as I confirmed that I was, in fact, in a jail cell and not a super-shitty hospital room like I'd hoped. Fuck. How was I going to get out of this mess?

"Naya? Are you awake?"

Noria's voice startled me from my state of semi-awareness, and I jolted upright and looked around for the source. My heart sank as I found it – she was sitting on the cot in the cell next to mine, her pale face pinched and her coffee-colored eyes round with concern.

"Shit," I muttered. My friend's little sister was in jail with me and a throbbing tattoo beat against the inside of my skull. "Noria, what are you doing in here?"

Noria smirked a little. "That asshole Brin threw me in here, to teach me a lesson after I punched him in the nose. But don't worry; I'll be out on bail in a little bit. I'm just glad you woke up before my family gets here."

Yeah, well I'm not, I thought grumpily, biting the words back as they would only hurt Noria's feelings. But by Magorah, I was *so* not looking forward to having her mother shoot death glares at me through the bars of my cell when she came to pick up her daughter. The idea was almost scarier than the fact that I was in jail.

Almost. After all, there's little else in this world more terrifying than an impending execution.

"So," I sighed, slumping against the concrete wall and trying to ignore the panic skirting the edges of my mind. "What'd I miss?"

"Aside from me punching Brin in the face?" Noria said proudly. I sent her a death glare of my own, and she deflated a little. "Oh, alright, alright. Nothing much, really. Com and I tried to argue with those other Enforcers about letting you go on account of the fact that you were just doing your job and you didn't hurt anyone aside from the rhino. The rabbit shifter lady defended you too. But unfortunately you Enforcers don't seem to have any respect for each other within the ranks, so they tossed both of us in here."

I winced at Noria's cutting words. "Yeah, well unfortunately the Enforcer's Guild is a highly competitive workplace. The less competition, the better your docket."

Noria was silent for a long moment as she pondered this. She'd declared a long time ago that she wanted to follow in her sister's footsteps and become an Enforcer, and I hoped my words would help dissuade her from that treacherous career path. Even though I loved what I did most days, I also didn't have too many other career options given my skill set and secrets. Noria, with her smarts and techie skills, had the entire world as her oyster. I really, *really* didn't want her to end up on the same path I was.

Especially since, at the moment, my path looked like it was coming to an end a lot sooner than I wanted it to.

"Would you do that?" Noria finally asked.

"Do what?" I blinked.

"Turn somebody else in who didn't deserve it, just so you could eliminate the competition." She bit her lip as she studied me.

"No. I wouldn't," I admitted with a sigh. For the most part I actually believed in justice, *true* justice. Not the half-assed, corrupted version practiced in society today.

As expected, Noria rewarded me with a huge grin. "That's exactly what I thought," she crowed. "You're way too far above that crap." The grin faded a little as a troubled look entered her eyes. "Naya?"

"Hmm?"

"Do you really think you're about to be executed?"

I sat up straight at the sound of her voice, so small and scared and unlike the brash, confident girl I knew. She was clutching the bars, staring at me with wide eyes, and I reached out, wanting to touch her hands and reassure her. But before I could, the door at the end of the hall opened, and a guard marched down the hall with Noria's mother in tow.

I sighed, slumping back against the mattress again. So much for companionship. I silently endured the expected death glare from Noria's mother as she collected her daughter, then gingerly lay back on my rock-hard cot. It was wrong, but I missed having

Noria in the cell next to me. It was comforting to have a comrade in here to distract me from my fear, especially since I knew that when I next emerged from this cell, I would be walking to my death.

Without Noria to distract me, my aches and pains made themselves known, increasing from a dull ache to sharp, throbbing pains in the bones of my face and my ribcage. Dread pooled in my stomach as I realized that my injuries were more severe than I'd thought. I was going to have to shift to heal them.

Normally, shifting was no problem for me. Because I was half-mage and had more natural magic at my disposal than a regular shifter, I could change forms faster and more frequently. But I'd just used a boatload of magic disintegrating that rhino shifter, and I'd already been short on sleep and food then. I was past the point of exhaustion now.

Is there even any point in healing myself? I thought despondently, my eyes tracing the cracks in the concrete ceiling. *If I'm going to be executed tomorrow?*

Of course there is, a voice in my head argued fiercely. *You're the only one who gives a fuck about solving the silver murders. You can't just give up and die. Don't allow your fear of what could be to put you into an early grave.*

Tears sprang to my eyes at that last line – it was something Roanas told me often, especially when coaxing me into trying a new maneuver early on in my training. He'd taken me in when I was still a cub, after my mother died and my aunt had kicked me out of the clan, and of all the things he'd taught me that phrase stuck with me the most. It was his way of saying not to give in to my fear of the unknown – just because something could go wrong didn't mean that it would, and if you didn't try at all you'd never reap the rewards.

Magorah, what was I supposed to do now that he was gone?

The door at the end of the hall opened and footsteps rang across the concrete. I sat up, swiping the tears from my face in case I had a visitor. Sure enough, a hulking thug of a human with a bulbous nose and a shock of red hair dressed in leathers stopped in front of my cell. His wide mouth stretched in a grin, displaying the gold tooth that winked where one of his canines should have been.

Oh lucky me. It's my favorite person in the world.

"Deputy Talcon," I said coolly, sitting up straight. The pain in my ribs flared, but I ignored it, unwilling to show him any sign of weakness.

"Sunaya." He dragged the last syllable out, then made tsking sounds as he wagged a meaty finger at me. He was built like a troll, nearly as wide as he was tall, the bulging muscles of his arms displayed by the sleeveless black shirt he wore. "I heard you were cooped up down here, so I thought I'd come down and see how my favorite Enforcer was doing." He raised a long, paper-wrapped package clutched in his fist. "Want a sandwich?"

I wanted to tell him to fuck off, but my stomach growled so loudly in response to the food that he laughed before chucking the sandwich through the iron bars of the cell. It landed in my lap, and I fell on it greedily, the shame in my gut unable to trump the gnawing hunger in there.

"Good little panther," he cooed as I ripped open the wrapper and inhaled the sandwich. My nose told me it was safe, a simple if unimaginative combination of turkey and cheese, so I wasted no time in chowing it down. I had to swallow my pride if I wanted to have my strength for tomorrow.

"Got any water to go with that?" I asked nonchalantly, wiping my mouth with the back of my hand.

His eyes narrowed at my blasé response to his goading. "You always were an ungrateful little bitch," he said darkly, his lower lip curling.

"Sure, and you always were a disgusting, fat fuck."

His eyes bulged, and he lunged toward me before he remembered that there was a row of iron bars separating us. I watched with satisfaction as he stood there, taking in deep breaths through his flaring nostrils, a vein pulsing in his temple. Good. The bastard deserved to stew a little, especially after all he'd put me through.

"So," I said, folding my arms across my aching ribs. "What brings you down from your cushy office upstairs? Got tired of jerking off to my ID photo?" I'd been down here enough times to know I was in the holding cells in the basement of the Enforcer's Guild. Shame burned the lining of my stomach as it occurred to me that my peers had likely all watched Brin and Nila haul my unconscious ass down here, but I forced myself to push it aside. There were more important things to worry about than my bruised pride.

"As a matter of fact, I did." His lips stretched into a cruel smirk as he regarded me with his beady eyes. "It's been awhile since you last came in, so when I heard you were in the building I decided to come and see that pretty face of yours in person again." His eyes gleamed with lust, and a small shiver crawled down my spine. "So much better than a picture."

"You know," I drawled, doing my best to cover up the disgust coating my throat, "if you pull out your dick here and try to shoot a load at me now, you might actually be able to hit me since I don't have an amulet to incinerate you with anymore. Why don't you try it and see what happens?" I bared my fangs, daring him – if he whipped out his dick now I had a real shot of reaching through the bars and ripping it to shreds with my claws before he could react. After all, it wasn't like I had anything to lose now, and I partially blamed him for the situation I was in.

Talcon's lips pressed into a thin line. "You've got a real smart mouth for someone who's facing execution, *hybrid*." I flinched as he spat the word, the contempt in his voice so much like my aunt Mafiela's that my heart shriveled inside my chest. "Don't pretend that little trinket is what saved your ass today. We both know what really happened, and you're going down."

I lifted my chin, refusing to let him see the fear churning inside my gut. "I look forward to seeing the look on your face when the mages test the amulet and are forced to vindicate me." Not that that was going to happen, of course – in fact, I sincerely hoped the Mage's Guild decided *not* to test the amulet when I spun my bogus story for them tomorrow, because if they did I was most definitely toast.

Uncertainty flickered across Talcon's face for just a moment, and then he scoffed. "Yeah, right. You were always good at bluffing. But you know," he said, a sly smile curving his lips. "I could help you escape in exchange for a little something-something."

I arched an eyebrow. "What, you want your sandwich back? I don't think it's any good to you at this point, but I'm sure I can figure something out." I stuck a finger in the back of my throat and pretended to gag.

"Oh, don't bother with that." Talcon's sausage fingers reached for his fly. "I've got something much better for you to choke on."

"Fuck you." I instinctively reached for the chakram pouch strapped to my thigh, but there was nothing there but my leather-clad leg. Dammit. Was I ever going to get my weapons back?

"I'm not sucking you off for my freedom, Talcon. You probably couldn't give it to me anyway."

"You never know," he purred, wiggling the zipper on his pants.

I rolled my eyes. "Please don't make me bite that thing off."

His expression turned downright ugly. "Fine," he said,

baring his teeth. "I was just giving you the opportunity to enjoy a last moment of pleasure before your death."

"Couldn't you drag your mind out of the garbage for once and do some actual work?" I threw up my hands, tired of this bullshit. Why the fuck did the Enforcer's Guild give the deputy position to such a total ass? Just because he came from an old human family with money didn't mean he deserved the job. "Instead of standing around here holding your dick, you could be out there solving those silver murders and getting some real recognition for a job well done."

Something flickered in his eyes, and for a moment I thought I'd actually dented his pride. But the look disappeared as quickly as I'd seen it, and he shrugged, a patronizing smile on his thuggish face.

"I never figured you for one to believe in conspiracy theories, Sunaya. Guess it's a good thing you're finally getting put down, or I'd have to fire you myself. I look forward to seeing you at your hearing tomorrow, *hybrid*."

Fury raced through me like wildfire, but I snapped my mouth shut as Talcon turned and walked back down the hall, wanting him gone more than I wanted to fight. The relief that coursed through me as I listened to his receding footsteps was quickly eclipsed by despair as I slumped back down onto my cot. What the fuck was I supposed to do now? Sit here and wait to die? I'd always imagined being taken out while I was on the job, protecting an innocent or bringing down a criminal. Death by execution, for something I was born with and couldn't control, had never been part of the plan.

Before I allowed the bitterness coating my tongue to spread throughout the rest of me and sap my strength, I pulled off my clothes and used the bit of energy I'd gotten from Talcon's sandwich to shift. A hot white light engulfed my body as it stretched and changed shape, and when it faded away I'd transformed from a tall, lean woman into a black panther. Only my bottle-green eyes remained constant, regardless of what shape I was in. I always figured the mages who created us did that on purpose, so shifters would be easily identifiable.

My claws scraped against the ground as I stretched, my sleek form rippling, and I let out a satisfied sigh as the last of my injuries knit themselves back together. Now that I was in beast form and the pain of my injuries had gone, some of the despair and anxiety began to lift from my heart. Curling up on the cold concrete, I rested my chin on top of my paws and allowed sleep to finally take hold of me. Once I got some rest I would focus my mind on getting out of this mess alive. After all, I was twenty-four and had my whole life ahead of me. Not to mention a series of murders to solve.

"SUNAYA BAINE?"

The sound of an unfamiliar male voice woke me from a fitful sleep. I cracked an eye open to see a man standing above me, his slim form draped in a long, khaki coat. Though it was dark in the jail at this time of night, my sharp eyes were able to pick out the porkpie hat clutched in his left hand, his slicked-back dirty blond hair, and his horn-rimmed glasses, the last of which sparked a memory.

You're a reporter, I wanted to say, but then I remembered that I was in my panther form. Yawning, I stretched, my claws producing a scraping sound as they gouged into the concrete floor. The human took a nervous step back, clearly not a fan of my sharp implements. To amuse myself, I rose up on my hind legs, hooking my paws through the bars of my cell as I met his gaze. His eyes widened as his back clanged into the cell bars behind him.

"Y-you are Sunaya Baine, aren't you?"

Satisfied at the tremor in the man's voice – I never was much of a fan of reporters – I nosed my clothes into the shadowy portion of my cell and changed back into human form. His sigh of relief and the scent of fresh sweat rolling from his pores were telling – this man was afraid of shifters in general, not just me.

"I am Sunaya Baine," I said once I'd pulled my clothes back on and stepped back into the dim light. I leaned against the bars and looped my hands through them lazily, affecting a pose of nonchalance. He eyed my hands warily, as if he expected me to claw him at any second, and I found myself annoyed at his skittishness. "Can I help you with something?"

"Yes," he said, drawing his air of professionalism back around him. He pulled out a notepad and a pen from one of the pockets of his greatcoat and looked up at me with a polite smile over his glasses, his pen poised. "My name is Hanley Fintz, and I'm a journalist for the Herald. I heard about your unfortunate predicament, and would like to interview you."

I arched a brow. "Bit late for interviews, don't you think?" Not that I knew what time it was, since Brin and Nila had stripped my body of anything actually useful, such as my watch. The fuckers had even taken my Enforcer bracelet, the symbol of authority I'd worked so hard to earn. But judging by the fact that the lights down here were still dimmed, it must be night above ground.

The reporter shrugged. "From what my sources tell me, your hearing is set for early this morning. Since they're likely to rule against you, I have to take what opportunities I can get to talk with you before it's too late."

In other words, this schmuck had bribed one of the guards upstairs to let him into the jail cell so he could interview me. Did absolutely no one understand the meaning of 'work ethic' anymore? Pressing my lips together, I eyed the reporter distastefully, not sure that he didn't deserve a beating just as much as the guard upstairs, though unlike the guard he was just doing his job.

A long silence stretched. Eventually Fintz cleared his throat. "Come now, surely you can tell me *something*," he coaxed. "I would like to paint you in the most positive light possible, which is not very hard. If you have to die, at least you can die a martyr in the fight against the oppressive mages who rule us."

His voice was low and urgent, infused with passion. But the hungry way he eyed me seemed less sincere. Releasing the bars, I took a step back, holding my hands up defensively.

"Look," I told him. "If you want to paint me as a martyr or a hero or whatever after I'm six feet under, that's your business. But I'm not dead yet, and I'd appreciate it if you'd stop looking at me like some vulture waiting for me to gasp my last breath, so you can swoop down and start feasting on me."

The man recoiled a little, his pointy nose twitching. "Well that's vulgar."

"Yeah, well you know what else is vulgar?" I leaned against the bars again to pin him with an accusing stare. "The fact that nobody in this town seems to give a damn about all the shifters who are dying of silver poisoning. If you really wanted a juicy story, you'd be investigating that, starting with my mentor's murder, not trying to prod me for bullshit quotes about standing up to the system."

"I would love nothing more than to investigate these poisonings you speak of," Hanley said sulkily. "But unfortunately, Mr. Yantz decides who and what I investigate and what stories are printed, and he is simply not interested in publishing that story."

"Of course not." I bared my fangs in disgust. Petros Yantz, the CEO and Chief Editor of the Herald, had turned the once-prestigious paper into little more than a glorified gossip rag. He was one of the primary reasons I detested reporters. "Why don't you go and tell your boss to fuck off for me, before I find a reason to break out of this cell and come harass *him* in the middle of the night."

"I see." His eyes glittered as he returned his pad and pen to his pocket. "I'm sorry you feel that way. I suppose I'll just have to contact your family for quotes instead. Do have a good night." He placed his hat on his head, then turned and walked away.

I snorted at his parting shot, lying back down on my cot. It was doubtful he would get anything more interesting than a 'Good Riddance!' from my aunt Mafiela if he asked her how she felt about my death, and though some of my cousins might have nicer things to say about me, I doubted she would let them speak to the press.

Closing my eyes, I tried to take advantage of whatever time I had left before my hearing to get some sleep. But now that I'd been awakened, my mind kept buzzing with all the thoughts jockeying for position inside my head. The predominant fear, of course, was how the hell to ensure Roanas got avenged and the silver murders got solved. Even if I did manage to avoid execution, which was very unlikely, I would face a long sentence, most likely of hard labor in the mines. Plus I would be stripped of my magic, and at my age that would reduce my mind into a puddle of mush. No matter how the judge decided to punish me, I would have zero opportunity to conduct an investigation myself.

Of course, I could always ask Comenius and Noria to look into it for me... except I didn't want to risk their lives on this. Comenius had a daughter abroad who he helped support with the money he earned from his shop, and Noria was simply too young to be involved in all this. Even if neither of them were susceptible to silver poisoning, that didn't mean the killer wouldn't try to take them out if he – or she – discovered they were hot on his trail.

I guess there's always Rylan, I thought bitterly, twirling an inky curl of hair around my index finger as I stared up at the ceiling. My cousin would be more than happy to look into the murders, if only so he could point the blame back at the Mage's Guild and gain one more nail to hammer into the coffin he was trying to create for them. But there was no way for me to get a message to him – mindspeech could only take you so far, and frankly it had been a miracle that Roanas had reached me at all. It was intended to be used in close proximity between shifters while we were in animal form, not as a mental telephone system.

You could probably send him a message if you used your magic.

The thought was almost as intriguing as it was frustrating. If the flashy display of power that landed me in this cell was any indication, I could probably do a whole lot with my magic if I could just figure out how to access it on demand, instead of in a panic. Closing my eyes, I tried to feel for the telltale spark that always lit inside me before an outburst, but there was only a void where it should have been.

My hands clenched into fists as helpless rage overtook me. I wanted to break something, or smash my fists into something satisfying, but I would only break my hands against the concrete walls and then I would have to expend even more energy healing myself. It was so unfair that the mages in this town got to use their magic to elevate themselves above us, while mine only served to drag me down and get me in trouble. The only time it was ever useful was when I was in mortal danger.

Maybe it'll flare up again when the executioner tries to cut off your head.

A kind of dark hope lit in my chest at the thought. If my magic did come to life, I might be able to direct it long enough to make some kind of escape. And if not, maybe I could at least take a few of the slimy bastards with me before I died. Then I would truly be a martyr, just like the reporter guy said.

With that grim, yet oddly comforting thought clutched to my chest, I closed my eyes and waited for the sun to rise so they could come and take me away.

5

An hour after the sun rose, I was clapped in irons and dragged upstairs to the Hall of Justice, which was located on the third floor of the Enforcer's Guild. I'd been in this room, with its stark walls, soaring ceiling and cold, unforgiving benches a handful of times – it was where Enforcers were tried and convicted for their crimes, and it wasn't used often.

Behind the judge's bench stood Maronas Galling, the Captain of the Enforcer's Guild, and on the floor, seated at the prosecutor's bench, were Deputy Talcon and Director Chartis, the Chief Mage's representative and head of the local chapter of the Mage's Guild. The guards escorted me none-too-gently toward the defendant's bench, but not before I saw Comenius and Noria seated in the gallery amongst the handful of people – mostly reporters – who'd chosen to attend. Comenius's face was grave, whereas Noria's heart was in her eyes, her hands twisting nervously in her lap as she watched me. I tried to give her an encouraging smile, but she only bit her lip, her eyes shimmering with fear.

Sighing, I turned away from my friends, knowing that

looking at them would only make me more anxious. Instead, I glanced down at my shackles, and my heart plummeted at the sight of the shimmering runes carved into the iron. I'd seen such runes used once before on a mage, in order to restrain his magic.

So much for trying to take the executioner down with you.

Finally, the Captain stopped shuffling his papers around and looked down at me. He was a commanding figure, with close-cropped steel hair and a matching beard covering his square jaw. His broad shoulders looked as if they bore the weight of command well enough – which they had before he'd let the Main Crew turn everything to shit. Nevertheless, my heart sank at the look of disappointment that flickered briefly in his dark eyes before hardening.

As the moment passed he called the room to order, then turned toward the prosecutor's bench. "Deputy Talcon, do you have the list of charges?"

"I do indeed," Talcon said, rising from his seat. He was dressed in a neatly pressed dark suit, which made me feel inadequate since my hair was a rat's nest and I was still dressed in yesterday's clothes.

"Sunaya Baine has been called before this court today on the charges of possessing magic without a license, and of using magic without a license to kill a shifter. These charges are substantiated by witness statements." I gritted my teeth at his smug tone.

"May I see the statements, please?"

"Of course." Talcon handed a sheaf of papers to Captain Galling.

Captain Galling read the statements out loud. They were from Brin and Nila. My embarrassment was eclipsed by simmering rage that grew with every word. The bastards hadn't bothered to show up on time to save those bunnies, but they didn't have any problem burying me for doing so.

Magorah help me, but did they have no sense of decency at all?

"Well?" Galling asked when he'd finished reading the statements. "Do you have anything to say in your defense, Miss Baine?"

I bit back the scathing remark I *wanted* to say and cleared my throat. "Yes, Captain." My voice was surprisingly steady despite the adrenaline pumping through my veins. "I'd like to point out that I was wearing a protective amulet on my wrist during the attack. Its magic must have activated in response to the rhino shifter's attempt to kill me. That is far more logical than the idea that *I* killed the rhino myself."

"That's a very good story," Director Chartis drawled, drawing my attention toward him. His dark green eyes, which matched the robes he was wearing, assessed me lazily, almost as if he couldn't be bothered with prosecuting me. Nevertheless, he somehow found the energy to press on. "But unfortunately it does not match the evidence. I tested the amulet myself yesterday, and it held no traces of recent magical residue." He drew the amulet out of his sleeve, and I gritted my teeth as he dangled it tauntingly at me. "I'm afraid that means, in plain language, that it hasn't been used recently."

A murmur spread through the crowd and fear crackled through me like a live current. So much for my shitty cover story.

"Besides," the Director continued, "the amount of magic required to disintegrate a rhino shifter would have reduced an amulet of this size and strength to ash. As you can all see, it's quite intact."

"Alright, settle down, settle down," the Captain ordered the room. He looked down at me wearily. "I'm afraid that unless you have anything more to say in your defense, I'm going to have to convict you of using illegal magic."

"The penalty of which," the Director reminded the room, as if he needed to, "is death."

The Captain hesitated. "I think under the circumstances we should be able to reduce it to hard labor in the mines, don't you think? It was self-defense, after all."

The Director shook his head. "Whether or not it was self-defense is completely irrelevant," he said dispassionately. "The death penalty is mandatory in such cases, especially since the accused is too old to be trained. She cannot be allowed to run amuck with her magic unchecked."

Rage boiled up inside me so fast I swore steam came out of my ears. How dare this man stand there and dismiss my life so casually, as if I were a rabid dog that needed to be put down! I opened my mouth to rip him a new one, but I was cut off by a voice in the back.

"Captain Galling, I would like permission to speak."

The sound of rustling fabric filled the air as everyone, including me, turned around to see Comenius standing in the gallery, his jaw set, determination gleaming in his cornflower blue eyes. The Director and Talcon began to protest at the same time, but Captain Galling held up his hand for silence.

"Speak," he commanded.

Comenius took a deep breath and squared his shoulders. "It is my belief that Miss Baine has committed an act of magic worthy of a mage, due to the fact that she is half-mage herself. Because of this, I believe that she should be allowed to appeal to the Chief Mage himself, rather than simply tried and executed in a courtroom that is strictly meant for Enforcers."

It was a testament to the strength of my willpower that my jaw didn't crash straight to the floor. Appeal to the Chief Mage? Was Comenius mad? The Chief Mage wasn't just the ruler of Solantha – he governed the entire state of Canalo and was one of the most powerful mages in the Federation of Northia. Even if he could help me, I doubted he would have time – he barely ever emerged from his palace, busy with whatever matters of state and magic he was usually concerned with.

Maybe that's the point. If the Chief Mage is so busy, it'll be a while before he's able to see me. Weeks, maybe even months. During that time I'm sure to find a way to escape.

"That's ridiculous," Talcon sputtered, his face growing red as he jumped to his feet. His fists clenched at his sides as he faced the Captain. "Sunaya is no more a mage than I am!"

"On the contrary," the Director said, sounding somewhat reluctant, "she would have to be at least half-mage to have pulled off the display of power the reports suggest, whereas you are a full human, Deputy Talcon."

I would have laughed at the murderous look Talcon shot Chartis, if the situation hadn't been so dire. In any case, the Director was completely unruffled by Talcon's outburst. It dawned on me that he might not actually care about the proceedings either way; he was just here to make sure the Chief Mage's laws were enforced.

"What are you suggesting, then, Director Chartis?" Captain Galling asked, his brow furrowing. "Should we execute Miss Baine, or allow her to appeal to the Chief Mage?"

The Director sighed, running a hand through his wavy dark hair as if the idea of being tasked with making an actual decision was just too bothersome. "You can certainly order her execution if you want," he told the Captain. "But if the Chief Mage found out that he was circumvented by not allowing him to respond to an appeal, I imagine he would be most displeased."

"Very well." The Captain banged his gavel, and as he looked down at me I swore there was a twinkle in his eye. "We shall refer the matter to the Chief Mage for a final ruling. You are all dismissed."

I wasn't exactly dancing a happy jig when the guards escorted me back to my cell, but my heart did feel significantly lighter now that the Captain had granted me a reprieve. With the way bureaucratic red tape liked to pile up in this city, I was unlikely to get my audience with the Chief Mage for some time, maybe even a month if I was lucky. That was plenty of time for me to figure out how to escape, I thought as the cell door clanged shut behind me.

My best bet, of course, was to contact Rylan and have him get me out of here. He'd happily take me underground in an instant, and since he and the others had already proven successful at evading capture, I was relatively certain that I could, too.

The only drawback was that I would have to pledge myself to the Resistance, something I had been avoiding for as long as Rylan had been trying to recruit me because I was afraid of how they would view me if they found out I was half-mage. But since that cat was out of the bag, there was really nothing to lose now, was there?

Decided, I sat cross-legged atop my cot and waited for Comenius and Noria to come and visit me. We hadn't had a chance to say more than two words to each other after my hearing, and I knew that they would be anxious to see me. It was only a matter of time before Noria wore the guards down with her insistence.

Sure enough, the door at the end of the hall opened several hours later, and I heard the telltale clop of the heavy uniform shoes the guards wore. But instead of three pairs of feet, as I'd expected, I heard four.

"Time to go, Baine." Two sets of guards stopped outside my door, dressed in the blue and black uniform that marked all of Privacy Guards' employees – a security firm that contracted out to a variety of government agencies and businesses, including the Enforcer's Guild and the Mage's Guild. The guard who spoke to me held up the same set of rune-protected cuffs from before, and a current of anxiety ran through me as I eyed them.

"Time to go?" I echoed as the cell door opened. I presented my hands and allowed the guards to cuff me – there was little point to fighting back at this stage. "Go where?" I had a feeling he wasn't referring to the visitors' room.

"To Solantha Palace, of course. The Chief Mage is expecting you."

I reeled as the guards pulled me from the cell, two flanking me with their meaty hands clamped firmly around my upper arms, one leading the way, and the other bringing up the rear. Apparently no chances were being taken with me – the guards on either side of me were shifters, and the one up ahead smelled of burnt sugar, indicating that he was one of the low-level mages Privacy Guard employed for situations like this.

"Y-you're taking me to the Chief Mage *now*?" I spluttered, digging my heels into the floor like a petulant child. Not that it did me any good as they marched me out into the main hall – the heels of my boots simply screeched against the scuffed tile, drawing the attention of every Enforcer in the hall.

"That's right." The mage guard leading the way spoke without turning his head.

"But that's ridiculous," I protested as they led me down the front steps and into a horse-drawn carriage waiting at the curb. My heart sank as I saw the Chief Mage's personal emblem emblazoned on the side of the carriage, a large blue shield with a golden rune composed of a series of interconnected brush strokes – the traditional symbol for magic with a few embellishments added that I imagined were unique to the Chief Mage – painted into the center. "He doesn't have time to see me now."

"I wasn't aware you were so in tune with the Chief Mage's

schedule." The mage guard arched a brow at me as the two shifter guards escorted me into the cab, which had dark, cushioned seats and was large enough to seat six. I gritted my teeth as all four of them settled into the cab around me, resentment oozing from my pores as the mage guard rapped on the inner roof of the carriage, telling the driver to get moving. The carriage lurched into motion, but I didn't budge since I was squeezed in between the two hulking shifter guards. I glared up at them both, but they didn't even deign to look at me – they just stared straight ahead.

Guess a lowly shifter-hybrid like me didn't merit their attention.

Biting back a sigh, I relaxed against the cushiony seats as much as I was able and settled in for the ride. Solantha Palace was located in the Mage's Quarter, an affluent neighborhood located in the upper left quadrant of Solantha, a thirty-minute carriage drive from Rowanville. I'd been to the Mage's Quarter a handful of times on Enforcer business, but I'd never had any cause to visit the Solantha Palace. It was the seat of power for the Mage's Guild and the residence of the Chief Mage. The idea of stepping behind those magically reinforced castle walls and into the domain of the most powerful mage in Solantha was enough to make the hairs stand up on the back of my neck even on a good day.

As the carriage bumped and jostled over the city streets, I stared out the window and tried to recall what I knew of the Chief Mage. Admittedly, it wasn't much. He'd only taken up the mantle a few years ago, and I'd been out of town during his inauguration ceremony so I didn't even get the chance to see him. Dammit, but what was his name?

Iannis ar'Sannin.

Ah. I remembered now – he was from Manuc, a small country thousands of miles from here. I wasn't sure why he'd come to the Northia Federation or how long he'd been here, but apparently he did the Federation Council some huge favor, which was why they'd appointed him as the Chief Mage of Canalo. There had been a lot of worried talk amongst all the races that he would change things for the worse, but so far the status quo seemed to have held. Since that effectively meant that my taxes still went to supporting a group of selfish mages that didn't give a rat's ass about my interests and were a breath away from executing me, I didn't consider that a good thing.

The cityscape around us changed from small roads between cramped apartment buildings and shopping centers to wide, open streets lined with townhouses. Rows of strange trees with blue trunks and star-shaped flowers that sparkled in the sun drew my eye, but I only scowled at their magically engineered beauty. Similarly, the front lawns of the houses we passed were graced by multi-hued and strangely shaped shrubbery not designed by Mother Nature. I shook my head at the sight of a poplar tree in another yard whose trunk had been dyed a brilliant fuchsia. Instead of blossoms, tiny golden bells hung from its branches, and as we passed the tree actually *waved*, sending a tinkling of bells through the air. Just another display of mages flaunting their superiority – except this time they were competing against each other instead of us lowly shifters and humans.

Eventually we passed through that neighborhood as well, and into an area where elegant houses and mansions butted up against the coastline, vying for the coveted view of Solantha Bay. I swallowed as I caught sight of Solantha Palace jutting above the others in the distance, and darted my eyes back to my lap, knowing soon enough I'd be seeing it up close and personal.

The journey ended all too soon, and as the guards pulled me from the carriage sweat broke out at the edges of my temples and in the palms of my hands. My eyes darted around, hardly able to appreciate the old, elegant décor of the neighboring houses around me, or the magnificent view of the Firegate Bridge that spanned the length of the bay in the distance. I was far more aware of the late afternoon sun beating against the top of my head, and the palace that loomed directly in front of me – a sprawling white stone edifice with red tile capping the roofs and turrets. The beauty of the ornate carvings in the stone and the sparkling glass windows were lost on me as I was marched through the meticulously trimmed gardens and up a wide stone staircase – all I saw was a monument to the absolute power and greed that had corrupted so many of the mages in this city, and it filled me with a simmering resentment that made me forget about my anxiety.

That resentment only grew as a servant dressed in blue and gold – the Chief Mage's colors – opened the door to receive us, and the guards led me into a large, elegant foyer. The sun shining in through the large stained glass windows splashed colorful patterns on the wood-inlaid flooring, and tasteful oil paintings of landscapes hung from the walls. The décor was warmer than I expected – my mind had conjured stone and marble and crystal – but it still spoke of a lush extravagance that was undeserved, in my opinion.

There was a reception desk in the center, manned by an old mage, but we didn't approach it. Another mage dressed in the grey robes of an apprentice was already descending the grand double staircase that curved around the foyer to greet us.

"Hello," the young mage greeted me in a stiff voice. "My name is Elgarion ar'Manit. I am Director Chartis's apprentice, and I've been sent to escort you to the audience chamber." His dark eyes glittered with disdain as he took me in. "He will be pleased you've arrived so promptly."

"I was actually thinking I may have arrived too soon," I responded coolly, lifting my chin to look the mage in the eye.

Just because I was quaking in my boots didn't mean I had to let any of these people know I was intimidated. "Surely the Chief Mage has more important things to do than bother with someone as insignificant as me?"

Elgarion wrinkled his nose. "Yes, that was my opinion too," he agreed with a hint of annoyance. "But for some reason he's taken an interest in your case and demanded to see you immediately."

An interest in my case? Just what the hell was that supposed to mean? A chill went through me as Elgarion turned and led the way up the right side of the staircase. The last thing I needed was the most powerful mage in the city taking more than a passing interest in me, especially when the man was known for holing himself up in this admittedly gorgeous palace to perform magical experiments. I wasn't interested in escaping my death sentence only to end up as a lab rat.

The apprentice led us down a carpeted hallway, and as we passed by several open doorways I caught glimpses of crystal chandeliers, rich, colorful drapes and carpeting, and parquet floors. The number of rooms bordered on ridiculous – the Chief Mage could house a third of Solantha's homeless population based on what I'd seen so far.

I bet that would just mess with his magical energy, I sneered inwardly. *Having a bunch of humans and shifters running around breathing his sanctified air.*

The hallway branched off into a separate wing of the palace, and my nose wrinkled as the scent of magic intensified abruptly. *This must be where the Chief Mage does most of his work,* I thought apprehensively as Elgarion stopped outside a set of double doors made of dark, heavy wood.

"Prepare yourself," he told me sternly. "We are about to enter the audience chamber."

Well la-dee-dah, I thought crossly as he turned to open the doors – and then nearly swallowed my tongue as I was ushered into the room. I was expecting something smaller, like a fancy office, but this chamber was more like a hall. Tall, gleaming mahogany columns held up the soaring ceiling, and the walls, of pale pink granite veined with gold, gleamed in the warm glow of multiple lamps. A long blue and gold carpet carved a path through the center of the parquet floor, and the guards escorted me to the other side of it, where a tall man dressed in dark blue robes awaited us behind a large desk made from the same pale pink granite as the walls. Standing off to his right was Director Chartis, who stared imperiously down at me, his arms tucked into the folds of his dark green robes.

As I was hauled before the Chief Mage, I shoved aside my awe and anxiety and conjured up the simmering resentment from earlier so that I didn't show weakness. And then I met the eyes of the man who held my fate in his hands.

"Iannis ar'Sannin, the Chief Mage of Solantha," Elgarion announced, as if the Chief Mage needed any introduction. I fought the urge to roll my eyes as the apprentice bowed low. "Sir, I have brought the prisoner you requested."

As if, I thought irritably. *All you did was meet me at the door and walk me up a flight of stairs.* The guards had done most of the work, and as usual, a mage was taking the credit.

The Chief Mage said nothing as he studied me impassively, and I stared back, not knowing what else to do. *He's handsome,* I thought, and was immediately annoyed with myself. But it was true. Hair the color of dark cherry wood framed his oblong face, and though his nose was a little too long to qualify as classically handsome, his sharply defined cheekbones and strong jaw still placed him firmly in the good-looking camp. But it was his eyes that were truly arresting – they were an iridescent violet, unlike anything I'd ever seen in my life. The only people I'd heard of who had eyes like this were the Tua, a magical race of beings who lived an ocean away, and were so reclusive they were rarely seen unless they chose to show themselves.

Umm, hello??? You're standing before a high-level mage who can change his appearance at will. He could make his irises rainbow-colored if he wanted to!

I snorted, both at the image and at myself for getting caught up by the Chief Mage's looks. Without his magical glamour he probably looked like any other human on the street. This display was just another way of trying to show that mages were better.

The mage in question arched an eyebrow. "Is there something that amuses you about this situation, Miss Baine?"

I bristled at his cool, slightly condescending voice, which carried a whisper of a musical accent. "I'm just wondering why you don't drop the glamour and show me what your real face looks like." I shrugged. "No reason to impress the criminal, right?"

A flicker of surprise disturbed the austere expression on his alabaster face, but before I had time to gloat at the reaction I'd caused, the guard on my left punched me in the kidney. Hard. A gasp flew from my lips as the left side of my body exploded with pain.

"Show some respect!" the guard growled.

Like hell. "That. Fucking. Hurt!" I snarled, baring my fangs at him. Before he had a chance to hit me again, I raised my knee high and brought my boot crashing down on his foot, scraping my heel along his shin as I went. The big bastard howled, and I used the opportunity to jump away from him. The guard to my right moved forward, and I swung my right elbow up as he closed in, smashing it under his chin. He staggered back into the third guard, who had to pause mid-rush to catch the guy. The sharp ring of steel caught my attention as the fourth guard drew his sword and aimed it at me, prepared to deliver a killing blow.

Fuck, I thought as I turned to face him. *I could really use my crescent knives right now.* They were great for catching an opponent's weapon. I raised my manacled hands, thinking the best I could hope for was that his sword would slice through my chains so I could regain full use of my hands, because my magic sure as hell wasn't going to step in and save me this time.

"ENOUGH!"

We all froze as the Chief Mage slammed his open palms against the stone desk, the sound reverberating off the granite walls. His violet eyes burned with cold fury as he turned to the Director, who'd stood off to the side next to his gaping apprentice the entire time, watching the fight. "Get them out of here." His voice was as frigid as Solantha Bay in the middle of a snowstorm.

"Yes sir." Director Chartis motioned toward the two guards who were still standing to collect me, and I bared my fangs at them, fully prepared to be dragged back to my cell kicking and biting.

"Not her," the Chief Mage snapped before they could lay a hand on me. "The guards."

The Director froze. "You want me to remove the *guards*?" he sputtered. "After that violent display from this... this beastly girl?"

"Are you questioning my ability to defend myself against a hybrid?" The Chief Mage asked coolly. His face had turned to stone again, no hint of the emotion from earlier, but that was okay – I was furious enough for the both of us. How dare he refer to me so dismissively!

"N-no," Chartis faltered, glancing at me uncertainly as I glared at both of them. "It's just... this is against protocol."

"I'll remind you that I'm in charge here," the Chief Mage said mildly. "Now have these guards escorted outside, or I will have *you* escorted out as well. And if that happens, rest assured you will not be coming back."

The Director's face paled at the threat. He nodded tightly at his boss, and turned to shoot me a death glare before waving the guards out the door. The sound of the double doors closing behind them echoed through the chamber with an awful sense of finality.

Before the Chief Mage could address me again, a hidden door to his right slid open, and a brown wolf shifter with yellow eyes prowled into the room.

"Ah, Fenris." The Chief Mage turned to greet him. "You are late."

I narrowed my eyes as the wolf shifter settled next to the Chief Mage and regarded me balefully. I glared back at him, disgust rising up in me at the sight of a shifter, any shifter, relegating himself to little more than a mage's pet.

"I would not be so quick to judge a book by its cover."

I blinked, startled as the wolf shifter's deep voice echoed in my head. I hadn't actually expected him to speak to me, and what was he talking about anyway? Was he reading my mind somehow?

"Director Chartis," the Chief Mage said, drawing my attention away from Fenris. "Please read the charges."

"With pleasure, sir." Chartis pulled a sheet of paper from the sleeve of his robe, then listed off the same charges that Talcon had read, back at the earlier hearing. But this time, instead of being filled with anger, a kind of hopelessness stole through me. The Chief Mage didn't look like he had a single ounce of compassion in his magical bones. What made me think that the outcome of this appeal was going to be any different?

"I see." The Chief Mage drummed his long fingers on the table as he regarded me with those strangely colored eyes. I fought the urge to squirm beneath his piercing gaze, and instead lifted my chin and stared back at him as if I could see into the depths of his stone heart.

Not that I actually could. But as Talcon had so sweetly informed me yesterday, I *was* good at bluffing.

"Why was Miss Baine not identified as a magic user during the mandatory school testing?" the Chief Mage asked, never taking his eyes from me. "According to her file she attended a state-run educational facility."

I blinked. The man had read my *file*? Maybe he really *was* interested in me. My insides squirmed uncomfortably at the thought.

Chartis cleared his throat. "She did, sir, and the tests were run. As to why they failed, I cannot say, but her status as a magic user is beyond reasonable doubt now. It's an open-and-shut case."

Fenris growled at that, and I glanced down at him, curious as he turned his glare on the Director. Was the Chief Mage's pet shifter actually on my side?

Maybe he's not so bad after all.

"I'm not quite so eager to rush to judgment," the Chief Mage said, giving the Director a mildly disapproving frown for his trouble before turning his violet gaze back on me. "What do you have to say about all this, Miss Baine? Why was your magical talent not discovered during your school years?"

"Why don't you tell me?" I challenged. Truthfully, though, that question had been burning in the back of my mind for many years. I'd never understood how I had managed to slip past the magic testing even though my magical outbursts, when they happened, were so powerful. Quite frankly it was amazing I'd been able to go undetected all these years from everyone. "It's your test. I don't know, and don't care."

"I'm not entirely certain I believe you, Miss Baine." The Chief Mage steepled his fingers. He studied me as if I were an interesting puzzle that had been presented to him as a way to pass the time. "And I find that unlike you, I do care. I don't like the idea of citizens slipping past the test so easily, especially one with a magical talent as strong as yours. I'll need to study your case further to determine exactly how it was done and to make sure it does not happen again."

"Study?" I echoed as images of me being strapped to a metal table under a set of bright lights danced through my mind. "As in, like, an experiment?"

To my surprise, the Chief Mage's lips curved, a hint of amusement sparkling in his eyes. "Rest assured that no part of your body will be altered. Experimenting on humanoid subjects is a long banned practice, in any case."

"Right." I let out a breath. *Because I fully expect you to follow the letter of your own laws.* However, something about him made me wonder whether or not he really did hold himself to the same standards he was subjecting everyone else to.

"Argon, have her taken to a secure location where she can be kept until I am ready for her," the Chief Mage ordered the Director. "Also, remove the shackles from her wrists. They won't be necessary any longer."

"Sir," the Director protested, though I wasn't sure whether he objected to removing my shackles or the fact that the Chief Mage wasn't calling for my head. But a single frown from the Chief Mage silenced him.

"Very well," he sighed, coming forward to remove my shackles. I held my wrists out to him with a cheeky grin, and he glared at me as he passed a hand over them, muttering some kind of incantation. The shackles glowed briefly before they dropped from my wrists into his outstretched hand. "Don't think this is some kind of vacation, Miss Baine. You will be brought to account for your actions soon enough."

I smirked as he and Elgarion escorted me out of the room to

the guards waiting in the hall beyond. Maybe that was true, but I had another day to live, and that was good enough for me. The longer I stayed alive, the greater my chances of escape. And once I was out of this forsaken place, I could solve the poison murders and join the Resistance to overthrow the mages once and for all.

6

I'm not sure why I expected to be led to a five-star chamber instead of a sparse tower room with rough-hewn furniture and iron bars fitted over the single window. Maybe it was because every single room I'd seen in this palace was dripping with wealth and grandeur, and I assumed they could have spared one of those rooms for me. But in any case, there I was, twiddling my thumbs as I sat on my narrow mattress, wondering what I was supposed to do with myself now.

At least I have a nice view, I thought sullenly as I gazed out at the glittering bay. My eyes followed one end of the Firegate Bridge to the other, the metal, which was enchanted to look red, contrasting starkly against the pale blue sky. A mirror to the Bay Bridge on the other side –though that one lacked the gorgeous coloring – it was the pride and joy of Solantha, a feat created through a combination of magic and human engineering, and proof that humans and mages *could* work together to create things if they really wanted to.

If only mages thought that way all the time, I mused. But they only collaborated with humans when it served their purpose, and from what I'd heard, they'd only collaborated on the bridges because a human engineer had brought up the project and designed the schematics. The long-lived mages were the opposite of innovative, and would have never undertaken such a project without human involvement.

Shaking off my melancholy thoughts, I returned my attention to the beauty of the bridge itself. My eyes traced its sleek line all the way down to the other side, then traveled further along the coast where a small island rested smack dab between the two bridges.

Forget the view, I thought to myself, shuddering a little. *At least I'm not over there.* That little spot of land was Prison Isle, where Solantha's convicts were sent to serve their sentences. I'd gone over there once, to question a prisoner regarding a bounty I was chasing, and the memory of the heavy scent of depression combined with filth and squalor suddenly made me appreciate my little room. Sure, it was basically a closet with a bed and a dresser inside it, but it was a hell of a lot safer and cleaner than any of the cells on Prison Isle.

My stomach growled, calling attention to the fact that I hadn't eaten anything since that sandwich Talcon had given me. I frowned, wondering where I could find the kitchen. Elgarion had informed me that I had free run of the palace and could go into any room that wasn't locked, but he hadn't given me a map or explained where anything was. Hell, I didn't even know where the bathrooms were around here, which would be great to know because I could really use a shower. My hair was getting a little greasy, and I still smelled of alcohol, ash and old sweat.

Stripping off my leather jacket, I left it atop the dresser and wandered down the spiral staircase in my tank top and leather pants. It didn't take me too long to find a servant, who directed me to the bathroom in the East Wing with a beady eye and a warning not to linger too long.

I quickly found out from peeking into a few of the rooms

that the East Wing was where all the nice, well-behaved people got to stay, as it was practically brimming with sumptuous bedrooms. Which must have been why Snappy over there had told me to make it fast, because I wasn't a guest, but a glorified prisoner.

Then again, most of the rooms were empty, so maybe the Chief Mage really did stick his guests in the tower. It would definitely discourage return visitors, and since he didn't seem to be interested in entertaining, I wouldn't put it past him.

Thankfully, even reprobates like me were allowed to use the bathrooms, and I was pleasantly surprised to discover a claw-foot tub with running hot water. I hadn't been sure there would be hot water, since every single source of light I'd seen in the castle was fueled by spelled candles, indicating a lack of electricity. I figured the mages probably just spelled the water hot themselves when they used the facilities. But even though the Chief Mage, like most of his kind, refused to use technology himself, apparently he wasn't above using his magic to achieve the same effects to provide hot water for everyone. I frowned, wondering whether he'd enchanted the water pipes himself or if it was something the Mage's Guild maintained. From what little I understood of magic, using it to run hot water through such a huge place was no mean feat.

My grumbling stomach urged me through my bath faster than I liked, and with a fluffy white robe wrapped around my body I headed back up to my tower room to dress. As I was debating whether or not I should wear the same pair of underwear for the third day in a row, it occurred to me that I should look in the dresser. Maybe the last 'guest' had left behind something I could wear.

My eyes nearly popped out of my skull when I opened the top drawer. There was a lot more than just someone's discarded granny panties inside here – the drawer held several pairs of underwear and tops. A chill went through me as I pulled out a pair of basic white panties and held them up to my hips – they were exactly my size. The black tank top I pulled out was the same, as were the stretchy black cotton pants I pulled out of the second drawer.

What the fuck? Had the Chief Mage ordered clothing for me? There was enough here for at least a week's worth of outfits. The only reason I could fathom as to why these would be here, was because he'd already been planning to keep me here for an extended length of time.

The thought filled me with a combination of hope and apprehension. Hope, because it meant I had at least a week to figure out how to escape this place, and apprehension because I had no idea what the Chief Mage had planned for me. Maybe he was lying, and he really did plan on using me for one of his experiments. I had no trouble envisioning his face hovering over me while I lay on a table, his cold violet eyes observing me clinically as he used his magic to scramble my intestines or something.

The very thought made me lose my appetite.

I should refuse these clothes, I thought, staring down at the underwear in my hands with disgust. Putting them on would be like accepting a gift, and the last thing I wanted was to be beholden to the Chief Mage in any way.

Never be too proud to take advantage of the resources around you. Roanas's voice echoed in my ears. *A silver rope might burn, but you can still use it to climb out of a pit.*

Tears stung the corners of my eyes, and I dressed hurriedly. If I allowed myself to dwell on my thoughts too long, I would lapse into the grief hovering like a dark cloud above my head, just waiting for the right opportunity to burst. I couldn't allow myself the luxury of a breakdown, so I pushed down the emotion and did my best not to focus on it.

I found a door that led from the East Wing onto the grounds, but as soon as I tried to step across the threshold an invisible barrier pushed me back. I grit my teeth as I tried again, and then a third time, to no success. *Wards.* I grimaced, noting the runes carved into the molding. It was unlikely they'd been keyed specifically to me, but clearly they wouldn't let anyone who wasn't cleared exit the building, and I was definitely on the *Not Authorized to Leave* list.

Determined, I searched the palace for other exits, but every time I tried to pass through a door or window the same invisible barrier pushed me back. This explained why none of the mages or servants that passed me in the halls seemed to care what I did or where I went – there was no chance of me escaping unless the Chief Mage decided to change the wards. An hour later, I was tired, pissed *and* hungry, so I decided to wander down to the kitchen and find some food.

Despite the lack of a map, it wasn't hard to find the kitchen – all I had to do was follow the scent of baking goods down a set of stairs that led from the foyer to a raised basement.

I moved down a stone corridor and took a right, then smiled as I found myself standing in a large, commercial-style kitchen. The space was pretty open, with all of the wood and coal-powered appliances flush against the far wall, and several large counters placed near the front where the kitchen staff chopped, kneaded and mixed various ingredients. The smell of roasting chicken and baking bread filled my nostrils, and I closed my eyes, inhaling greedily.

When I opened them, a woman in a chef's hat and coat stood in front of me with a scowl, a wooden spoon propped on her wide hip. "Can I help you?"

"Umm, yeah." My stomach growled, and I gave her my best puppy dog smile. Which, in retrospect, might not have actually worked since I'm a feline. "I haven't eaten all day and I'm looking for some food. Do you have anything to spare?"

The woman's eyes narrowed as she looked me up and down. "You're that hybrid, aren't you? The one Lord Iannis has under observation?"

I grimaced inwardly, both at her use of the word *hybrid* and the fact that she'd called the Chief Mage *Lord*. By Magorah, did that man really need a reason for his head to get more inflated? But then again, it *was* a proper title for him.

"Yes, that's me," I said brightly. If I was going to own it, I might as well wear it proudly.

"Fine. Wait here."

I frowned as the woman disappeared into the pantry, eyeing the freshly baked bread and roasted chicken sitting on the countertop not ten feet from my elbow. Why was she going to the pantry when there was perfectly good food here?

The answer became obvious when she bustled back out into the kitchen again, a hunk of brown bread in one hand and a wedge of cheese in the other. "Here," she said, thrusting them both at me as if she couldn't wait to be rid of them.

"Thanks," I muttered, testing the bread with a squeeze of my fingers. It was rock hard, and the cheese was liberally speckled with mold. "Didn't realize I had the words 'garbage can' tattooed on my forehead."

The woman completely ignored me, and I sighed, slinking out of the kitchen with my proverbial tail tucked between my legs. It seemed as though the kitchen staff and servants had all been given the 'hate on sight' order when told about my presence, and I wondered whether the Chief Mage himself was to blame for that, or one of his lackeys. Magorah knew I'd pissed off practically everyone in the audience chamber, so it could have been any one of them.

I really have to work on my diplomacy skills.

I sat on the floor in the hall with my back against the wall and nibbled on my five-star fare, my ears alert as I listened to the kitchen staff gossip, hoping to catch any clues about the shifter murders. But all they talked about were their families and friends, tomorrow's menu – which nearly made me cry because it sounded delicious and would probably be off limits to me – and which of the servants were boinking each other. The latter could have been interesting if I were able to use it as blackmail, but I seriously doubted the Chief Mage could be bothered with that kind of thing.

He's bothering with you, isn't he? My heart stuttered a little as I remembered the way he'd looked at me, as if he could actually see beyond my tough shell and into the real me. Sure, the idea scared the shit out of me, but the idea of someone actually knowing my secrets and accepting me instead of writing me off as a failure or a problem was highly appealing.

Then I looked down at what was left of my rock-bread and snorted. The Chief Mage didn't give a flying fuck about me beyond the puzzle that I presented to him. Clearly my pre-heat hormones were starting to filter in and were addling my brain. I still had several months before I actually went into heat, but my body usually ramped itself up for the occasion, building up so that by the time it came I would be a horny, ravenous monster.

It was one of the only things I hated about being a shifter. The fact that it only happened twice a year was no consolation.

I went back into the kitchen and nagged the cook for some more bread and cheese, and then took my crappy meal back upstairs so I could roam the halls. Eventually I found a deserted storage area full of broken furniture and tools. It didn't take me long to clear a space. I sat down on the floor and closed my eyes, pulling in slow, deep breaths through my nostrils and exhaling them gently through my mouth. It took longer than usual, but the meditative exercise had the desired effect – my heart rate slowed, my nerves stopped zinging, and the thoughts clamoring in my head gradually faded away, leaving me with a sense of peace.

It was time to train.

I put myself through a set of simple hand-to-hand forms, starting with the basic ones and moving on to lengthier, more complex movements. Doing the forms was as instinctive as breathing – I'd been practicing Kan-Zao, an ancient martial art developed in Garai, ever since Roanas had taken me in. He'd learned the art himself from a Garaian adept while living abroad, and had been a master in his own right.

Finished with the forms, I looked around the storage room for something I could use for weapons practice. My crescent knives or chakrams would have been ideal, but I would settle for any implement that could be fashioned into a staff or blade. If I did find a way to break out, I would likely have to go up against some of the guards, and I needed to be prepared for that.

I was just contemplating the idea of breaking off the legs of an old chair and fashioning them into stakes I could hide in my boots when I heard movement at the door.

"What are you doing in here?" Elgarion asked, stepping into the room. His dark eyes narrowed as he surveyed the space, no doubt noticing that I'd moved things around.

I folded my arms and arched a brow. "I thought I was allowed to go wherever I wanted, so long as the door wasn't locked?"

Elgarion pressed his lips into a thin line. "That's true, but it seems like you're looking for something."

I blinked. I was still holding the chair in my hands... upside down. I righted it hastily and set it back down on the dusty stone floor. "I was just taking a break from training."

"You mean self-defense?" A smug look crossed his face as his eyes scanned my form, lingering on the sheen of sweat that marked my forehead and exposed arms. "I wouldn't waste your time on that, hybrid. You're not going to live much longer, and any mage could easily best you regardless of your physical skills."

"Are you interested in my 'physical skills'?" I purred, closing the distance between us. Elgarion took a step back as I fluttered my eyelashes at him, wanting to wipe the smug look off his face for once. "Is that why you're following me around?"

"W-what? No!" His pale skin flushed, and I heard his pulse speed up. "I'm just doing my job! I would never have such lascivious thoughts, especially about a hybrid like you."

I ignored that jab as I leaned in closer to him. It helped that I knew I was getting to him, but I was also getting used to the insult.

"I'm sure you feel better telling yourself that," I said, giving him a slow wink. "But you know what I think?"

"What?" He sounded slightly out of breath.

I straightened, raking his body with a scathing look. "I think you're just an untried boy who hides behind his magic and his textbooks and doesn't know anything about the real world," I sneered. "If you think magic can protect you from everything, kid, then go ahead and try to beat me. I've had to take down a mage or two in my line of work, and I guarantee you'd be child's play compared to a fully-trained mage."

His face turned beet red, and I waited with baited breath to see what he would do next. It was true that I'd brought in a few mages, but they had been low-level ones, and I'd been armed with protective amulets and weapons. Not to mention that I didn't really know how well-trained Elgarion was – since he was born into a mage family he would have been using magic his entire life, unlike me. Right now I had no amulets or weapons, only my natural-born talents, and I was interested in seeing whether or not my magic would work to defend me within the palace walls.

Of course, my magic would only activate if he actually tried to kill me. So maybe this wasn't the smartest idea.

In the end, he merely bared his teeth at me in an impressive mimicry of my own sneer. "I have better things to do than deal with a lowly hybrid like you," he said haughtily. I stifled a snicker as he turned on his heel and walked off with his nose in the air. These mages all walked around with sticks up their asses, and all it took was a little poke for them to go rigid.

With a shake of my head, I closed the door behind me, and continued my search for a weapon.

SIX HOURS LATER, I wearily trudged back down to the kitchens in search of food. I'd trained until I'd exhausted myself, then dragged my butt back to my tower room to try and sleep, but between the crushing sense of loss that filled me whenever I was left alone with my thoughts and the hunger pangs that gnawed at my stomach, getting shut-eye was impossible. So I waited until I was sure that dinner had been served and cleaned up, then crept back downstairs so I could sneak some food from the larder that wasn't rock bread and fuzzy cheese.

As I expected, the kitchen was deserted, not even a mouse hanging around to observe my theft. There was no food sitting on the countertops, so I broke into the pantry in search of something palatable. It didn't take me long to strike gold – a loaf of relatively fresh bread on one of the shelves, and a piece of smoked salmon wrapped in butcher's paper.

"Who knew fish and bread could make someone so happy," I muttered as I alternated between stuffing mouthfuls of food into my mouth and into a paper bag I'd found. I could have stayed

there all night scarfing down food, but even *my* damaged sense
of self-preservation told me it would be unwise to linger.

I crammed as much food into the bag as it could possibly
hold, and walked out of the pantry with a spring in my step and
a smile on my face. Sure, this wasn't a five-star meal, but it was
better than stale bread and cheese, and I was looking forward to
hightailing it back to my room so I could enjoy it.

Unfortunately, someone was waiting for me in the kitchen.

"Just what do you think you're doing?" the guard leaning
against one of the countertops asked. He was the human one
who'd escorted me to the audience chamber earlier along with
the others, and from his cocky stance and the gleam in his eye, it
was clear he was looking for some payback.

"Getting some food." I pulled the loaf of bread out of the bag
so he could see it. "A little bread, a little meat. Why, you
want some?"

He narrowed his eyes. "I don't know," he drawled, drawing
his short sword from its sheath. "Seems like you're stealing to
me. I'm gonna have to teach you a lesson for that."

He charged me, raising the sword up with both hands as he
moved in with a slashing strike, obviously thinking he had the
upper hand since I was unarmed. But I'd prepared for this. I
pulled the brass drawer handles I'd pilfered from one of the
broken dressers from my jacket pocket and slipped them around
my knuckles as I dodged the blow. He whirled around, tracking
my motion, his shoes scuffing loudly against the stone floor, and
attempted another slashing strike.

This time, instead of moving away I moved in, bringing up
my knuckles so I could catch the blow with my drawer handles,
just as I would have done with my crescent knives. Unfortunately the handles didn't cover my hands as well as the knives
did, and I winced inwardly as the blade grazed my fingers, sharp
pain slicing into my flesh.

"What the fu–" he began, his eyes wide with confusion, and I wasted no time, pulling one of my makeshift stakes out and stabbing him in the joint where his arm connected to his torso. He fell back screaming as he crashed into one of the counters, his hand flying to the bloody stake embedded in his flesh, and I smirked. Even if he pulled that thing out right now – which wasn't a good idea – he wouldn't be able to use his sword arm again to fight me.

"What's going on down there?" a male voice shouted, and I winced. The sound of footsteps thundering down the stairs outside had me looking around frantically for an escape route, but there wasn't one, and before I knew it three more guards had filed into the kitchen, their swords drawn.

"So much for showing mercy," I muttered, glaring at the now-whimpering guard slumped against the counter. If I'd killed him he wouldn't have screamed, and I wouldn't be in this mess right now. Served me right.

"You!" the guard in the lead shouted, jabbing the point of his sword at me. "You tried to kill Harry!"

"Are you kidding?" I threw my hands up in the air, fully prepared to argue for my life, but the guards simply rushed me, in no mood to talk. I flung my second stake in their direction to distract them and leapt over the counter where Whiny – or was it Harry? – was still sobbing his delicate little heart out, making a beeline for the exit.

The sound of metal sang through the air, and the tip of a short sword plunged into my upper back. Blood poured from my searing shoulder, and I cried out as one of the guards slammed me into the wall, a dark-haired guy with cold eyes and cruel lips.

"Well, well, well," the assassin-guard mocked, his cruel lips curving into an even crueler smile as he pressed his body against mine. "Cat got your tongue?"

I bared my teeth at him, which was less intimidating than

it sounds because I didn't even have enough energy to elongate my fangs. I was tapped out in every way possible, and the guard knew it as he pressed his hard chest against mine, wrapping his hand around the blade of his sword. The scent of his coppery blood mingled with mine as the blade cut into his hand, and I swallowed at the manic gleam in his eye. This guy was nuts, and should never have been hired by Privacy Guard, let alone the Chief Mage. I was almost certain that the Chief Mage himself would never have allowed this guy on his payroll if he knew the guy carried around this kind of bloodlust.

"I don't see why the other guards are so afraid of you," he sneered, his dark eyes boring into my own. "You're nothing but a pussy, after all."

I slammed my knee into his crotch, then smashed my foot into his face when he doubled over and sent him skidding across the stone floor. Battle-fever rushing through my veins, I grabbed the blade and yanked it out of my shoulder, then made another dash for the door. Somehow I cleared the entrance, but I didn't make it more than two feet into the hallway before the remaining two guards tackled me to the ground. I grunted as my cheek smashed into the stone floor, and several ribs cracked as the weight of both men slammed into me.

"You're going to pay for that, bitch!" One of the men rolled me over and straddled me – I wasn't sure which one, because my vision was blurred with tears of pain and fear. I held my arms above my face as he rained blows down upon me, his huge fists smashing into my forearms, my neck, my chest. Tears streamed down my cheeks, from the utter agony of two hundred plus pounds sitting atop broken ribs pounding against my neck and chest so hard I couldn't breathe. But I clenched my teeth, refusing to give him the satisfaction of so much as a whimper.

Unbelievable, I thought dimly through the crashing waves of pain. *I'm a shifter hybrid who incinerated a rhino yesterday, and I'm going to die in a cold, dark basement at the hands of a human.*

Roanas would be disappointed if he knew I'd failed so quickly.

That thought galvanized me, and I reared up, pulling strength from a reserve I didn't know I had to flex my claws. I wrapped my bloody, torn fingers around the guard's neck, taking satisfaction as I dug into his meaty flesh. His eyes bulged as I squeezed, my claws tearing into his skin, and I held on tight as the other guard rushed forward to kick me.

If I was going down, at least I was taking this bastard with me.

"What is the meaning of this!" a deep, familiar voice shouted, and the guard who was about to kick me in the head froze. I froze too, my hands still wrapped around my attacker's neck, as a tall, bearded man dressed in dark clothing descended the basement stairs, his yellow eyes glowing in the darkness of the hall.

It was Fenris, in human form.

The breath I was holding left me in a rush of relief, and I collapsed. Unfortunately, so did the lout I was choking to death, and it didn't appear that he was going to move any time soon. Groaning, I attempted to shove the guy off me, but my arms might as well have been feathers – they had absolutely no strength left in them.

"Sir," the guard who was still standing began. "We heard screams and came down here to find the hybrid –"

"Don't call her that," Fenris growled, dropping to his knees beside me. He shoved the guard off me carelessly and pressed his fingers against my neck to feel my pulse. "Sunaya, what happened here?"

Tears blurred my vision all over again at the compassion in his voice. Finally, there was someone here in this forsaken place who wanted to help me, who didn't look at me with suspicion and malice.

"I just came down here for some bread and fish," I croaked, the tears sliding down my cheeks faster now that nobody was there to beat them out of me. "That's all I wanted."

"Resinah forgive me," Fenris muttered, sliding his hands beneath my shoulders and my knees. "I should have seen to this."

An alarm bell went off in my head – Resinah was the female goddess mages prayed to, and not one that shifters ever referenced – but then Fenris lifted me into his arms. Pain screamed throughout my entire body, and I forgot about everything except the agony. My vision blurred again, a dull roar filling my ears, and I wasn't sure what happened after, but the next thing I knew I was being laid out on a table.

By Magorah, I thought, a sharp burst of panic ripping through me as the Chief Mage's face swam into view. *They're going to experiment on me now!*

But when his hands touched me, they were surprisingly gentle. I stilled as a sense of peace stole through me, washing away the panic, and looked up dreamily into Iannis's face. And as he looked down at me, his brows drawn together, lines bracketed around his mouth, I could almost imagine that he cared.

"Sleep," he said, his deep, slightly musical voice like a balm to my battered soul, and I went under without another thought.

7

A knock on the door disturbed me from a deep, dreamless sleep. I sat up, disoriented as I looked around the small, round room with its chest of drawers and single, barred window. It took me a moment to remember that I was in Solantha Palace, and that I was kept here so the Chief Mage could study me like a lab rat. My stomach tightened as I scoured my brain for memories of last night, but all I could dredge up was a sense of agony, and the image of the Chief Mage's face hovering above my head, backlit by a bright, white light. Had he started experimenting on me already?

"Sunaya?" the knocking on the door persisted, and my right ear twitched as I recognized Fenris's voice. "Are you awake?"

Another memory tickled the back of my mind at the sound. "I'm coming," I called, swinging my legs from the side of the bed. It was then I noticed I was dressed in a simple white nightgown I'd never seen before in my life.

Someone had *definitely* tampered with my body last night, even if it had only been to change my clothes.

But if the Chief Mage had drugged or spelled me in some

way, my body didn't know it. Energy sang through my muscles as I got to my feet and crossed the room, and I felt like skipping.

He must have given me some kind of weird pick-me-up spell.

But when I opened the door to see Fenris standing on the other side, the memory of him rushing toward me down the basement steps slammed into my brain.

"Oh." I clutched the side of my head as I stared at him. He was dressed in dark red instead of black today, but otherwise he was the same tall, muscular man with the dark brown beard and yellow eyes who'd called off my attackers. "You saved me last night."

"Glad your memory is in working order." He arched a brow, then lifted the plate of food in his hands. "Hungry?"

"Famished." The sight of the cold chicken, mashed potatoes and biscuits made my stomach ache so fiercely I thought it might devour itself. I snatched the plate from his hands before I remembered my manners. "Umm, do you want to come in?"

"That was the idea, yes."

I stepped back to let him enter the room, and that was all of the attention I could spare – I plopped down onto my bed and immediately inhaled the food on my plate.

"Mmm," I mumbled appreciatively when I was done. "You got any more of this?" The plate of food had taken the edge off my hunger, but I hadn't eaten a decent meal in forty-eight hours, at least not by shifter standards. Our high metabolisms needed more food than the average human.

Fenris frowned. "I should have thought to bring more. You need the nourishment after your ordeal."

"Is that why you're here?" I asked, gesturing to my empty plate. "Have you been assigned as my personal maid or something? Because somehow that kind of task seems beneath you."

Fenris scowled. "Actually, the Chief Mage sent me here to let you know that he wouldn't be able to meet with you until later this afternoon. I decided to bring you some food on my way, so that you wouldn't get yourself in trouble in the kitchens again."

"What does the Great Lord Iannis have to do that is so pressing he had to push back our morning meeting?" I rolled my eyes. Was I supposed to be grateful to Fenris for rescuing me when it was his master's fault I'd been nearly beaten to death in the first place?

Fenris arched a brow. "As a matter of fact, he's still recuperating from last night. He expended a lot of energy healing your injuries, which were rather extensive."

My jaw dropped as the fragments of memory from last night finally fell into place. "You brought me to the Chief Mage and had him *heal* me?"

"It seemed the least he could do, since you'd been starved and beaten while under his protection," Fenris said mildly. "Or at least that's what I told him when he asked me why I hadn't brought you to the infirmary instead. Would you rather I had left you lying on the floor?"

He scowled at me, and I flinched, the truth of his words ringing in my ears. "No. But it doesn't mean that I'm going to grovel at your feet for the supposed 'favor' you've done me. After all, you're the pet of the mage who's keeping me here."

Fenris's jaw tightened. "I'm no one's pet."

"Well then why are you here with him?" I narrowed my eyes. "You seem like a decent guy, so he must have some kind of hold over you. Do you owe him a debt? Because there are other alternatives to indentured servitude –"

"I am not a slave, Sunaya," Fenris cut me off, his voice clipped. "I know this might be hard for you to believe, but Iannis and I are good friends. I stand by his side, as he would stand by mine."

"Is that why you sit at his feet?" I snapped. "Like a dog? Because you two are *equal*?"

Fenris's expression turned downright thunderous. "I know that you're frustrated with your own situation, but believe me when I say from experience that Iannis is not what you think. If I sit by his feet as a wolf, it's because it's advantageous to the situation, nothing more. We respect each other, and he has more than earned my loyalty."

I raised my eyebrows at the conviction that burned in his voice and eyes. He certainly seemed sincere, and yet..."If he's so great, then why am I still trapped up here in this tower like a prisoner instead of back on the streets? He should have already determined that I'm not a threat to the public."

"Because you appealed to Iannis directly, and he does nothing by half-measures. He'll keep you as long as he has to, in order to ensure you're not a threat and can be released safely back into society."

Disgust filled me at Fenris's choice of words. "Yeah, well this isn't just about me, buddy." I poked him in the chest. "I was in the middle of investigating a series of shifter murders that no one is taking seriously when I was carted off to jail. If I don't go free, the murderer is going to keep killing and he'll never be brought to justice."

"Murderer?" Fenris's dark brows winged up. "What murderer?"

I gave him the abbreviated rundown of the situation, and by the time I finished he was frowning again. "I haven't heard anything about this," he said, stroking his beard.

"Yeah, well that's because whoever's behind all this likely has someone from the media in their pocket." I scowled. "Surely you don't think that's out of the realm of possibility, do you?"

"Well, no," Fenris admitted, "I suppose I could try looking into it myself, but I'll need to find more evidence than just your word before bringing it to Iannis."

"Well take your time then," I drawled, leaning back against

the wall as Fenris turned for the door. "It's not like lives are at stake or anything."

Fenris shot a reproving glare at me over his shoulder. "The Chief Mage expects you in his study in the West Wing at one o'clock, so please make sure you are well-fed and ready by then." His expression softened. "I've instructed the kitchen staff that they are to feed you properly. Feel free to mind-message me if you run into any trouble."

He closed the door on his way out, and I stared at the brass doorknob for a long time. Had I just gained an ally? Or was there an ulterior motive here that I was too blind to pick up on?

AFTER A LONG, hot bath, a huge breakfast, and a nice nap, I leisurely made my way over to the Chief Mage's study in the West Wing. Sure, the kitchen staff might have handed me my stack of pancakes begrudgingly, and the mages who passed me in the halls still looked down at me from their snooty noses as they went about their business, but I was so happy to have a full belly and a clear head that I couldn't find it in me to be resentful.

Unfortunately my good mood didn't last – anxiety began to creep in on my sense of contentment as I approached the carved mahogany door that led to the Chief Mage's study. Though I was mostly disabused of the notion that I was going to be strapped to a table and magically mutated, I was hyper-aware that whatever happened beyond those doors once I stepped through them could very well determine my fate.

I curled my fingers around the cold brass doorknob, then hesitated. I could loiter out here for a few minutes, couldn't I? I mean, the longer I stayed out here, the longer I could postpone my inevitable death.

Don't be a scaredy cat, Naya. Put your chin up, shoulders back, and walk in there like you own the place.

Right. I couldn't let the Chief Mage see that I was intimidated. Taking a deep breath through my nostrils, I followed my own advice, turned the knob and stepped into the Chief Mage's study.

It was a large room, with plenty of light filtering in through a broad, multi-paned window to the left, the rays of the afternoon sun spilling across the swirling blue-and-gold patterned carpet that covered the length of the floor. To the right, in front of a blue marble hearth with a crackling fire, lay Fenris in wolf form. He rolled to his back and regarded me lazily with one yellow eye, apparently reluctant to move from the hearth, and a smile tugged at the corner of my lips despite myself.

"Miss Baine. You've arrived." The Chief Mage's voice drew my attention to where he was standing behind a large wooden desk that was clear except for a couple of leather bound books. Shelves filled with more books loomed behind him, and he looked as intimidating as ever, with his cold eyes and enigmatic expression. If I'd expected him to regard me any differently after spending half the night up saving my life, I was wrong – he studied me with the same amount of clinical interest he would one of the books on his desk. And though I knew I shouldn't be disappointed, I was.

"Unfortunately." I watched him warily as he came around the desk, a set of dark purple robes flowing around his tall frame. They accentuated the breadth of his shoulders, and the lavender sash that belted them together drew the eye to his trim waistline. Unsure of what to do with myself, I automatically defaulted to parade rest, spreading my legs slightly apart and clasping my hands behind my back, shoulders straight.

"You are a rather rude individual," the Chief Mage observed, eyeing me up and down critically as if I were a knife on display at a weapons shop rather than a living, breathing person. I caught his scent for the first time – a pleasant combination of sandalwood, musk, and of course, magic – and catalogued it for future reference. "And troublesome, as well."

"Troublesome?" I glared up at him. "I could say the same of you."

He arched a brow. "You're the one who made an appeal to me. I'm simply doing my job."

That's a laugh. "I didn't realize your job consisted of cooping starving, sleep-deprived hybrids up in your palace and siccing psycho assassin-guards on them for daring to pilfer a loaf of bread from the kitchen."

He frowned. "Psycho assassin-guards?"

"*She's referring to the guard who stabbed her in the shoulder with his sword.*" Fenris's voice echoed in my head, and I assumed Iannis's too, by the way he glanced over at Fenris.

"I already have one of my staff looking into the matter," the Chief Mage said dismissively. "Rest assured it will not happen again."

"Forgive me if I'm less than assured," I said sarcastically, folding my arms across my chest.

The Chief Mage frowned. "You doubt my ability to keep you safe?"

"I doubt your ability to keep *anyone* safe," I challenged, taking a step forward. "Instead of taking an interest in lowering the crime rate in this city, you're up here enforcing your cruel, antiquated policy against me. Forgive me for not giving you my vote of confidence."

To his credit, the Chief Mage didn't react to my aggression; he stood his ground and regarded me with a disapproving frown. "It's my job to ensure the laws that protect our country are enforced in Solantha," he said sternly. "Uncontrolled magic wreaked havoc on this country during the Conflict. It is necessary to regulate the use and existence of magic, so as not to have a repeat experience."

I scoffed at that old party line. "That's just an excuse you mages use not to share power and influence with anyone else. If you're so worried about people like me running wild with our magic, why don't you set up a state-funded program to train us?"

"The amount of resources needed –"

"Don't even *try* to tell me there isn't enough gold." His eyes widened angrily as I cut him off. I knew I should probably be afraid, but I was too riled up to care. "Magorah knows you and everyone else in the Mage's Quarter are swimming in it. The real problem is that not one of you actually cares enough to take the time to train us, do you? That's why you only give us the choice of having our magic wiped, or execution, whenever you find one of us out."

The Chief Mage's violet eyes glittered. "It's a logical approach," he said stiffly.

"It's a *cruel, heartless* approach." I took another step forward, into his personal space, and his nostrils flared as he looked down his long nose at me. The hair on my arms stood up as magical energy sang through the air, and for the first time real fear crackled through my nerves. But I couldn't back down, not now. "That's hardly any choice at all, since nearly all the people who go through the magic wipe end up with permanent mental damage. By the time the mages who perform the wipe are finished, most of the victims would have been better off dead." Tears pricked the corners of my eyes. "One of my childhood friends, Tanya, failed the test when she was just twelve years old. She was from a human family, and her magical ability was weak, so her family chose to put her through the magic wipe. By the time they were done with her, she could hardly remember her own name, and to this day her family has to care for her because she can't function in society well enough to hold a job. So don't tell me how necessary these oppressive laws are. You're worse than murderers, all of you!"

"How dare you!" the Chief Mage snapped, his cheeks coloring. My eyes widened as he took a step toward me, the folds of his robes brushing against me. Magical energy crackled around us, little blue-white bolts that wriggled like worms in the air. "Your accusations border on the ridiculous; magic wipes don't cause mental damage when done properly. Your lies –"

He stopped mid-sentence as Fenris, who at some point had shifted to human, laid a hand on his arm. "She's not lying, Iannis."

The magical energy around us faded, and I let out a small sigh of relief as the Chief Mage turned his deadly glower from me so he could look at Fenris. "She has to be."

Fenris shook his head. "Director Chartis handles most of these reports, and it's unlikely he would have passed anything like that along to you," he told Iannis. "I researched this recently, and from what I understand, approximately three quarters of all magic-wipes result in permanent damage to the subject."

The Chief Mage was silent for a several seconds. "Seventy-five percent?" His voice was dangerously frigid now. "That's intolerable. I've performed several magic wipes myself – any properly trained mage should be able to do it without causing permanent harm. Who is performing these spells?"

Fenris eyed him warily. "You'd have to ask Director Chartis. But if I were to guess, it's likely low-level mages, or even apprentices."

"Are you kidding me?" I shouted, balling my hands into fists at my sides. I wanted to punch the Chief Mage in the nose, but I settled for shoving my face into his instead. "You've been letting inexperienced mages perform mind-altering magic on us? You lazy, incompetent bastard!"

"Enough!" The Chief Mage raised a hand and blasted me

with a pulse of magic. I staggered several steps backward before I found my footing and froze as our gazes collided again – his violet eyes glowed with rage. "You are not the only one in this room capable of reducing another being to a pile of ash," he said in a soft, deadly voice. "I would advise you to remember that when you speak to me, Miss Baine."

"Fine." I swallowed hard, then firmed my chin and shoulders, forcing my body not to tremble. As angry as I was, the man standing in front of me was the Chief Mage for a reason, and I did *not* want to fuck with him if I hoped to make it out of this place alive.

"Good." The anger abruptly disappeared as his face returned to stone. "I'm going ask you a series of questions. My magic will tell me if you are lying, so I suggest you be truthful."

I resisted the urge to scoff, unsure whether I believed that. But in the interest of staying alive, I decided to answer his questions truthfully. I could always test his claim later, when he was less likely to want to incinerate me.

"Excellent." He turned around, reaching for something on his desk, and when he turned back I saw he had a manila file with my name on it open in his hands. "You are the daughter of Saranella Baine, correct?"

"Correct." A pang went through my heart at the mention of my mother's name. It had been fourteen years since she'd died, but I still missed her fiercely.

"Did she ever mention your father to you? His name, his rank, his country of origin?"

"Not once." I swallowed against a lump in my throat. "I think she figured that if I didn't know my father was a mage, I might not tap into my powers until I was old enough not to be subjected to testing any longer."

"An interesting theory, but quite incorrect," the Chief Mage said, almost conversationally. My nails dug into my palms – did he not realize how insensitive he was being? "You were eight years old when you had your first test?"

"Yes," I murmured, my mind flying back to that day. I remembered how terrified my mother had been, how she'd sobbed and clung to me and wished aloud that she could keep me home from school that day. I'd been scared too, not so much because of the test but because my mother was crying. That was the only time I'd ever seen her shed tears. She'd been a kind and compassionate woman, but tough as nails, and the moment of weakness still shook me even as a memory. "I passed."

"Obviously." The Chief Mage flipped a page in my file and scanned it. I gritted my teeth. "Had you shown any signs of magical aptitude before then?"

I frowned, thinking back. "I conjured some rainbow butterflies at my third birthday party," I recalled. "My cousins thought it was the greatest thing they'd ever seen, and my mother nearly had a heart attack. None of my aunts ever brought their kids back to our house again." My heart ached for the hurt and bewildered child I had been. Whether I liked it or not, she still lingered as a ghost in my heart, waiting in vain for someone to accept her.

"Were they real butterflies?"

I blinked. "Huh?"

The Chief Mage frowned impatiently at me. "Were they real butterflies, or just an illusion?"

"Oh, they were real," I insisted. "I caught one in my hand and felt its wings fluttering against my palm." Happiness burst through the ache of that memory, and I paused, surprised that I actually had a joyful memory of magic in the recesses of my mind.

The Chief Mage's eyebrows arched. "At only age three? Are you sure?"

"Yes."

"Impressive," he muttered, scanning my file again. Warmth filled my chest at the accidental compliment, but I pushed it down. "And yet you passed the test."

I sighed. "I don't understand it either."

He studied me for a long time. "Your mother died when you were ten years old, correct?"

"Correct." It had happened so long ago, and yet at the mention of it, I still remembered the way her hand had felt in mine, so weak and clammy as she'd drawn her last breaths. She'd been taken by a rare shifter disease that destroyed the immune system – a true tragedy, as she'd barely reached a hundred years of age, only a third of a shifter's normal lifespan.

"And you were taken in by Shiftertown Inspector Tillmore after that?"

I cleared my throat. "Not right after. My Aunt Mafiela kept me until I was thirteen. That was about as long as she could stand me before throwing me out in the streets. Roanas caught me stealing bread from a vendor in the town square, and took me in, instead of prosecuting me."

As a general rule, I tried not to think about those nights I'd spent huddling in cardboard boxes in alleys, scrounging for food wherever I could and staying out of sight as much as possible. Even though I was a child, the other shifters had considered me taboo because of my hybrid status – they all knew that I was only half-shifter, even if they didn't know I was half-mage rather than half-human. If my aunt Mafiela had chosen to keep me, things might've been different, but her throwing me out on the streets was a declaration to all that I was tainted, unworthy.

The Chief Mage's eyes flickered. "Mafiela Baine... she is the matriarch of the Jaguar Clan, correct?"

I nodded.

"Did she know that your father was a mage when she revoked your status as a clan member?"

"I'm not sure." I clenched my jaw on the lie. Much as I hated my aunt Mafiela, the fact that she hadn't immediately reported my shifter-mage hybrid status to the Mage's Guild was her saving grace. I couldn't throw her under the train, at least not for this. Iannis stared silently at me for a long moment, and I wondered if he really *could* tell that I was lying.

"Being a hybrid and born out of wedlock were reason enough for her to give me the boot. She felt no particular loyalty toward me once my mother died."

"Does Shiftertown not provide any sort of assistance to the needy?"

"Most of the taxes paid by everyone in this city go into *your* coffers," I snapped. "What little money Shiftertown gets to keep is used for city maintenance." The same went for Rowanville and Maintown.

The Chief Mage frowned. "Maintenance? The Mage's Guild is in charge of civic upkeep. That is one of the reasons why we charge taxes to begin with."

I laughed. "Yeah, well you ought to take a closer look and see where that money is actually going, because it's sure not being used for city improvements or welfare."

"I believe we are going off topic now." The Chief Mage's frown deepened. "So Inspector Tillmore took you in. Did he know about your magic?"

I sighed. "Roanas knew everything there was to know about me." There was no point in hiding it, since he was dead. Grief smarted at my eyes, and I cleared my throat, blinking. The man had taught me everything I needed to know, and it was his recommendation that had gotten me into the Enforcer's Guild in the first place. "He took me in when I was thirteen years old."

"Despite your inability to control your magic?" The Chief Mage arched a brow. "A selfless act indeed."

"Roanas taught me how to defend myself so my magic

wouldn't have to," I growled. "And I was always safe when I was with him. He did the best he could."

"I suppose so," the Chief Mage murmured. His eyes narrowed as he studied me for a long moment, before he set the file aside.

"Hold out your hands." He stepped toward me, his own hands outstretched.

A shiver rippled down my spine as I eyed him, a sense of déjà vu filling me. This was exactly what the other mages had done when they tested me, and even though I knew there was no harm in having it done again, since everyone in Solantha probably knew I was half-mage, it still made me nervous.

"Your hands," the Chief Mage repeated, his voice tinged with impatience.

I placed my hands in his reluctantly, watching as his long fingers curled around them. He turned my hands over until my palms rested face up, then stroked my wrists with his thumbs. Another shiver rippled through me, but this one was warm and tingly, and I sucked in a sharp breath through my nostrils. His scent filled my nose, and my cheeks heated as I became incredibly aware of how close we stood together.

If Iannis noticed my sudden discomfort, he said nothing, simply continued to stroke his thumbs across my wrists in small circles. The warm tingles gradually grew stronger as they ran up and down my arms, like an electric current looping between us, and as the scent of burnt sugar thickened around us I realized that current was actually magic.

His eyes opened, and a pang of disappointment went through me as he dropped my hands. "Not a single spark," he murmured, eyeing me curiously.

"What does that mean?" Fenris, who'd been standing nearby, asked. His brow was furrowed as he studied me.

"It means that someone has put a block on her magic, likely her father."

"My father?" I echoed. Anger bubbled up in my stomach at the implications. "Why would he do that? So I'd be helpless to defend myself?"

"On the contrary," the Chief Mage corrected me. "He would have done this to keep you hidden, so you would pass the tests without arousing suspicion." He sounded intrigued. "Whoever your father is, he must have been a high-level mage to have accomplished such a sophisticated spell."

"Gee, I'm so proud," I snapped, folding my arms across my chest.

Annoyance flickered in the Chief Mage's eyes again, but he ignored my sarcasm as he walked around his desk. I watched, curiously, as he opened a drawer and pulled out a fountain pen. "Hold out your hand."

Bewildered, I did so, and he placed the pen in the center of my palm. I inspected it to try and see if there was anything special about it, but there were no runes or strange markings of any kind on the surface. "What am I supposed to do with this thing?"

"Make it levitate."

I scowled at him. "Exactly how am I supposed to do that?"

The Chief Mage shrugged. "The same way you do it every time. Reach for your magic, and direct it."

Sighing, I closed my eyes and did as he asked, searching for that glowing light in the center of my being that appeared whenever I had a magical outburst. But as usual, there was nothing but a void, and when I opened my eyes the pen was still in my hand.

"It didn't work."

The Chief Mage only arched a brow, and reached for my hand as if to take the pen. But instead, he wrapped his fingers around my hand. Instantly, ice crackled up my forearm, spreading rapidly to my shoulder with no signs of stopping. Panic burst in my chest as a deep, painful cold engulfed my arm. I knew that if it reached my heart I would die.

As soon as I had that thought, the magic inside me flared to life. Heat flooded my body, and blue-green flames raced up my arms. The ice melted instantly, water sluicing down to the floor to be absorbed by the expensive carpeting.

"As I suspected." The Chief Mage dropped my arm, a satisfied look on his face. "Your magic only works when you believe your life to be in danger."

"I could have told you that!" I balled my hands at my sides, my heart pumping furiously. "You didn't need to almost kill me!"

The Chief Mage's lips thinned. "Don't be silly, Miss Baine. I would have stopped the ice before it reached your heart. It does me no good if you die before I complete my investigation."

"*Not. Re. Assured.*"

As I half-expected, the Chief Mage ignored that too, instead leaning forward to peer into my eyes. "Fenris," he murmured, "Jaguar shifters, they typically have yellow eyes, do they not?"

"They range in color, actually, but a golden color is the norm." Fenris shrugged. "They're also one of the few big cat feline species that have melanin coats as well as lighter coloring, explaining why Sunaya's coat is black when so many of the Baine jaguars are not."

"I personally prefer the term panther," I said coolly. It was a misnomer, but it was simpler than identifying myself as a 'black jaguar'.

"Hmm." The Chief Mage glanced back at me. "Your father may very well share your eye coloring, then."

I rolled my eyes. "Are you seriously going to try and identify my father, a *mage* who can change his appearance, by his eye coloring?"

"Of course not," the Chief Mage said mildly. "But it's something we should consider, nevertheless."

"You know," Fenris said, "if her father had claimed her at birth, which would have been the honorable thing to do, Sunaya would be a mage in good standing by now."

Huh. That was interesting. In theory Fenris was correct – the issue of being born illegally with magic mainly applied to humans, which made sense as all mage families originally descended from normal humans. Full-blooded shifters, on the other hand, were never born with magic other than their innate ability to shift, making me an extremely rare case. I gritted my teeth as the realization swept over me that my father could have claimed me as his daughter and I would have been allowed to train as a mage, sparing me years of heartache and difficulty.

The Chief Mage arched a brow in Fenris's direction. "Your point?"

"My *point* is, I don't think it's just to punish Sunaya for her father's neglect, which is the only reason she can't control her magic properly. In my opinion, he is more deserving of punishment than she is. He knew the consequences of leaving her to fend for herself, and yet did nothing aside from putting a spell on her to seal her magic away. A spell that, in the end, did not save her."

I expected the Chief Mage to scoff at this, but he said nothing for a long moment, simply staring at me. I forced myself not to fidget, wondering what was going on behind those strange violet eyes. Was he actually considering letting me off the hook in favor of pinning responsibility on my father? If that was the case, I would have to give Fenris a good, long smooch for his suggestion.

And maybe I had enough gratitude in my heart to give the Chief Mage a pat on the head, too.

"Your father will not escape justice," he said finally, and then glanced at the clock on the wall. "Unfortunately our time is up for now, as I have other obligations to meet. Return here at the same time tomorrow, and we will resume our study."

"Yessir." I sketched a mocking bow and carted myself back to my room, wondering if the Chief Mage really was going to find my father, and if he did, whether or not I would finally get to meet the bastard face to face.

8

I spent most of the afternoon training, burning off my frustration as best I could with the forms and exercise routines my mentor had taught me. Practice reminded me that I was still missing my crescent knives and chakrams, and I wondered where they had gone off to. I really hoped Brin and Nila hadn't decided to keep them for themselves, or sold them off to other Enforcers. They were valuable weapons, both gifts from Roanas. The chakrams were especially valuable, because they were spelled to return to my pouch after they'd been thrown.

Perhaps *I can ask Fenris to try and get my weapons back for me.*

Huh. That might actually be a good idea. Even if he held on to them for me, that was better than leaving them to the Enforcer's Guild. Heck, I might even be able to get him to convince the Chief Mage to let me wear them – the guards would think twice about messing with me then.

With that thought in mind, I left my makeshift training area and went to find Fenris. A human servant told me he was in the West Wing, so I headed in that direction, passing through the balcony that overlooked the foyer as I did so.

"What do you mean, we can't see her!"

I froze at the sound of Noria's strident tones, and looked over the railing to see her standing below, arguing with the mage who served as the receptionist for the palace. Her cloud of red curls bounced around her face in time to her wild gesticulations. Next to her stood Comenius, who looked slightly uncomfortable about her outburst. Both were dressed in white from head to foot – mourning colors – and my heart sank into my toes as I realized what that meant.

Roanas's funeral.

Rage began to build inside me. Why had nobody told me he was being buried today? Even if I couldn't have attended the funeral myself, I would have liked to pray for him, perhaps even hold a rite on my own.

"I'm sorry, but Sunaya Baine is a *prisoner*," the mage sniffed haughtily. Ire bubbled up inside me as he wrinkled his long, slightly crooked nose. "And as such, she is not cleared for any visitors at this time."

"That's preposterous!" Comenius protested, his handsome features tightening into a scowl. "Even Prisoner's Isle allows their inmates visitors, and Sunaya hasn't even been sentenced."

"I don't know why you're wasting your time here," the mage sneered. "With her volatile behavior, it's only a matter of time before the Chief Mage has her executed –"

The animosity building inside me finally came to a head. I vaulted over the balcony, twisting around in the air before landing in a crouch directly in front of the mage.

"What was that you were saying about my volatile behavior?" I asked, baring my fangs at the snotty old mage. His wrinkly skin turned sallow, his beady eyes widening as much as they were capable.

"Naya!" Comenius and Noria exclaimed at the same time.

The mage's bushy grey eyebrows quivered as he scowled at

me. "Just what is the meaning of this, young lady? Are you threatening me?"

The guards standing by began to close in, and I stepped in front of my friends to shield them, not wanting them to get caught up in another altercation with these brutal bastards.

"*Fenris,*" I called out mentally. "*Could use a little help here.*"

"Sir, we apologize for the intrusion," Comenius said swiftly from behind me. I turned to see him grab Noria around the waist and begin steering her towards the door. "We'll just be on our way now –"

"No!" Noria actually stamped her foot. "I'm not leaving!" She flung herself at me, and I staggered as she wrapped her arms around my waist like a child would do to a mother who was trying to leave them behind somewhere.

"Noria," I muttered, trying to extricate myself from her grasp as the guards drew closer, one of them testing the draw on his short sword. I didn't want to give the guards an excuse to work off some of their aggression on her. "You can tone it down a notch."

"May I ask what's going on here?"

Relief sang through my veins at the sound of Fenris's voice, and I turned to see him standing at the top of the stairs, watching us with a bemused expression.

"Oh hey." I waved nonchalantly, as if I didn't have a human girl dangling from my waist and a bevy of guards ready to pounce on us. "I'm just greeting some visitors."

"This vile hybrid threatened me!" the reception mage shouted, pointing toward me with a trembling finger.

Fenris's brow darkened as he descended the staircase. "I don't care for your choice of words, Canter," he said sternly, the guards backing away as he approached.

"Who is *he*?" Comenius murmured in my ear, watching

wide-eyed at the way Fenris managed to intimidate everyone else in the room. "Isn't he a shifter?"

"Yeah, but he's friends with the Chief Mage," I muttered back. "And also his right-hand man. So everyone seems to listen to him."

"That's strange," Noria mused, also watching with narrowed eyes. "The Chief Mage giving a shifter that kind of power, while oppressing the other shifters under his rule?"

I shrugged, but the words struck me nevertheless. It *was* strange that Fenris had so much influence over the guards and even some of the mages around here, even if he was a friend of the Chief Mage's. Moreover, I still didn't understand why the two of them were friends in the first place, especially since the Chief Mage certainly didn't show me any kind of preferential treatment. What made Fenris so special?

Canter seemed to recover from his momentary panic attack, and drew his robes around himself imperiously. "I don't see what business it is of yours what I call her," he sniffed, "but in any case that's not the point. These two hooligans," he jabbed a finger towards Comenius and Noria, "came in demanding to see the prisoner, and I denied them on account of the fact that she isn't cleared for visitors."

Fenris simply arched a brow, folding his arms over his broad chest. "I wasn't aware that anyone had to be 'cleared' in order to receive visitors around here. Would you care to show me where such a policy exists?"

Huh. Good point.

Canter's sallow cheeks reddened. "T-the Chief Mage s-said so," he stuttered, and Fenris took a threatening step toward him, baring his fangs in a rare show of temper.

"You should know better than to lie to me," he said in a soft voice. "Even if I couldn't tell by your scent, it's a simple enough matter for me to ask the Chief Mage myself. And I'm certain he would tell me that no such policy exists."

"Huh," Noria said. "Can shifters really smell when someone is lying?"

I grinned down at her. "It's one of our many superpowers, kid," I said, bumping my shoulder playfully into hers. Fenris shot me an annoyed look, but I didn't care – I was just happy to have my friends with me.

"Your insinuations are insulting," Canter snapped, but the scent of fresh sweat rolling out from his pores was telling – the man was a liar, and a bad one at that. "I refuse to stand here and be mocked like this."

Fenris shrugged, gesturing to the chair behind the desk that was stationed in the foyer. "Fine, then sit and be insulted instead," he said. "But either way, I see no reason why Sunaya can't have a short visit with her friends."

In the end, we were taken up to one of the "conference rooms" right off the balcony landing, which was essentially a parlor furnished in gold and green, with low couches and chaises and elegantly carved wooden furniture.

"Don't think you aren't under observation," Fenris warned me, and left us to our own devices.

Suddenly nervous, I grabbed a gold-tasseled pillow and fidgeted with it as I sat. Noria and Comenius sat on the love seat opposite me.

"What?" I finally snapped, noticing the way their eyes brimmed with curiosity and reproach. "Why are you guys staring at me like that?"

"Well –," Noria began.

"No." Comenius laid a hand on her knee. "You can't say it like that."

"Like what?" Noria protested. "You don't even know what I'm about to say."

But I did. It was written clear as day on her freckled face. "You don't think I'm suffering enough," I said flatly.

Noria's shoulders sagged, and she looked at me with a combination of guilt and anger. "Well, yeah."

"Not that that we're upset about it," Comenius rushed to assure me. "It's just that –"

"Oh who are you kidding?" Noria snapped, shoving Comenius's hand off her knee. "Of course we're upset about it. Or at least I am! I've been lying awake all night, thinking you're being magically tortured and interrogated and experimented on, only to find out that you're clothed and fed and perfectly healthy, and walking around as if you own the damned place." She leveled a glare at me that was so fierce I actually shrank back a little in my seat.

"Look," I said, scowling at Noria. "Just because I'm not chained to the wall in a dirty cell somewhere doesn't mean I'm okay. I can't set foot outside these walls until the Chief Mage decides to release me, and at the rate he's going that might not be until next year."

Noria glanced around at the fancy furnishings of the room. "I'm not entirely sure that's a bad thing," she said dubiously, her eyes lingering on the expensive-looking paintings that hung on the walls. "The Chief's got excellent taste, for a mage." She wrinkled her nose.

"Yes, well, that didn't do me much good when I was nearly beaten to death by the guards last night."

"What!" Comenius shouted as Noria's face went pale. "What do you mean, nearly beaten to death?"

"And by those guards?" The shock in Noria's voice was evident. "There must have been an army of them if they were able to take you down."

"I don't know about an army," I said dryly. "But there were a few." I gave them a quick rundown of the incident, explaining that I'd basically been starved all day and had little energy left when the guards had jumped me in the kitchen. "If it weren't for Fenris, I'd probably be dead."

"*Verflixt*," Comenius muttered and I blinked – it was rare for him to swear. His pale blue eyes burned with emotion. "I'm sorry, Naya. I should have known, should have done something –"

I shook my head. "There's nothing you could have done," I said gently, hating the guilt that was written all over his face. "And remember, had you not thought of appealing to the Chief Mage, I'd likely be dead. It's okay, anyway. I'm all better now."

"I can see that." Noria studied me, her dark eyes glittering with suspicion. "From what you've said it sounds like you were injured really badly. Whoever healed you must have been really good."

I shifted uncomfortably in my seat. "It was the Chief Mage, actually."

Comenius's jaw dropped. "Iannis ar'Sannin *himself* healed you?"

I groaned. "It's not a big deal, guys. Fenris brought my bleeding, broken body up to his room and demanded he do it."

"Still," Comenius mused. "He could have simply ordered any one of his mages to do it. This is very interesting."

"What it is, is *concerning*," Noria said, leaning forward. "Naya, you aren't like, becoming friends with these people, are you? Just because the Chief Mage wiggled his fingers and did some magic mumbo jumbo on you doesn't mean that he's your best bud now. If anything, it's *his* fault this happened to you in the first place."

"You think I don't know that?" I scoffed, leaning back against the cushions and crossing my legs as if my pulse hadn't suddenly kicked up a notch at Noria's accusation. "No one knows better than me I'm like a mouse under his paw. He's a cold, calculating bastard who doesn't give a flying fuck about me, and I plan on putting as much distance between myself and this place as I can, as soon as possible. We are *not* friends."

"Good." Apparently satisfied with my declaration, Noria sat back. "Now we can get on with the rest of our visit."

I arched a brow. "And that is?"

"The silver murders." Comenius pulled a new issue of the Shifter Courier from the inside of his tunic.

I took it from his outstretched hand, my eyes narrowing as I read the front-page article, which was about another shifter death.

"Surely this should spark some kind of investigation, no?" I asked after I'd read the article. The victim was the daughter of a wealthy shifter merchant – surely *that* had to merit some attention.

Comenius pressed his lips together. "I'm not so sure. I disguised myself as a reporter and attempted to interview the family, but I was ambushed by several thugs not far from the house. I suspect they had been following me."

"By Magorah." I reached for Comenius's hand, but stopped myself. "Are you alright, Com?"

"I have a few tricks up my sleeves." A small smirk played across his lips, but his expression quickly grew serious again. "I managed to palm this from them." He drew a tiny cloth pouch from the inside of his sleeve and handed it to me. "Strange, that human drug dealers would be hanging around Shiftertown."

I opened up the pouch and took a sniff. "This is cerebust. It only works on humans." Scowling, I sniffed again to see if it was cut with anything, and a few grains of the drug flew up my nostrils. A strange, giddy feeling flew through me, and I dropped the bag, stunned.

Thankfully Comenius snatched it out of the air before it spilled all over the carpet. "Naya? Are you alright?" He peered into my eyes. "Your pupils are dilating."

"I... I think I'm a little high." Panic overtook the strange euphoria, and sweat broke out across the line of my brow. "That's not possible. Shifters don't get high." Cerebust was a recreational drug used by humans, but like most drugs it didn't work on shifters. Our metabolisms run too high – we might get a slight buzz from an actual hit, but a few flecks of cerebust in my nostrils should *not* have had any effect on me.

"As I thought." Comenius's eyes blazed triumphantly as he returned the little pouch to its hiding place up his sleeve. "Someone has treated this drug with a chemical or process that makes shifters susceptible to it." He folded his arms as he sat back.

My mind reeled at the implications. "But that doesn't make any sense," I protested. "Surely I would have heard if there were drug dealers running around Shiftertown? That kind of thing can't be kept a secret for long." But my heart sank as I realized that for the last couple of months I'd spent most of my time between tending bar in Rowanville and taking on what few Enforcer jobs I could. It had been many moons since I'd spent any length of time in Shiftertown.

Comenius shrugged. "It could be a relatively new thing," he said. "Something that's still being tested on the market. But it *is* interesting that this is being peddled by humans."

"Sure," I said, waving my hand impatiently. "But I don't see what this has to do with the silver murders."

"Think about it, Naya." Noria leaned forward, excitement gleaming in her dark eyes. "You said that when you examined Roanas's glass, you didn't detect any silver in it. And yet he died of silver poisoning."

My jaw dropped as the implications of that dawned on me. "Are... are you saying that you think the *cerebust* is being laced with silver?"

"That would certainly explain why you were affected by it,"

Comenius pointed out. "If it was a small enough dose, the silver would weaken you just enough to allow the drug to affect your system. And since you'd be high, you wouldn't even notice."

"So whoever's manufacturing the drug, could also be behind these poisonings." My mind was racing now. "That rhino shifter –"

"Could have been overdosing on a silver-laced drug," Noria finished for me. "Unfortunately we'll never know since you incinerated him, but Comenius and I have been looking through the papers and have found evidence that Rhino-boy wasn't the only shifter who's had a psychotic break like that in the last few months."

Antsy now, I jumped up and started pacing in front of the fireplace. "I have to get out of here," I said, shoving my hands into the pockets of my jeans. "There's no way I'm going to be able to solve these murders if I'm stuck behind these walls."

"Don't be in such a rush, Naya," Comenius said hastily. He rose to his feet as well, squaring his shoulders as if prepared to restrain me. "We haven't conclusively determined whether or not there actually is silver in the cerebust. Noria has an alchemist friend who is going to run some tests –"

"He's a *chemistry* student," Noria corrected, shooting him a testy glare. "Alchemy is magic."

Comenius snorted. "Well *excuse* me."

I couldn't help it – I laughed. "My incarceration seems to have had a positive influence on you," I told him. "I've never seen you so sassy before."

He sobered a little. "You haven't been incarcerated yet, Naya. And if I have my way, you won't be."

Tears pricked at the corner of my eyes, and I swallowed against the lump in my throat. "Thanks," I whispered. "You guys are the best friends I could have." I threw my arms around

Comenius, then reached out and snagged Noria as well for a group hug.

"We know," Noria said, the grin clear in her voice. "And that's why I sent a message to Rylan asking him to break you out."

"Noria!" Scandalized, I broke free of the hug, my eyes darting around wildly. I expected the guards to come rushing in any minute, to cart her away so that she could be questioned about the Resistance's whereabouts. "You can't say that shit in here, not when we're being monitored!"

"Don't worry," Noria said, pulling something from her pocket. "As far as they're concerned, we haven't been saying anything at all for the last ten minutes of our conversation."

She tossed the object in her palm to me, and I caught it, then held it up to the light. It was a small, handheld electronic device with a glowing blue light, and it smelled of magic. "What the hell is this thing?"

"It's a jammer," Noria said proudly, folding her arms across her chest. "Interferes with magical wavelengths when it's activated, which I did before we started talking about the murders. Anyone listening to us via a magical spell wouldn't have been able to hear a damned thing. I've already tested it out a few times, so I know it works."

I gaped at the tiny gadget, amazed. "How the hell did you manage to come up with something like this?"

Comenius scowled at Noria. "She's been experimenting with combinations of magic and technology with a college friend of hers who happens to be a mage," he said. But though the disapproval in his voice was clear, I detected a glimmer of admiration in his eyes. "It's going to get her killed one day, if the Mage's Guild finds out."

I arched a brow, impressed. "You actually found a mage who was willing to collaborate with you?"

Noria shrugged. "He's in my college, so he's pretty progressive."

"I'll say." Though the Academy was technically open to anyone, it was mostly a human-centric institution, with a few shifters attending as well. Mage students were practically unheard of, as most of them simply moved on from their apprenticeships to positions in the Guild, or as freelancers. Very few cared about taking courses or learning skills outside of magic. "What's your mage friend taking?"

Noria's expression turned guilty. "Chemistry."

"Noria!" Comenius's head looked like it was going to explode. "You can't be serious. You're taking the cerebust to a mage?"

Noria glared at him defensively. "He's not like the others," she told him. "He actually believes in equality among the races, which is why he's willing to work with me. He believes magic should be accessible to everyone."

"You know that if it's found out that he's helping you he could be punished, right?" I couldn't believe what I was hearing. "Noria, I can't believe you would put someone in danger like that, just to experiment with a few gadgets!"

Noria's face crumpled under the weight of my disapproval. "I thought you of all people would understand, Naya. We need change, and it's never going to happen if we don't pursue things like this. Isn't that what we're all after?"

Guilt clawed at me as I took her by the shoulders and looked her in the eye. I was being the biggest hypocrite in the world, and I knew it. "Of course it is, but I can't stand the idea of you getting hurt. Your sister would murder me."

Noria frowned. "Why would she do that? This has nothing to do with you – I'm doing this of my own volition." She shrugged my hands off her shoulders as anger sparked in her dark eyes. "What, you get to take credit for my rebellions now? I have my own thoughts and ideas, Naya, and no one else is responsible for them. You're not the only one willing to fight, you know."

"She doesn't mean it that way, Noria." Comenius gently placed his hands on the girl's shoulders, trying to calm her. "She's just worried about you."

"Yeah, well she shouldn't be." Noria tossed her hair and gave me an imperious look. "I can take care of myself. And for once, I'm going to take care of you, too. It shouldn't take Rylan long to get my message, and when he breaks you out of here, remember that I'm the one who saved the day."

"Noria –" I reached for her as she turned away, but she was too quick, and she slipped out of the room in the blink of an eye. I sagged, the weight of guilt and defeat crushing my spine. "By Magorah, Com. What have I done?"

Comenius took me in his arms, and I rested my head on his shoulder, soaking up the comfort he offered. "She just wants to be like you and Annia," he said softly.

"I know," I said miserably. "But I want a better life for her than what we have, and instead she keeps pushing herself closer to the edge. And now because I keep trying to push her back, she hates me."

"She doesn't hate you." Comenius pulled back, and reached down to grab something off the coffee table – the jammer. "If she did, she wouldn't have left this for you." Smiling, he placed it in my palm. A warm tingle spread through my body as he closed my fingers around it. "Keep it with you, for now. I don't know how it works, but I'm sure you'll figure it out."

"Don't go," I murmured as he stepped back.

His pale eyes shimmered with sadness. "You know I'm needed back at the shop," he told me. "And besides, I'm reasonably sure the Chief Mage would not be pleased to find he has an additional houseguest."

I scowled. "Fuck the Chief Mage."

He arched a brow. "That would be an interesting way to escape your death sentence."

I sputtered. "I'm not –"

"I know," he said, squeezing my arm gently. "But I wouldn't blame you if you took advantage of his interest in you. Think what you want, but there *is* a reason he hasn't killed you yet."

"Yeah, because I'm a puzzle he hasn't had the chance to solve yet," I muttered. "As soon as he cracks me, I'm gone." But I couldn't help but wonder whether or not there was any truth to Comenius's words.

Comenius only smiled and shook his head. "Stay safe, Naya." As he left me alone in the room, my head and my heart were swirling with so many thoughts and emotions I thought I would burst.

9

I spent the rest of the day caught up in a maelstrom of confusion, guilt, and anxiety that made me envy humans for their ability to drink their problems away. I was worried about Noria, worried about Rylan, worried about the shifter murders and my complete inability to do anything about them.

And on top of it all, I was also worried about the Chief Mage's intentions toward me.

What if Comenius is right? I thought as I flopped down onto my bed, my belly full of beef stew and bread – yesterday's leftovers by the smell of them, but at least I was getting fed. *What if the Chief Mage's interest is more than clinical?* I thought about the fact that even though he was cold and dispassionate, he'd also shown me some kindnesses. I was out of those magic-suppressing shackles, he'd expended his own magical energy to heal me, and he was going out of his way to find my father.

Going out of his way? Are you kidding me? Finding your father is part of his investigation... he's definitely not doing it for you.

A knock on my door derailed my train of thought, and I sat

up as the scent of the visitor reached my nose – it was Elgarion. My heart rate sped as I crossed the room to answer the door – what did the Director's apprentice want with me now?

I opened the door to see him standing in the hall with a candle in his hand. Ice filled my veins as I caught sight of the two guards standing behind him.

"What do you want?"

"The Chief Mage commands your presence," Elgarion said stiffly. His dark eyes glittered in the candlelight, and I knew he was still thinking about the way I'd embarrassed him back in the storage chamber the other day. But I could hardly hold onto that thought – I was still stuck on the fact that the Chief Mage had sent for me in the evening, far earlier than I expected to see him again.

"Where?" I demanded as I reached for my jacket. My makeshift crescent knives and stakes were still in the pockets, and I was *not* going anywhere near those guards without them. "And why?"

"To his quarters," Elgarion told me. "As for why, I cannot say. But he does not like to be kept waiting."

As if I give a fuck about that, I wanted to snap, but I kept my mouth shut and followed Elgarion. He led me past the Chief Mage's study and further back through a maze of corridors until we reached a door near the end of the West Wing.

"The Chief Mage will join you shortly," Elgarion said, opening the door to reveal a large sitting room.

"Wait." I hesitated, my foot on the threshold. "There's no one here?"

"The Chief Mage insisted that this be a private meeting." Disapproval was stamped all over Elgarion's stony face.

"Then why did you bring these guards along?" I asked, incredulous.

Elgarion stiffened, then drew his robes around him. "Good night, Miss Baine."

I gaped as he swept back down the corridor with the guards in tow, as the truth suddenly dawned on me. Elgarion, the apprentice to the Director of the Mage's Guild, *was afraid of me.* Feeling smug, I grinned after Elgarion's retreating shadow before I sauntered into the room.

The smugness faded as I looked around the large, empty chamber, which, while decorated in the Chief Mage's colors, was cozier than I expected. The wall to my left was lined with bookshelves, and the one on my right was dominated by a large bay window that offered a beautiful view of the Firegate Bridge stretching across Solantha Bay. Couches made of dark, heavy wood and upholstered in blue and gold were grouped around a marble hearth where a roaring fire crackled. The flames illuminated the gold threading woven through the plush blue carpeting covering the floor, which sank under each step I took.

As I wandered over to the window to look out at the view, I realized that there were very few smells beyond the Chief Mage's own scent and Fenris's. He probably didn't invite visitors here often. The realization only made me even more uncomfortable. What was so urgent that he had to call me in the middle of the night to his private chambers, that couldn't be said in front of the guards?

The thoughts that question sparked caused my cheeks to flush and my palms to grow uncomfortably warm. Which was great timing, because the door to my left, at the far end of the room, opened, and Iannis stepped through.

"Sir." I turned on my heel to face him, feeling incredibly off-balance. He was still dressed in the same robes from this morning, but his cherry wood hair had been freed from the confines of its queue, flowing freely around his oblong face, the ends flowing over his broad shoulders. The loose waves gleamed in the firelight, and I fought down a sudden urge to reach out and touch them. Was his hair as soft as it looked?

If that's not the fastest way to get yourself incinerated, I don't know what is.

"Sir?" He arched a brow as he came to stand next to me. The firelight behind him cast his features into shadow, making him look even more enigmatic and mysterious than usual. "Could it be that your time in the palace is actually teaching you some manners?"

I flushed. "My apologies," I quipped. "I should have addressed you as Almighty Dictator."

He frowned, not at all amused by my sarcasm. "I don't understand why you aren't fearful of me."

I scowled, crossing my arms over my chest. "Do you *want* me to be afraid of you?"

For the first time, hesitation flickered over his features. "I demand respect," he said firmly. "Respect and order are the only means to ensure a functioning society."

"Maybe," I snapped. "But respect still has to be *earned*, and force alone isn't enough for you to get it. Perhaps you should try actually *empathizing* with your people."

The Chief Mage was silent for so long that my skin started prickling beneath the weight of his stare. What the hell was I doing, telling the Chief Mage how to run his city? Was I *trying* to get my head chopped off? A bead of sweat rolled down my spine.

"I'm leaving tonight," he finally said, "which is why I summoned you. I won't be able to meet with you tomorrow as I originally anticipated."

"Leaving?" Dread pooled in my stomach at the thought of being cooped up in this palace for who knew how long. I knew I should probably be excited – my chances of escaping increased tenfold with the Chief Mage gone – but the truth was I wanted him to wrap up his 'investigation' of me, and if he left that would only drag things out. "Leaving where?"

"That isn't really any of your business," he said mildly, "but I'll only be gone for a day, so you needn't worry that your stay will be extended too long."

"Oh." I let out a sigh of relief before thinking better of it, then flushed as he arched his brow at me again. "So, what's it gonna be? Are you going to try and turn me into an ice sculpture again?"

"Hardly. Now give me your hands."

I hesitated as he offered his own, palms up, just as he had last time. With my conflicting hormones and emotions growing stronger by the day, I wasn't certain that touching him was a great idea. But I also wanted to get this over with, and if that meant he had to hold my hands like we were two toddlers playing a rhyming game, then so be it.

I placed my hands in his, and my pulse sped up as his long fingers curled around them. That same warm tingle spread through me, just as before, but this time it was accompanied by a familiar heat pooling in my lower belly that could only be described as attraction. I struggled against the feeling as he circled his thumbs across the insides of my wrists – didn't the man know that was an erogenous zone? – and tried to clear my head.

"You need to relax," he murmured.

My cheeks burned. Did he know? "I d-don't think I can." By Magorah, I sounded like a schoolgirl all over again, squirming under the attention of my first crush.

"Close your eyes," he suggested. "Focus on the magic flowing through you, rather than me."

I did as he suggested, doing my best to ignore the feel of his skin against mine and his scent, which seemed to grow more intoxicating the more time I spent inhaling it. It took me a moment, but eventually I zeroed in on the current of magic humming through my veins, and began to mentally trace its path through my system.

A sudden shock jolted me from my trance, and I gasped, my eyes flying open as power surged through me. It crackled through my nerves like lightning, and rippled down my arms. Cold fear shot through my veins as our joined hands began to glow, and I braced myself for the Chief Mage to explode into a cloud of ash as the rhino had done.

Iannis's face tightened, his eyes glued to our hands with fierce intensity, and he sucked in a sharp breath through his nostrils. The glow from our hands dissipated, and the air began crackling around him instead, the way it had when I'd riled him up before.

I took a step back, shock and relief mingling in my veins. "Did... did you just absorb all that magic?"

"For now," he said through gritted teeth. His voice was edged with pain, and suddenly I was filled with guilt. He shouldn't be suffering like this, not as a result of helping me –

I paused mid-thought as he grabbed a potted plant sitting on a side table and released the surge of magic he'd taken from me into it. The tiny shrub instantly exploded into a full-blown tree, unfurling rapidly, the roots spreading across the parquet and the tree branches making scraping sounds as they spread across the ceiling. I gaped, open-mouthed as white flowers bloomed from the branches right before my eyes.

"Well." The Chief Mage regarded the tree wearily. "The servants are going to have an interesting time removing this."

I gaped at him. "Was that an actual attempt at *humor*?"

He frowned. "I'm a mage, not an automaton, Miss Baine."

"Coulda fooled me. I wasn't aware there was a difference." I folded my arms, but I didn't have it in me to glare at him the way I usually did. I couldn't deny that I'd seen flashes of humanity peek out from beneath his cold exterior, though I'd go to my grave before I'd admit that to him.

"I sometimes wonder whether or not you truly have a death wish, or if you simply can't help but insult anyone who you perceive as stronger than yourself, in an attempt to make yourself feel less inadequate."

"Excuse me?" I couldn't believe what I was hearing. "Are you accusing me of being a *coward*?"

"On the contrary. A coward would never dare to insult and defy me the way you do at every turn." He advanced on me with a scowl, and I took another step back. My shoulder blades brushed against the wall, and I stiffened. "If not for the fact that you direct so much animosity towards me, I could almost admire it. But it does make me wonder how you've managed to survive this long with your attitude. You appear to give very little thought to consequences before you jump into action."

"Can we move on to the part where you tell me what the point of this 'experiment' was?" I was not at all comfortable with his analysis of my personality. "Why exactly did you feel the need to siphon enough magic from me to create a tree in your sitting room?"

"The tree was an unintended side effect," the Chief Mage admitted. "I should have foreseen the magical surge and brought a more appropriate receptacle for the excess. As it is, I was not 'siphoning off' your magic, Miss Baine. I was releasing it from its bonds."

My eyes widened. "You... you freed my magic?" I mentally groped for that glow of power in my chest, and nearly toppled over in surprise when I actually *felt* it this time. "By Magorah. You really did!"

"Only partially," the Chief Mage warned. "So that you can learn to control it."

I frowned. The glow *was* weaker than what I experienced during the rare previous outbursts, but I'd chalked that up to the fact that I wasn't supercharging myself to deliver a death blow to anyone. "Why not give me access to the whole thing?" I protested. "It's *my* magic."

"Again, I want you to be able to control it. If I give you access to all of it at once, you may find yourself overwhelmed, especially since there is no one to teach you how to direct it. With the small amount I've given you, you should be able to grasp some rudimentary basics." His features tightened momentarily. "I did not want to leave you entirely defenseless while I was gone, in view of the incident in the kitchen."

I softened a little at that, before I remembered that I'd still seen those same guards around the palace, shooting me death glares that promised retribution. "Are you even going to discipline those guards for trying to kill me?"

"Director Chartis is taking care of the matter."

I rolled my eyes. That meant the guards were going to get away with their outrageous behavior. "I want my weapons back."

The Chief Mage blinked. "What?"

"My weapons." I tapped my foot impatiently, though it didn't have the intended effect as the toe of my boot sank noiselessly into the thick carpet. "They were taken from me when I was arrested, and I want them back so I can defend myself."

The Chief Mage frowned. "I don't know anything about your weapons. In any case, that is what I gave you the magic for, so you can defend yourself."

I growled. "It's hardly going to be very helpful, since I've never been given any instruction on how to use it."

"And that is only because you haven't stopped talking long enough to allow me to give you some basic instruction."

I snapped my jaw shut. He was going to teach me to use my magic? Now?

"I still want them back."

He regarded me for several seconds as though he were weighing the pros and cons of allowing me access to sharp, deadly implements. "I will consider it. Now, give me your hands again. Time grows short."

10

S weat poured down my face as I held my hand palm up in front of me, concentrating with all my might. It was after midnight and I should have been asleep, but instead I sat cross-legged on my bed and focused on the spell the Chief Mage had taught me earlier. Moonlight spilled in through my tiny window, illuminating my palm as I stared at it – I was determined to master this thing before I fell asleep tonight.

Find your center, Iannis had said, and I drew in a deep breath, focusing in on the tiny glow within my chest. I touched the glow, and exhilaration raced through my veins. Magorah, but it felt so good to finally be able to do that! To be able to reach for my magic whenever I wanted –

The magical connection severed.

"Damn it!" I snatched up the pillow on my bed and flung it across the room. This happened almost *every* time. I got so freaking excited about using my magic that I lost my focus, and then it would disappear.

This wouldn't happen if Iannis gave you access to all *your magic.*

I sighed. There was no use thinking about that. Fact was, it was probably better that he didn't, because I seemed to have a knack for conjuring flame. Iannis said it was because of my fiery disposition – each mage had a natural bent towards certain types of magic based on their personality. Of course, when I'd asked him what his was, he'd told me that if I focused more on my magic and less on him then I might actually conjure a decent flame.

Cantankerous bastard.

Determined to prove that I could conjure a flame *without* the Chief Mage's help or the threat of mortal danger, I focused my attention inward again, closing my eyes so I could search for that tiny glow inside my chest. It winked into existence in my mind's eye, and as I connected with it, I channeled my thoughts into a single idea.

Fire.

Heat exploded above my palm. My eyes flew open, and I laughed at the sight of the dancing red flame. How fucking cool was that? I had a ball of fire bouncing around my hand. Talk about a killer weapon!

"Here, little flamey-flame," I cooed. The flame seemed to grow even bigger in response – though that was probably just a reaction to my thoughts as I doubted the thing was sentient. Grinning, I bounced it back and forth between my hands, marveling at the fact that though there was heat emanating from the flame, it wasn't burning me.

Headline: BURNED BY MAGIC: SUNAYA BAINE FOUND DEAD IN SOLANTHA PALACE AS THE RESULT OF UNSUPERVISED EXPERIMENTS WITH MAGICAL FIRE.

I snorted. Both the Herald and the Shifter Courier would have a field day with that one. But Iannis probably knew my own fire wouldn't burn me, or he wouldn't have given me this particular spell to practice on.

"*Naya!*"

Shock burst through me at the sound of my cousin's voice in

my head. The flame in my hand winked out instantly.

"*Rylan? What's going on?*" Fuck, fuck, fuck. Was he already here?

"*Look outside your window.*"

I turned to the window and peered out into the darkness, trying to spot him through the bars. At first I saw nothing but the gardens below and the bay stretching beyond the property, but then I spotted two huge condors heading our way... and there was a small, human form atop one of them.

"*Please don't tell me you're riding one of those birds.*"

"*Okay, I won't tell you. But I* am *here to rescue you.*"

I didn't think – I simply flew from my bed and straight down the stairs, heading for the nearest exit. Fear for my cousin's safety trumped the logic that told me there was no way to get past the wards which confined me to the palace. There was no way in hell some mage wasn't going to see them coming and shoot them down. Iannis wasn't an idiot – he would ensure that his home was well-defended from intruders.

I flung open the door at the bottom of the tower that led out into the back gardens and sprinted through. The wards gave me some pushback, singing my eyebrows and the hairs on my arms, but a burst of magical energy flared out from inside me, burning a hole through the barrier. The cool, salty evening air rushed across my face as I raced for the edge of the property, but I couldn't stop to enjoy it – Rylan was approaching far too fast.

"Go back!" I shrieked. I repeated the warning mentally in my head, slashing with my arms to indicate that they should *not*, under *any* circumstances, land. But it was too late – the two shifter-birds were already here.

"*Don't worry,*" Rylan assured me. "*We know about the barrier. We brought amulets that should help get us through.*"

I held my breath as they soared over the hedge separating the palace grounds from the street. The amulets that dangled around the birds' necks flared to life, and for a triumphant moment I thought they were actually going to work. But then they went black, and an energy field buzzed to life, encasing the palace in a glowing blue wall that surrounded the entire perimeter.

My heart plummeted into the soles of my bare feet as my would-be rescue crew squawked and shouted. They writhed frantically, trying to break free, but the energy field only crackled in response, holding them fast.

"*Stop!*" I shouted at them mentally. "*Stop struggling! I... I'll get you out!*"

"*How?*" Rylan's voice was tinged with fury and desperation. His yellow eyes blazed down at me as he writhed in the confines of the shield, his long black hair flying around his square face. "*They're coming!*"

I didn't need to turn around to know that – I could hear shouts from the palace, and doors bursting open behind me, no doubt mages coming to confront the intruders. There was no question in my mind that Rylan and his friends would be given a death sentence – they were already wanted for too many crimes against the State.

Not knowing what else to do, I sucked in a deep breath and plunged my hands into the energy field. Pain sizzled up my arms and through my entire body, and I shrieked at the magical back-lash, but I couldn't stop now. Desperation fueled the magical surge that crackled through my arms and into the magical field, and it parted just enough to release Rylan and his friends from its hold. They dropped like stones, the birds snapping out their wings at the last second, but Rylan wasn't so lucky – he crashed straight into the hard, unforgiving ground just inside the magical field, and my sensitive ears picked up the sound of crunching bones.

"Stop! Intruders!"

Two guards grabbed me as I tried to rush to my cousin's aid. I fought them furiously, but I'd used up too much magical energy to be effective, and I watched helplessly as two mages darted forward to capture Rylan. Thankfully, one of the shifter birds swooped down to distract, and the other one grabbed Rylan with his claws and hefted him into the air, past the rapidly closing magical field. The mages tried to blast them with energy bolts, but they were too slow, and the bolts were simply absorbed by the field.

I sagged with relief as I watched Rylan and his friends fly off into the distance, and prayed to Magorah that my cousin would be okay. My vision blurred with exhaustion as my adrenaline faded, so I wasn't quite able to make out the fuzzy figure that stepped in front of me.

"Miss Baine." Director Chartis's frigid voice briefly pierced through the fog of exhaustion. He sounded coldly triumphant, probably because he'd caught me in the act of what he saw as an escape attempt... not that he was completely wrong. "You will explain yourself this instant."

"Fuck you," I mumbled as the ground slid up toward me, and the guards' grip tightened on me just before I went under.

WHEN I AWOKE, the midday sun was streaming through my window, and hunger clawed so fiercely at my stomach that the ratty pillow beneath my head actually looked appetizing. I struggled up into a sitting position, feeling shaky, and tried to brace myself against the mattress, only to find that my hands were bound.

No, not bound. Shackled. Cold dread filled my stomach as I looked down at the runed shackles clamped around my wrists. Just when I'd finally gotten access to my magic, I'd lost it again.

Rage propelled me from my bed and across the room. I reached for the door handle, intending to break the door open, but the handle scalded me as I curled my fingers around it. I shook my burning hand and scowled at the knob, seeing the glowing blue runes I'd activated with my touch – they'd warded me in here. Locked me up like a common criminal... which in their eyes I was, but that didn't make me feel any better about it.

"Let me out!" I pounded against the heavy wooden door, shouting until my voice was raw and my hands throbbed. Eventually my rage gave way to exhaustion, and hopeless, bitter tears began to stream down my cheeks. I collapsed back onto my bed, staring up at the ceiling through a haze of defeat. I was locked in this stupid tower, and all because I'd tried to save my well-meaning but idiotic cousin from his botched rescue attempt.

Really, what had Rylan been thinking, charging in here like that? He'd done enough research to know there were wards around the palace, but clearly not enough to know how strong they were or he would have used more potent amulets. Either that, or whoever he'd bought those amulets from – probably someone on the black market – had bilked him. Either way it was sheer carelessness, and when I next saw him I was going to give him a good talking to.

Desperate for help, I mentally called for Fenris, and got no answer. I wondered if he was ignoring me, or if he was too far for me to reach by mind-message. He might have accompanied the Chief Mage on his trip, or was simply out on business of his own. Disappointment filled me, followed by a healthy dose of guilt and shame for even thinking to rely on Fenris in the first place. I'd never been so weak and helpless, not since my aunt Mafiela turned me out on the streets. Fear ballooned in my chest, forcing out all the air in my lungs and I couldn't draw in a breath.

My mind took me back to that time when I was twelve years

old and Aunt Mafiela had locked me in the closet for daring to steal food from her kitchen. She'd 'taken me in' shortly after my mother had died, which really meant she'd utilized me for slave labor, clothed me in her daughter Melantha's stained and too-small castoffs, and fed me meager table scraps. Of course that hadn't been enough for a growing girl like me, so she'd found me in the larder late at night, stuffing slices of ham into my face. Rather than relenting and giving me more food, she'd had me beaten instead, and then locked me in the small, dank closet beneath the stairs, left to spend the night with the rats.

And that was a light punishment.

I'd been trying hard this whole time not to let myself get lost in those dark memories, but the truth was that even though the conditions were better, being imprisoned in Solantha Palace felt a whole lot like the abuse I'd experienced at Mafiela's hands as a child. And the same fear I'd felt then dug its icy claws into my chest, dragging me down into the depths of despair.

Stop wallowing in self-pity. You're better than this!

I knew I was. But I didn't have the energy to prove it. Tears soaked my pillow as I tried to think of something, *anything* that would get me out of this place. But all I could envision was my head on the chopping block, the executioner's ax glinting in the morning sun right before he brought it down on my neck. I had no doubt that Director Chartis was going to do everything in his power to ensure that the death sentence hanging over my head was finally delivered.

Footsteps clopping against the stone floor in the hall drew my attention away from the clouds of misery in my head, and I sat up, hastily wiping the tears and snot from my face with my pillow. The door flew open, and Elgarion marched in along with a bevy of guards, who quickly surrounded me, two of them clamping their hands around my upper arms and dragging me to my feet.

"To the audience chamber," Elgarion said, tossing me a smug look. "Your judgment is long overdue, and it's about time someone finally put you out of your misery."

I tried to struggle as the guards marched me out of the room and down the tower steps, but I barely had the strength to fight off a mouse, never mind a troop of burly men. More tears pricked at the corners of my eyes, but I held them back with the last of my strength. If I was being taken to the audience chamber, did that mean that the Chief Mage was back, and ready to pass sentence? And that Fenris was there too, and simply ignoring my calls for help?

Elgarion flung the double doors to the audience chamber wide, and I squinted as the bright light assaulted my tear-swollen eyes. But by the time the guards dragged me across the carpet to stand before the Chief Mage's desk, my eyes had adjusted, and suspicion filled me as I saw that it wasn't Iannis at all who stood in the Chief Mage's place, but Director Chartis.

"You!" I pointed an accusing, if shackled, finger at him. "You're not the Chief Mage. What right do you have to call me here like this?"

Director Chartis splayed his hands on the desk as he leaned forward, leveling me with a stony glare. He was wearing gold and blue robes, the Chief Mage's colors, which made this whole thing even weirder.

"As the Director of the Mage's Guild, I have every right to call a hearing in a matter as urgent as this. I act in the Chief Mage's stead whenever he is away on business."

"He's supposed to be back today," I insisted, though my heart sank at the truth in his words. "Surely he would want to attend to this matter himself."

Chartis made a slicing motion with his hand, and a buffet of air slapped me in the face. My head snapped to the side, shock running through me as my cheek stung in response.

"Don't presume that you know the Chief Mage's mind simply because you've spent a few hours with him," Chartis said coldly. "I am his deputy, and I decide what matters are important enough for him to speak on."

I frowned. Something didn't seem right about this. Director Chartis was the one who'd recommended allowing me to appeal the Chief Mage in the first place, because he'd been afraid of the repercussions of not allowing me to speak to him. Yet now he was willing to go behind the Chief Mage's back?

"This is about the Resistance, isn't it?" I blurted. "You're in charge of monitoring their activities in Solantha, and you haven't gotten very far, have you?" That explained why he was willing to circumvent the Chief Mage – mages did not take failure very well at all.

"Silence!" He air-slapped me again, and my lip split open from the force of the blow. Anger burned in his eyes – the first real emotion other than boredom I'd seen from him, and it shocked me almost as much as the magical blows. "I will ask the questions, and you will answer them."

I licked my throbbing lower lip, blood coating the tip of my tongue as I eyed him warily. Spots of color rode high on his cheekbones, and his hands on the table were clenched into fists. There must be a lot riding on my answers.

"Who were the three shifters who attempted to breach the wards last night?"

"I have no idea."

He motioned again, and I staggered back under the force of another slap. "You will answer my questions truthfully."

"I don't know them!" I shouted, the anger rushing through my veins giving me renewed strength. "I'm an Enforcer, not a deserter! I don't know anything about the Resistance!"

Director Chartis walked around the desk slowly, his winter-green eyes gleaming. "I think you know more than you are letting on," he said. "Your cousin Rylan is a member of the Resistance. How can you claim to know nothing about them?"

"Rylan and I don't exactly talk much," I snapped. "Like I said, I'm an Enforcer. He wouldn't want to put me in a bad position."

"Oh really?" the Director sneered. "If you don't talk much, then how is it that he knew exactly what room you were in when he came to rescue you?"

I opened my mouth, and then shut it again. There was nothing I could tell him that wouldn't incriminate Rylan. Clenching my hands, I glared at him, wishing I could conjure a fireball so I could melt the self-satisfied expression off his face.

"You can't prove that Rylan was there last night. The shifters who tried to break in were gone by the time you showed up."

The Director scoffed. "Please! As if any judge or jury wouldn't believe my word over his." He pinned me with a cold glare. "Enough games, Miss Baine. You *will* tell me what I want to know, or else –"

"And just what is it that you want to know, Argon?"

My knees wobbled at the sound of Iannis's voice coming from the entrance to the chamber. Relief rushed through me as I turned to see him striding up the carpet, with Fenris in wolf form trotting at his heels. His expression was stony as usual, but the blaze in his violet eyes told a different story – someone was about to get a serious ass kicking.

And for once, it wasn't me.

"Lord Iannis." The Director bowed deeply, and I caught the scent of fear rolling off him. "I was simply questioning the prisoner –"

"In the audience chamber? Wearing ceremonial robes?"

Director Chartis flushed, drawing his gold and blue robes around himself, and it dawned on me that perhaps he was being a little *too* zealous about his Acting Chief Mage status. Was he plotting to steal the coveted title for himself?

"The Resistance made a rescue attempt on the prisoner last night," Director Chartis said stiffly. "I thought it best to get to the heart of this matter as quickly as possible –"

"Without even informing me that such an attempt occurred?"

"I –"

"No." The Chief Mage's voice turned dangerously soft as he took a step forward. "This is my city, my palace, and you do not have leave to make decisions like this without my knowledge. Over the past week I have been made aware of several instances where you have acted on reports without telling me of either the reports or the actions you took. This is unacceptable."

"My Lord," Director Chartis protested, "I was simply trying not to burden you with petty matters –"

"The fact that you have been using apprentices and low-level mages to magic-wipe citizens is not a petty matter!" The Chief Mage made a swift motion with his arm, and a wave of magic steamrolled over everyone in the room, forcing us all to our knees. Even Fenris was affected, though there was no terror in his yellow eyes, unlike the others. "And neither is the fact that you have taken no action against the guards who nearly killed my prisoner in the kitchen, yet now you have time to interrogate her. And in *my* audience chambers, no less." Magic crackled in the air around him, filling the room with dangerous tension and making it hard to breathe. "You have been undermining my authority at every opportunity, and I won't stand for it anymore. You are dismissed."

Chartis's face reddened as he jerked his gaze up from the floor to the Chief Mage's head. "You are terminating me from my position? You can't be serious!"

"I am." Iannis made another gesture with his hand, and the magic pushing us down to the floor abruptly dissipated.

"Guards, remove this mage from the chamber. He is banished from the palace, and his apprentice will be reassigned."

I got to my feet shakily as the guards dragged a raging Chartis out the doors. Elgarion followed behind his master, but not before shooting me a frigid glance that promised retribution – naturally this whole thing was *my* fault. But Fenris trotted up to me, rubbing his head against my legs, and I reached down to rub his thick brown pelt.

"You're alright?"

"Starving and shaky," I admitted, taking comfort from the warmth in his body, *"But alive."*

"I'll get you some food."

Nodding, I looked up to meet the Chief Mage's gaze. If I thought he'd be sympathetic to me, I was wrong – his frigid glare bore into me without mercy, filling me with dread all over again. Was he going to punish me?

"Thanks to a loyal servant who saw fit to send a report to me, your actions from last night have not gone unnoticed." He snapped his fingers, and Fenris returned to his side. "You will go back to your room and stay there until I tell you otherwise. If I find you wandering around before I summon you, you will be severely punished. Have I made myself clear?"

"Yes," I said, my voice as brittle as the rest of me. As I stood now, I wasn't sure I would be able to take another blow, physical or mental. So in the interest of self-preservation, I bit back any retort I might have made, executed an about-face, and left the room.

Hopefully Fenris would get me some food before the Chief Mage saw fit to summon me. Otherwise, the guards might come to my chamber and find me in a coma.

11

Servants arrived at my door with food shortly after I was sent to my room, and by the looks of things they were sent by Fenris – they brought in two roasted pheasants, a leg of ham, a heaping plate of potatoes and a bowl of greens that I didn't examine too closely. I dug into the food with enthusiasm, eager to replenish my energy, and by the time I'd licked every crumb and grease spot from my plates I was full, sleepy, and feeling a lot better about myself.

Sure, I still had no idea what the Chief Mage was going to do when he summoned me, but since he'd had my shackles removed and given me the ability to recharge, at least I wouldn't be completely weak and defenseless.

It was late afternoon, the sun beginning to dip toward the horizon outside my window, and the industrious part of me wanted to train, or study, or explore the palace – *anything* that might be useful. But since I wasn't allowed to do any of those things, I did what any self-respecting feline would do in my situation.

I curled up on my bed and slept.

When the knock on my door awoke me, night had fallen,

painting the room with shadows and moonlight. Yawning, I stretched lazily before I opened the door to find a single guard standing outside my room.

"What's up?" I covered my mouth with my hand to muffle another yawn, blinking at the guard.

"The Chief Mage requests your presence in thirty minutes." The guard looked me up and down with a disapproving frown. "He sent me to fetch you, so I suggest you make yourself look a little more... presentable."

"Presentable?" My first instinct was to tell the guard to fuck off, but then it occurred to me that I'd yet to look at myself in the mirror today. I probably had crusts in my eyes and pillow creases all over my face, not to mention bedhead. "Oh alright," I snapped. "Give me a few minutes."

I slammed the door in his face, then opened it again after I'd grabbed a robe and a change of clothes and headed down to the bathing room, skipping the bathtub in favor of a quick shower. Ten minutes later, I stood in front of the mirror dressed in a red tee and black sweats, feeling ridiculously inadequate as I finger combed my unruly black curls. Thankfully my face looked decent enough – the food and sleep had been enough to heal the simple cuts and bruises from Chartis's air slaps, and my bottle-green eyes were bright and alert – but I was woefully underdressed for an audience with the Chief Mage.

Oh please. As if you looked any better the last couple of times you were summoned. If he'd wanted you to wear better clothes, he would have had the servants provide you with some.

True. Clearly I was letting my hormones get the better of me again. Since when did I care what any man I wasn't trying to fuck thought of me? But I couldn't stop the sigh that escaped my lips as I studied my reflection. I'd been without my leathers and weapons for so long now, it was like a different person looking back at me.

A knock on the door interrupted my pity-party. "Miss Baine, the Chief Mage is waiting."

Grumbling, I wrenched the door open and stepped out into the hall. "Take me away, Captain."

The guard frowned at me, then led me through the torch-lit corridors in silence. He was nothing like the other guards, who'd been more than happy to taunt, glare and leer at me depending on their mood, and it made me wonder whether Fenris or the Chief Mage had specifically chosen him for that reason. I wasn't entirely sure how I felt about it – on the one hand it was nice not to have to put up with that shit, but on the other hand it was weird not to hear it.

Clearly I had masochistic tendencies.

The guard stopped in front of the doors to the Chief Mage's study, then opened them and stood back to let me in. "They're waiting for you, Miss Baine."

Sure enough, I stepped in to see Iannis sitting behind his desk, talking with Fenris who was lounging casually in the visitor's chair in human form. They both rose at the sight of me, Fenris coming around the back of the desk to stand by the Chief Mage's side. The sight reminded me of where Fenris's loyalties lay, regardless of how nice he was to me. The door closed behind me, and I swallowed against the ball of nerves in my throat.

"Hi." I clasped my hands behind my back so I wouldn't fidget with them.

"Hi." Fenris smiled at me reassuringly, but the Chief Mage remained silent and stony as usual. I held my breath, remembering his promise that I would not escape punishment. What was he going to do to me now?

"Right." I clasped my hands in front of me. "So, would you mind telling me what my punishment's supposed to be? Or did you call me here so you could study me in the hopes of finding new things to criticize?"

"Punishment?" The Chief Mage waved a hand dismissively. "There is no punishment. I just said that to satisfy our audience. This was simply a test."

My jaw dropped. "Excuse me?"

"Why don't you sit down," Fenris said gently, indicating the chair he had vacated.

Normally I would have refused, since I'm more comfortable standing, but in my shock I numbly obeyed. "What part of the last twenty-four hours was a test?"

"All of it." The Chief Mage took a seat as well, and Fenris remained standing next to him. "Your cousin making the rescue attempt, Chartis ordering you to come to a hearing, all of it."

I shook my head. "I don't understand."

"It had come to my attention that the Director has not been sharing pertinent information with me," Iannis explained, clasping his hands together and resting them on the blotter covering his desk. "I do have eyes and ears in the city, and I found out through them that your cousin was going to make a rescue attempt last night. I strengthened the wards to make sure that he would fail and left with Fenris to see what would happen during my absence. As I suspected, Director Chartis decided to take matters into his own hands without first alerting me to the problem."

A sense of foreboding filled me, and I leaned forward again. "Wait a minute. How did you know Rylan was coming?"

Iannis waved his hand dismissively. "As I said, I have spies. But if you're worried as to whether or not I am going after your cousin, I shall not bother just yet. The Resistance is hardly a concern – they're little more than a scattering of snakes hiding out in their holes in the desert country. There are more important matters requiring my attention at this time."

I gritted my teeth as my hands curled into fists in my lap. The way he spoke of the Resistance, as if they were nothing more than a cockroach beneath his boot, made my blood heat, and not in a good way. But I decided against mentioning it – I had to pick my battles, and there was no way I was going to win this one, not now anyway.

Instead, I directed my anger to a more pertinent matter. "You know that both my cousin and I could have been killed last night, right?"

"A possibility, but highly unlikely since I calibrated the wards to ensure they were not set to kill." His eyes gleamed as he regarded me. "I find it very interesting that you were able to breach the wards at all to free your cousin and his friends. That part of the plan was not anticipated."

I scowled, crossing my arms over my chest. "Well if you hadn't wanted me to do that, then maybe you shouldn't have given me access to my magic."

The Chief Mage shook his head. "The level of magic I granted you access to should not have been enough to allow you to bypass the reinforced perimeter. It should have barely been enough for you to breach the wards keeping you inside the palace walls."

I sighed. "So what? We already know that my magic bursts out when I'm in danger. Is it really a stretch that it would do that when someone I care about is in danger too?"

The Chief Mage arched a brow. "Has that ever happened before?"

"Well..." I racked my brain, then deflated when I couldn't find an example. "No." Only when my own life was on the line.

"The bond must have weakened more than you realized," Fenris remarked to Iannis, studying me with a frown of his own. "Either from your interference or because of something her father has done."

"Great." I stood up, tired of being peered at like a caged

mouse, and beyond sick of hearing about my father. "Now that this is all settled, can I go? Like, as in, back to my actual home?"

"Soon," the Chief Mage said. "I'm not quite finished studying you."

"Oh yeah?" I leaned forward, pinning him with a glare. "Well, I'm finished being studied!"

Iannis scowled, rising to his feet so he could tower over me. "I don't know why you're so reluctant," he began. "If I am able to complete my investigation, you could –"

"I don't care!" I slammed my palms against the table, making it shudder. "While you've got me cooped up in here, people are dying out there! There are shifters being murdered by silver poisoning, and nobody is investigating it no matter how loudly I yell, including you!" I poked my finger in his chest.

The Chief Mage's eyes blazed. "I haven't heard anything about these shifter murders, and I don't appreciate –"

"That's because Chartis and the Enforcer's Guild haven't told you about them, just like all the other things they've kept from you. You're corrupt, all of you!" I jabbed a finger in Fenris's direction as well, and he took a step back, his eyes widening. "And *you're* no better than any of them! I told you about these killings days ago, and you never even mentioned the matter to him, did you?"

Guilt flashed across Fenris's face. "I –"

I threw up my hands in frustration. "You know what, I don't want to hear about it from either of you. Any excuses you can make are meaningless to those dead shifters and their families. You all disgust me."

I turned on my heel and stormed out of the room, leaving them gaping after me. Fuck them all. If they weren't going to let me out of here, then I would figure it out myself, even if it meant I had to dig a hole to Garai in order to escape.

12

I spent the entire evening as well as most of next morning trying to decipher a spell book I had pilfered from the library, hoping I might learn something useful. An invisibility spell or instructions on how to remove or disable wards would have been nice. Unfortunately the book was written almost entirely in Loranian, the language mages used for spell casting, and it was damned near impossible for me to figure out anything it said.

I was drilling holes into the book with my eyes, a raging headache coming on, when Fenris knocked on my door. I thought about denying him entry, but the smell of roast beef and potatoes accompanied him, and I *was* hungry.

"Come in," I grumbled.

He entered, dressed in his customary dark tunic and holding the anticipated platter of roast beef. "I brought you lunch," he said cautiously.

Sighing, I put the textbook aside and took the plate from him. "Thanks," I muttered, not quite meeting his eyes. Part of me was embarrassed about my outburst yesterday, and the other part of me was still angry that he hadn't brought up the murders to the Chief Mage. Clearly he didn't take them seriously at all, which didn't make any sense since he was a shifter. Didn't he feel any sort of racial loyalty?

"So," he said, eyeing the textbook I'd placed on the bed next to me as I shoveled forkfuls of meat and potatoes into my mouth. "What are you reading?"

"I'm learning spells on how to boil peoples' brains from the inside out."

Fenris tilted his head sideways so he could read the title on the spine. "Well I imagine that would be quite tough, considering that this is a book on Agricultural Magic."

The tips of my ears burned in embarrassment... and then it dawned on me. "You can read Loranian?"

Nodding, Fenris reached for the book, then began flipping through it. "There's a lot of useful stuff in here about using magic to influence the weather, repel certain pests –"

"How do you know Loranian?"

Fenris looked up, a vaguely uncomfortable expression on his face. "I've spent quite a bit of time with Iannis these past years. You can't help but pick up a few things."

I frowned, sensing he was holding something back, but he broke eye contact, returning to the book, and I decided not to press.

"So are you here to help me bust out of this joint, or to give me more excuses from the Chief Mage as to why I can't leave?"

Fenris closed the book and set it aside. "I've come to inform you that Iannis is hosting a banquet, and that you and I are both required to attend."

My jaw dropped. "Me? At a banquet?" The Chief Mage must have lost his mind. I had little to no training in etiquette, and besides, I was still considered a criminal. "What is this banquet for? And who's attending?"

"A variety of Mage Guild members, from Solantha and

anywhere else in Canalo who can make it on such short notice," Fenris said with a shrug. "Iannis needs to choose a new Director for the Mage's Guild, so he's gathering the candidates together. It ought to be an interesting night, watching them drool over the position like a pack of wolves gathered around a choice haunch of venison." His features twisted briefly in disgust.

"Yeah, well you can count me out." I leaned back against my pillow, placing my hands behind my head and crossing my ankles. "No way am I hobnobbing with a bunch of snobby mages. Besides, I don't have anything to wear."

Fenris gave me a wry grin. "You won't have to worry about either of those things. We'll both be going in beast form."

"We will?" I frowned. "Why?"

Fenris shrugged. "I usually come in wolf form because the others underestimate me. It lets me observe and listen in where Iannis can't do so. As for why you're coming, I'm not certain, but I suggest you follow my lead and do the same. You might learn some useful things."

My mood lifted at that idea. Maybe I'd hear something that could give me a more solid lead regarding the shifter murders.

"Alright. I'll do it. When is the banquet?"

"Tonight."

I SPENT the rest of the day alternating between training and reading the primer on Loranian that Fenris produced for me – a pursuit that was both challenging and rewarding. By the time dusk began to settle over the horizon, I was a third of the way through the book, and had also deciphered a spell from the Agricultural Magic text that, in theory, would allow me to summon a spring rain in the middle of fall to water my crops.

Not that I envisioned ever needing such a thing. But still, the fact that I was even able to read it was a win for me.

Hungry, I wandered down to the kitchen to grab some food before the mages arrived, and then made my way to the banquet hall in panther form after ducking into my makeshift training room to change. It felt good to walk around as a beast, my paws padding silently across the parquet and carpets as I took in the castle using my panther senses. Though in human form my senses of smell and hearing were outstanding, they were even better as a panther – my ability to swivel my ears as well as detect odors through a secondary scent gland located above my upper teeth gave me an edge that my human form did not possess.

Strains of classical music emanated from the banquet hall, and I groaned inwardly, knowing it was going to be a fight to stay awake – classical music always put me to sleep. Hopefully whatever the mages said would be interesting enough to keep me alert. One of the double gilt doors was cracked open, so I nudged it a little wider with my shoulder and slipped inside.

I paused in the middle of the doorway to stare at the banquet hall. It had been transformed from a predictably fancy stateroom into a tropical jungle, replete with old trees with fat trunks and orchids hanging from their gnarly limbs. Dirt crumbled beneath my feet as I stepped, but when I pressed my nose to the ground I smelled nothing aside from the faintly soapy scent of floor cleaner.

It was an illusion, at least partially. A damned good one, too.

"Miss Baine." Iannis broke away from the center of the room, where he'd been observing the servants as they set up chairs and tables and long, rectangular serving areas with silver trays of food. "Good, you are on time."

"*Sure am.*" I did the ol' stretch and yawn motion, exposing my long, white fangs, which was usually an intimidating maneuver. Iannis didn't bat an eyelash. *"Where do you want me to go?"*

Iannis turned and pointed to a sturdy branch that jutted out from one of the trees and hung over the table. "You should find that vantage point sufficient for listening and observation. No doubt it will provide a thrill to some of the guests as well, to look up and see a black panther perched directly above them, ready to pounce." Dry humor tinged the last sentence.

"I'll do my best to be scary."

"Wait." He crouched down beside me as I turned to leave. "Before you go..."

He spoke a Word, and ran a hand down my sleek pelt from the top of my head to the base of my tail. Magic rippled through my body, and I yowled, springing away from his touch.

"What the fuck was that?" I shook my body like a dog as tingles raced through my nerves.

The left corner of Iannis's lips curled upward as he rose. "Just a simple glamour, Miss Baine, so the guests won't pay you undue attention. I suggest you get up in that tree now."

Huffing, I turned my back on him and did as he 'suggested', walking across the room to where the tree stood. I rose up on my hind legs to dig my claws into the bark, and though I was worried that the tree might prove to be an illusion too, it held steady as I scrambled up it and onto the branch.

Funnily enough, this is one of the ways jaguars like to hunt, I thought to myself as I settled onto the branch. We like to hang out in trees above watering holes and wait for prey to come and drink, then pounce. I crossed my paws beneath my chin and allowed my tail to hang over the side, swishing back and forth slowly enough to be subtle, while obvious enough to alert anyone paying attention that I was up in the tree. I did *not* need anyone here freaking out... though if I'd been perched above a pond they would have a right to.

I suppose this is as good as a watering hole, I thought to myself as I looked down at the arrangement of round, linen-covered tables being set up below me. From this vantage point I could probably take down just about anyone, though I doubted the Chief Mage would be pleased if I did so.

"Are you doing alright up there?"

I looked across the room to see Fenris standing by the serving tables, wagging his bushy brown tail at me. I swung my own tail back and forth a little faster in greeting, happy to see him.

"Just peachy. Though I wish I'd eaten more before we got here. Whatever's under those covered trays smells divine."

"I'm sure we can help ourselves to the leftovers once we're finished." Fenris's mental voice was tinged with a smile. *"In the meantime, stay where you are. Company is about to arrive."*

Sure enough, the mages began to file in one by one. Iannis stood by the entrance to greet them, and while he wasn't exactly the warm, welcoming host, he also wasn't incredibly cold either. I listened with half an ear as Fenris briefly gave me a rundown on each of the mages, including their name and position. Unfortunately the room was too well-lit for me to get a good look at any of them from a distance – my panther vision worked best in the dark – so I couldn't tell whether or not any of them had green eyes.

I thought you'd already concluded that you couldn't determine which one was your father by eye color alone, a snide voice in my head reminded me.

Yeah, okay, maybe. But that didn't mean I couldn't still look, just in case my father did happen to be among these men. There *was* a remote possibility that the mage who sired me resided in Solantha, after all.

Once all the guests were present and seated – approximately three hundred of them, both male and female – the staff started serving dinner. I tried to ignore the delicious smells of chicken cordon bleu, meat pies, roasted suckling pig, and other forms of deliciousness, and instead tuned into what these pompous bastards in their fancy robes were saying to each other.

"... Illusion is quite spectacular... I even think some of these trees are real..."

"I hear Lord Iannis is considering one of us to fill the Mage Commander's open position..."

"This roast duckling is just perfection. I need to instruct my chef to get the recipe from Lord Iannis's kitchen..."

"... does he often use beasts as decorations for his parties?"

I fought the urge to sigh, knowing it would draw attention. I was hearing absolutely nothing of interest. Lowering my head onto my paws I closed my eyes and prepared to take a catnap. By Magorah, but this was a colossal waste of time –

"I heard there was a bombing incident in Catharas."

My eyes popped open at the sound of a man's voice, and I looked down to see two relatively young mages sitting directly beneath my tree branch, sipping from glasses of wine and discussing bombings as casually as one might talk about the weather. Catharas was a city north of Solantha. While technically it straddled the border between state lines, it was still too close to home for me.

"Yes, well that's not very surprising," the other mage, a female, tittered. "The Resistance has been getting more reckless and crude in their attempts. It was a magic shop they bombed, wasn't it?"

"That's right." The first mage took another sip from his glass of white. "From what I understand, quite a few humans died."

The female mage sniffed. "Well, that can't bode well for them. The Resistance might be gaining popularity right now, but if they keep getting their sympathizers caught up in the crossfire, they may soon lose public support."

"True. If they go on like that, perhaps there will be no need to fight off the Resistance, and its base will simply dissipate."

Their conversation turned toward more mundane topics, and I tuned them out, mulling their words in my head. I couldn't deny the truth of them, and anger grew inside me at the idea that the Resistance was being careless enough to cause civilian casualties with their strikes. Could it be that Rylan had anything to do with these barbaric acts? I hoped not, but I resolved to have a talk with him about it the next time I saw him.

I KEPT my ears open the rest of the night for any more news regarding either the Resistance or the silver murders, but I didn't hear anything else of interest. Nearly two hours had passed since that last conversation, and my stomach was rumbling in earnest now. If I didn't get something to eat soon, I was going to crash the serving tables for leftovers, those mages be damned.

"Lord Iannis." A nasal voice interrupted my train of thought, and my ears swiveled in its direction. "I can't help but notice that you have yet to make a decision regarding the hybrid Sunaya Baine's sentence."

All other conversation in the room seemed to grind to a halt. I turned my head to locate the source of the voice, and saw that it was a bald mage with a handlebar mustache dressed in deep yellow robes. He was seated near the Chief Mage, clearly impossible for him to ignore.

"Yes, I have seen her wandering around the palace quite a bit," an older mage with a silver beard commented. "Does she not have too much freedom, for a prisoner?"

"I heard that she tried to break out the other night and nearly killed someone," another mage interjected. "Would that have happened if she were properly confined?"

"Forget confined," a rotund mage with carrot-red hair and a ruddy complexion chimed in. "She should be executed! Hybrids like her are a danger to society!"

I stiffened as the rest of the mages also began to clamor, tossing politeness to the wind to make their objections about my existence known to the Chief Mage. Who the hell did these pompous assholes think they were? My claws dug into the branch, shredding the tree bark, and wood shavings fell to the ground. The longer Iannis sat there and said nothing, the angrier I got. Was he going to cave to the peer pressure and let these bastards have their way?

"If you are all quite done," the Chief Mage said at last, raising his voice to be heard amongst the mages, "I would suggest that perhaps all of you are being hasty to dismiss the potential that Miss Baine represents."

"If you mean potential for disaster, then I don't think we're dismissing it at all!" the ruddy-faced mage protested. "In fact, I think you're taking this too lightly!"

Iannis leveled a glare at the mage, who shrank back slightly. "I don't take anything lightly, especially when magic is involved." His violet eyes moved amongst the crowd, meeting the eyes of every single mage present. "It may not have occurred to any of you, but Miss Baine could very well prove to be an asset in her own right if properly trained. There are other countries that allow hybrids, with few problems. A few of the states in our own country are experimenting with more liberal policies, and if Canalo is to keep up with the rest of the country, we need to be more progressive. Naturally, I would expect any mage who I appoint as Guild Director to share my view."

There was a lot of muttering amongst the mages then, some looking abashed, but many just plain resentful. "So what do you plan on doing with the hybrid, then?" Baldy finally asked. "Are you going to find someone to train her?"

"Yes." The Chief Mage clasped his hands in front of him. "That is one of the reasons I brought you all here tonight. I expect one of you to take on the task."

"You can't be serious!"

"I am," the Chief Mage said firmly, and my heart sank. He seriously wanted one of these jerks to train me? I doubted I would last a single day with any of them before one of us killed the other. If I happened to be the one who did the killing I would be executed, so it was a lose-lose situation for me either way.

A tense silence filled the room, so thick I could almost swim in it. "Well?" Iannis demanded. "Which one of you is up to the task?"

He called dozens of mages out by name, likely the ones he knew best, asking each one of they would train me. The ball of anxiety in my gut lessened a little bit with each refusal, and when he'd finally finished, I nearly slid off my tree branch as I went boneless with relief. Thank Magorah I wouldn't be subjected to any of their cruelty.

"Well, I have to say I'm highly disappointed in all of you." The Chief Mage frowned at the lot of them, and it occurred to me that he should have been angrier than he was. After all, if one of the purposes of hosting this banquet was to find me a trainer, hadn't this been a colossal waste of time? "I thought that surely one of you would have the fortitude to step up and take on this revolutionary project. It would appear my faith in you was misplaced."

Seriously? He was going to let them off with this light scolding? With the way he'd treated me, I thought he terrified everyone, but he seemed practically tame here. Maybe he was too easy on his mages, and that's why they were so irresponsible.

"Oh, very well." Iannis shrugged his shoulders and let out a small sigh – one of the most expressive things I'd ever seen him do. "I suppose if none of you are willing to train her, then I must take on the task myself."

I really *did* fall off the tree branch this time, and had to quickly right myself in the air so I didn't come crashing down onto my side. I landed on my feet, but nobody noticed my aerial maneuver because the mages had exploded into an uproar.

"A hybrid as your apprentice? That's preposterous!" the carrot-top mage shouted.

"There are plenty of worthy apprentices waiting for a master who would kill for that position!" This was Baldy, and his face was red with anger.

"What kind of example will this set for Canalo? Will every shifter in the state know that all they have to do is sleep with you in order to curry your favor?"

"SILENCE!"

Iannis's voice, magically magnified, shook the walls. Everyone clammed up instantly, and I stood stock still, the hairs along my spine standing straight up in the air. I wasn't sure if the energy crackling through my body was in response to the terror his glare inspired in me, or the fury and embarrassment that burned through my veins from the last mage's comment.

"Lysander," the Chief Mage said in a voice like boiling lava, addressing the silver-bearded mage who'd made the remark. "You have been around longer than most of the mages in this room, and know that I do not tolerate gossip and rumormongers, correct?"

"Y-yes, my Lord." Lysander bowed so low that the tail end of his beard touched the ground.

"Excellent." The Chief Mage's icy gaze swept the room. "Then you understand that *anyone* who repeats such a vile rumor, in my presence or outside, will be struck deaf and dumb *for the rest of the year*. Short of Miss Baine actually killing someone or causing extreme damage, I do not want to hear any more complaints about her. You are all grown mages and more than capable of defending yourself from a single hybrid shifter. *Do I make myself clear?"*

The mages all rushed to assure Iannis that he did, their heads bobbing furiously. I noticed that none of them were able to meet his eyes, though I stared openly at him. I should have been relieved at this turn of events, because it officially meant that I wasn't going to be executed, and was no longer a prisoner. But I was too confused to be grateful. What in the world was he thinking, taking me on as his apprentice? As much as I was loath to admit it, the other mages were right – there were many more apprentices out there who were more deserving of the position. Regardless of what Iannis said, the fact that he was favoring me would only encourage the rumors that we were lovers.

A hot flush spread beneath my fur as I realized what this meant – I would constantly have to endure whispers and speculative looks, not just from the mages but from everyone in Solantha. And what if this didn't end up working out? What if he dropped me like a piece of garbage, like my family had? I would be known as the scorned lover *and* the failed apprentice.

"You are all dismissed," the Chief Mage said, locking eyes with me. One by one, the mages filed out of the banquet hall, muttering and grumbling amongst themselves, until it was just Fenris and Iannis in the hall with me. Them, and my screaming thoughts, telling me to run as far and as fast from this room as I possibly could.

13

B olting from the room didn't work. All it took was a single Word from the Chief Mage, and I froze halfway to the door like a fuzzy black ice sculpture.

"As much as I'm certain you'd like to leave my presence and never return, we are not yet finished with this conversation, Miss Baine." Iannis's cool tones echoed in the empty hall. "We shall adjourn to my chambers for further discussion."

"*I don't want to go to your chambers!*" I snapped at him mentally. If he heard me, though, he didn't show it; he simply walked past me, his ornate blue and gold robes brushing against my fur before he disappeared through the doors. The spell dissipated and I growled, the beast inside me interpreting his "accidental" touch as an act of marking territory, which I did *not* appreciate.

"*Come on.*" Fenris paused beside me, regarding me with his yellow gaze. "*You may as well get this over with.*"

Huffing out a breath through my nostrils, I followed Fenris into the hall and back down to the Chief Mage's chambers. When we got there, Iannis was standing by the fireplace, holding a blue silk robe in his hands.

"Change," he commanded, his stern eyes on mine.

Heat flooded through my body as I stiffened beneath his gaze. I wasn't a prude, and had certainly never been shy about my body, but something about getting naked in front of the most powerful man in Canalo made the fur along my spine crackle.

"Miss Baine, I would prefer to have this conversation verbally." The Chief Mage held the robe aloft again, which shimmered in the firelight. "Please change back into your human form."

The *please* – which he'd never used on me before – reached past my embarrassment and softened me up. I did my customary yawn and stretch, then shifted back into human form. White light engulfed me as my legs and arms grew longer and my snout, fur and claws receded. Crouched on the carpet in human form, I reached up and snatched the robe from his grip, incredibly aware of the fact that I was not only naked, but practically kneeling at the Chief Mage's feet. I stood quickly and shrugged the robe on at the same time, the cool silk fluttering against my skin, and did my best to avoid Iannis's penetrating gaze. It didn't help matters that the blue silk smelled like him, and by the time I was done tying it around my waist I was decidedly hot and bothered. Worse, Fenris was in the room with his keen sense of smell, so at least one of these men *knew* I was hot and bothered.

As if things could get any worse.

"Alright, you boys have had your show," I said, trying to make light of the situation as best I could. I leaned my hip against the arm of one of the couches and crossed my arms. "*Now* can I go?"

"I didn't bring you here because I wanted to look at your body, Miss Baine," Iannis said mildly. But the gleam in his eyes and the pheromones coming off him told me that he had enjoyed looking. "I brought you here to discuss your apprenticeship."

That doused my fire as effectively as a hailstorm. "Yeah, I really like how you announced that to the Mage's Guild without even bothering to consult me first. Has it occurred to you that maybe I don't *want* to be your apprentice?"

"Sunaya –" Fenris began, his voice full of reproach, but the Chief Mage held up a hand.

"Has it occurred to *you*, Miss Baine, that perhaps you're being childish?"

"Childish?" I shouted as anger scalded my cheeks. "How is my desire to be consulted on matters regarding my future fucking *childish*? Maybe the problem is that *you're* treating me too much like a child, and not that I'm acting like one!"

"You are many things, Miss Baine," Iannis murmured, his violet eyes traveling up and down my body. "But a child is not one of them."

The heat in my cheeks spread to the rest of my body, and I wanted to sink into the floor. Thankfully, the Chief Mage blew right past his comment and back to the matter at hand. "Nevertheless, I'd like you to put your emotions aside for the moment and view this rationally. Aside from the fact that I'm bestowing an incredible honor on you –" he ignored my snort of disbelief, "– this is the only way I can grant you your freedom. I cannot simply set you loose in the world without proper training."

The argument ballooning inside me deflated abruptly. "Hang on. Are you saying that I'll be allowed to leave the palace?"

"You will be granted certain freedoms, yes," the Chief Mage confirmed with a nod. "Although, with these freedoms come responsibilities. You will have to work hard and study every day, and in addition you will be expected to conduct yourself like a mage at all times. You will need to observe proper etiquette and curb your overly emotional attitude, and we will need to get you a proper set of robes –"

"Whoa. Hang on there." I held up a hand and took a deep breath through my nose. "You are out of your fucking mind."

"I fail to see –"

"Yes, as usual, you fail to see how anyone could possibly have an objection to your viewpoint." I planted my fists on my hips. "But I do. Just because I was born half-mage doesn't mean I'm ready to embrace the lifestyle! I've lived my entire life as a shifter, and I'm not going to change that overnight because you wave your hand and command it to be so." I waved my own hands as I spoke, and his eyes narrowed at my mockery. "If being your apprentice means I have to put on robes and walk around like I have a wand up my ass, then you may as well send me straight to the chopping block, because I would rather *die* than live the emotionless, passionless existence you mages do."

The Chief Mage's eyes flashed, and he took a step forward. "The fact I do not display my feelings all the time does not mean I don't have them," he said tightly. "Rather, I would say I exhibit remarkable control for not lashing out at you, even though you mock me at every turn."

Guilt sank its razor sharp claws into my chest, and I fought the urge to shrink back beneath his glare, which held more than simple anger. Could it be that I'd actually hurt his feelings?

That's ridiculous.

And yet, I couldn't deny the truth in his words – any other mage would have happily executed me at the first taste of my flippant tongue. But Iannis hadn't, and I'd refused to give him credit for that.

"L-look," I stammered, my emotions off balance, "even if I did agree to be your apprentice, I don't see what the point is, since my magic is too unpredictable to train."

The Chief Mage scoffed. "That's nonsense. You're the daughter of an extremely powerful mage. There is no reason that I wouldn't be able to cultivate your talents and turn you into a powerful mage in your own right."

I froze. "How the hell would you know that about my father?"

"Your magical signature is very strong and distinctive, which considerably narrows the field of possibilities."

"Oh yeah?" My heart jumped with excitement. "Well who's on the list?"

The Chief Mage folded his arms. "I don't see why I should divulge any details to you, since you're not willing to be apprenticed."

Damn him. "That's blackmail, and you know it."

"*Blackmail implies that he's holding damning information over your head, which he is not.*"

I glared at Fenris. "I don't care how you put it, it's still coercion and I don't like it."

The Chief Mage simply shrugged. "Like it or not, that is the situation. If you want to know who your father is, you must complete your apprenticeship first. Or at the very least, make significant progress."

Fury blazed in my chest, and I took a step forward. Fenris chose that moment to put his body in between us, and shift back into human form.

"I think perhaps we should change the subject," he told the Chief Mage. I frowned, noticing that Fenris was fully clothed. How did he do that? Did he have some kind of charm that allowed him to retain his clothing? If so, I needed to get my hands on it, stat. "After all, there is still the matter of the poisoning to be dealt with."

My ears went on full alert. "Poison? What poison?" Was another shifter dead already?

The Chief Mage wrinkled his long nose. "Fenris detected hemlock in a drink that was served to me," he said, sounding more annoyed than anything else. "A rather amateur assassination attempt, considering that I am immune to most poisons, but it must be punished nonetheless."

Fenris inclined his head. "I would appreciate if you could lend me your lie detector wand so I may go question the kitchen staff. They might have seen someone or something, or one of them may even be responsible."

The Chief Mage nodded, drawing out a long, wooden stick from his sleeve. "Report your findings back to me," he told Fenris.

"Why do you need a stick to tell you whether or not someone's lying?" I asked. Any shifter worth their salt could smell a liar – no magic necessary.

"The stick is more reliable," Fenris said lightly, but his face tightened, and I knew I had struck a nerve. He nodded stiffly at both of us and left.

The door closed behind him, and I shifted uncomfortably on the balls of my feet, self-conscious about the fact that I was alone with a man I was attracted to... a man who had just seen me naked. He regarded me silently, his violet eyes glittering, but with the firelight reflected in them he seemed warmer than usual, less dispassionate.

"I like how at the first sign of an assassination attempt on yourself you rush to have Fenris investigate, but you've yet to do anything about the silver murders," I snapped, more to dispel the sexual tension in the room than anything else.

"There you go again," Iannis said softly, taking a step toward me. His eyes darkened, and I backed up unconsciously to try and maintain some distance. "Throwing barbs and insults in my face, after I've extended you an honor that most apprentices would kill for. What do you hope to accomplish by this, I wonder? Can it truly be that you have a death wish?"

"No." My shoulder blades brushed the tomes on the shelves

behind me, and I stopped moving. "I just don't like being told what to do by someone who thinks he's better than me."

Iannis placed a hand on either side of my head, bracing his weight on the shelves as he leaned into me. I sucked in a sharp breath, and my head spun as I inhaled his masculine scent. My heart was pumping so hard I thought it would punch a hole through my chest, and I fisted my hands at my sides to keep from quivering beneath his penetrating and unmistakably hot gaze.

"I would be the first to admit I know nothing about how to fight with crescent knives and chakrams," he murmured, his warm breath caressing my cheek. "But make no mistake, when it comes to magic, I am your better in *every* way."

My breath caught as he lifted a lock of hair from my shoulder, rubbing the glossy black curl between the pads of his thumb and forefinger. "W-what are you doing?"

"Reminding you who is in charge." He wrapped the curl around his finger, his eyes never leaving mine. "I could twist up the fibers of your being just like this strand of your hair, and you would die a painful death. Instead, I'm struck by this odd compulsion to help you, despite the fact that you push me away at every turn." His lips curled up at the corners. "Strange that at this moment, we're the closest we've ever been to each other, and yet for once you're not pushing back."

My cheeks flushed as a tingle spread up my arms and down my body. Part of me wanted to shove him away, but I was caught up in the strange spell of this moment, fear and desire chasing each other through my veins as if to see which one could overwhelm me first. My lips parted instinctively, and I wet them with my tongue, imagining what it would feel like if his lips were pressed against mine instead. I knew I should fight these feelings, but our bodies were far too close, his masculine scent surrounding me and making it hard to reason. All I could think about was the heat spreading through my lower belly and how the silk of the robe was suddenly harsh against my skin.

His nostrils flared, and for a moment I thought he might actually kiss me. But instead he cleared his throat and took a step back.

"I think it's best we both retire for the night," he said, voice clipped. "We'll adjourn tomorrow evening for your next lesson, so try not to get into too much mischief before then. You are dismissed."

Nodding, I fled the room, anxious to put some distance between us so I could sort out the confusing jumble of thoughts jockeying for position in my head. It wasn't until I'd gotten back to my room that I realized I was still wearing his robe. I spent the rest of the night with his scent clinging to me, in and on and all around me, and ached for something I didn't even think I wanted.

14

I t took me most of the night to fall asleep, and I didn't wake until the early afternoon sunlight struck my eyelids through my bedroom window. I sat up, rubbing my gritty eyelids as I tried to gather my muddled thoughts, and froze at the sensation of cool silk gliding against my skin. Looking down, I groaned as I saw that I'd fallen asleep still wearing Iannis's blue robe – I was *not* going to walk around the rest of the day with his scent clinging to me.

I quickly changed into a pair of cotton pants and a loose fitting shirt, and trotted down the winding staircase toward the East Wing so I could grab a bath. On my way down the corridor, I ran into Fenris.

"Sunaya!" Fenris smiled. "I was just coming to find you."

Dread pooled in my stomach. "What is it now?" Couldn't I ever have a day to myself?

Fenris chuckled at the pained expression on my face. "Don't look so sullen, Sunaya. I've simply come to show you to your new quarters."

My eyebrows winged up. "New quarters?"

He nodded. "As the Chief Mage's apprentice, that dingy

tower room isn't appropriate for you anymore. He instructed me to help you get settled into your new room."

"Oh. Well then." I made a grand gesture with my arm. "Please, lead the way."

I followed Fenris the rest of the way to the East Wing, a bounce in my step. Maybe this whole apprentice gig wasn't so bad after all. He led me to the end of the wing and showed me into a corner room at least four times the size of my tower cell, with a huge four-poster bed draped in green silk dominating the far side and a sitting area with a fireplace directly in front of me. The room was decorated in pale greens and earthy browns, with a generous amount of light spilling in through three rectangular windows framed with gossamer curtains. The glossy wooden floorboards creaked beneath my weight, covered strategically with plush rugs in certain places, but otherwise left bare to gleam in the natural light.

"Wow." I couldn't help the grin that burst across my face. "This is definitely a step up." I threw open a pair of double doors, then froze at the sight of all my clothes hanging neatly from the racks of the biggest walk-in closet I'd ever seen. My attire took up perhaps a quarter of the available space, and boxes stacked neatly in the center of the room took maybe another quarter.

"By Magorah," I whispered. "You... you had my stuff delivered?"

Fenris shrugged. "Iannis suggested that I look into it, actually. Good thing, too, because your landlord was preparing to have you evicted. Two servants brought your things over this morning." He grinned as he produced a set of keys from his sleeve and tossed them to me. "They even managed to recover your steambike."

Tears stung the corners of my eyes, and I flung my arms around Fenris's neck. "Thank you so much," I murmured, so ridiculously grateful to have my things. I would be able to wear my own clothes again, and if the servants had brought over everything, even carry a weapon!

Fenris stiffened briefly, but quickly relaxed and patted me on the back. "It's no trouble at all," he said. "I'll leave you to get acquainted with your room."

I spent the next few hours organizing my things, unpacking all the stuff in my boxes and rearranging my clothes until they were on the racks the way I liked them. I filled the empty book-case that stood by one of the windows with my books – a combination of martial arts theory, history texts, and novels that were strictly for pleasure reading – and the second one I filled with my smaller weapons, such as knives and throwing stars. The bigger weapons, such as my staff and swords, had to go in the closet.

Finished at last, I took a long, hot bath, dressed myself in a pair of leather pants and a long-sleeved red top, and tucked two knives into my boots. As an afterthought, I grabbed one of my short swords, similar in style to the ones the guards used, and secured it around my waist with a belt and sheath.

Yep, I thought as I gazed at myself in the full-length mirror installed in the walk-in closet. My curly black hair tumbled around my shoulders, and my tanned skin glowed with good health. I was finally starting to feel like my old self again.

"Going somewhere?"

I nearly stumbled as I walked out of the closet – Fenris had popped his head back in.

"Am I not allowed to?" I demanded, folding my arms across my chest. "Surely now that I'm an apprentice I can come and go from the palace?"

Fenris nodded, stepping into the room. "Iannis has allowed you four hours of free time per day in which you may do whatever you wish outside the palace walls, in addition to any time you may be sent out to run errands."

I clenched my jaw at that. "So I'm still a prisoner?"

Fenris sighed, running a hand through his thick, dark hair. "Can't you at least take this one as a win, Sunaya? The Chief Mage doesn't want you putting yourself at risk until you are properly trained."

I tossed my hair over my shoulder. "I've been taking care of myself for a long time," I told him. "But I guess I'll accept the terms. Still, it would be nice if I could get my lost weapons back. Not to mention my Enforcer bracelet." I tapped my naked wrist.

Fenris winced. "Yes, about that –"

Dread turned my stomach to lead. "They're gone?"

Fenris nodded. "Iannis asked me to track them down, but the Enforcer's Guild doesn't have them."

My nails bit into my palms as I clenched my fists. "Brin and Nila. Those bastards."

"We're still looking for them," Fenris insisted. "With enough time, we might –"

"Stop." I held up a hand, my heart aching. Those weapons had been among my most prized possessions. "You can at least get my Enforcer's bracelet back, can't you?" I felt sick to my stomach at the thought of losing that, too. It would mean the end of my livelihood, especially if I ended up not making it as a mage.

Fenris nodded. "That should be possible. If we can't get the original back, we can order the Enforcer's Guild to issue you a new one."

I sighed as a modicum of relief trickled through me, then changed the subject. "Did you find anything out last night with that lie detector wand thingy the Chief Mage gave you?"

Fenris scowled. "Unfortunately not," he admitted, rubbing

the back of his neck. "None of the kitchen staff appeared to know anything, and the wand didn't twitch at all when I questioned them, so they weren't lying. It could have been one of the mages at the party, or theoretically one of the servants of the dignitaries who are staying here as guests. It's tough to narrow down."

"That doesn't sound very reassuring." I pursed my lips, wondering how effective that wand really was. Why did Fenris rely on it? Surely his nose was good enough.

"It's not. I'm going to do some further investigation into it." He pulled a book from his sleeve and handed it to me. "This is a basic primer on magic, one of the few not written in Loranian. Iannis found it last night and asked me to give it to you, so you could practice in your room when he's not available. I suggest you be very careful and make sure no one is nearby when you are practicing, especially if you are going to perform a new spell. It wouldn't do at all if you accidentally hurt someone."

"Thanks." A spark of delight lit in my chest as I took the book, something that would not have happened a week ago. Strange how my outlook on magic had changed in such a short time, now that it was more accessible to me.

Fenris showed me how to activate the pre-spelled wards set around the perimeter of my room, which I could use to keep anyone from entering while I was performing magic. He then left me to my own devices. I stared at the book for a little while, tempted to start working now, but the outdoors called me more strongly than the spells did. I slid the book onto one of my shelves, between a paperback on Garaian History and a mystery novel.

It was time to go and see how my city had fared without me.

I GRABBED a few scones from the kitchen, then hopped on my

steambike and headed towards the Port. I was in a ridiculously good mood, and it wasn't just the fresh air on my face or the sights and sounds of the city that surrounded me as I rode through the streets. The staff and guards had all been fairly pleasant to me as I'd left, addressing me as 'ma'am' or 'miss', and no longer gave me dirty or suspicious looks. The mages, for their part, hadn't changed their level of animosity, but only the way they expressed it – instead of sneering at me they scowled, beaming hatred or jealousy my way when they thought my back was turned. They thought their bad vibes would bring me down, but instead they only widened my smile and lifted my spirits. Any day I could wiggle the stick up those stuffy bastards' asses was a good day in my book.

The bell tinkled as I opened the door to Comenius's shop, which looked exactly the same as it had the last time I'd walked in here. Of course, that had been less than a week ago, so I shouldn't have expected anything different, but still, the normality brought me comfort.

"Naya!" Noria dropped the coins she'd been counting back into the register and dashed around the counter as she caught sight of me. I laughed as she flung her arms around me and hugged her back, relieved that she wasn't mad at me. "I'm so glad you're here! How did you get out? Did Rylan rescue you after all?"

"No." I clamped my lips shut on the scolding I wanted to give her for sending Rylan into a trap in the first place – she'd only been trying to help, and in the end the Chief Mage had simply used the situation to his advantage. "I was released."

"Really?" Comenius popped in from the back of the shop, his stern face all smiles. I embraced him as well, inhaling his comforting sage and thyme scent. "How did you manage that?"

I stuck out my tongue at him. "The Chief Mage made me his apprentice."

"WHAT?"

For the next ten minutes I was peppered by a barrage of questions, which I answered as best I could. Comenius was stunned, but happy, while Noria was flat-out confused.

"But I don't understand," she whined plaintively when I'd finished explaining to her that I was going to have to live at the palace until I'd finished my apprenticeship. "He's the *enemy*, Naya. How could you?"

"Not all mages are the enemy," Comenius pointed out mildly. "After all, you're working with a mage at the Academy right now, are you not?"

Noria pouted. "Yeah, but he's not the *Chief* Mage." She worried her lip for a moment. "He's still working on analyzing that drug. He's pretty busy between classes and his own projects right now, but I hope he'll have something for us by next week."

I nodded, sobering a little as my mind turned back to the murders. "Has there been any other news?"

Comenius shook his head. "No murders since the last one reported by the *Courier*."

I ran my tongue along my upper teeth, frustrated. "That's supposed to be a good thing, but..."

"You feel like you need more leads, and you don't have anything," Comenius finished. His frustrated look told me that he commiserated, which made me feel a little better. "I know what you mean, but until we get an answer back regarding the drug, I don't have anything concrete to go on."

"You know," Noria said, her brow puckering thoughtfully. "You could easily take this chance to run off to the Underground and join up with the Resistance, now that you're free. I don't see why you've got to be beholden to the Chief Mage."

I scowled. "Noria, I support the Resistance too but I've already had a taste of what it's like to be a captive criminal, and I don't like it. I'm much happier on the other side of the table where I get to catch the bad guys, and I can't do that if I'm a wanted fugitive."

Brackets formed around the edges of Noria's mouth. "But what if those bad guys aren't really bad guys, but just people exercising rights that have been unjustly taken away from them? Like you with your magic?" She jabbed her finger into my chest. "I've been thinking about this for a while, and I'm not sure that being an Enforcer is actually a good idea. All I'd be doing is supporting our corrupt regime. When I'm done with college I'm joining the Resistance."

I bit back a groan at Noria's defiant look. This is what I got for trying to convince her not to be an Enforcer – an even *worse* career decision.

"Have you spoken to Annia about this? Or your mother?"

" Annia's still out of town on a mission." Noria wrinkled her nose. "But I don't have to talk to her. I'm old enough to decide for myself."

"Yes, but I'm sure she'd still want to hear about it." I laid a hand on her shoulder, gentling my voice. "She's your sister and she loves you, just like we all do."

Noria looked away. I sighed, then continued. "Besides, my reluctance to become a criminal isn't the only reason I'm sticking around. I've got to solve these murders. Not to mention that having inside access to the palace will allow me to pass on useful information to Rylan."

"Oh." Noria perked right up. "Well, I guess that's okay then."

"Still, though," I amended, my frown returning at the thought of Rylan. "I can't say that I'm too happy about the Resistance's methods of, well, resisting."

Comenius raised his brows. "What do you mean?"

I relayed the conversation I'd heard from the two mages back at the banquet about the terrorist attacks, and by the time I was finished both Comenius *and* Noria were scowling.

"There's no way that's true," Noria insisted, her dark eyes burning.

"At the very least we don't know the full story," Comenius declared, ever the conservative. "The mages could have been embellishing their story, or even leaving key things out."

"Exactly!" Noria planted her hands on her hips. "You can't trust anything they say."

"Well, that's definitely possible." I paused to consider that, thankful that my thick hair hid the tips of my reddening ears. Was it possible that I was succumbing to the brainwashing effects of the mages' propaganda? "Still, I can't completely discount what I heard until I know more."

"Hmph." Noria wrinkled her nose. "I think you've been doing a little too much listening, and not enough looking." She returned to her post behind the counter. "I'm going to go do something productive. You should too."

"Yeah," I said slowly as Comenius shot me an apologetic look. "I guess you're right." It was time to do more looking, that was for sure, and not just on my part. I was going to get the Chief Mage involved with this even if it killed me. It was about time someone other than me did something about this whole mess.

ON MY WAY back to Solantha Palace, I stopped by the Shifter-town Cemetery to visit Roanas's grave. It was located outside the Twenty-First Street Temple, a tall, grey stone building where shifters went to pay their respects to Magorah. I bypassed the temple itself, avoiding the reproachful gazes of the carved animals perched on the corners of the building, and headed to the cemetery in the back.

The cemetery was a wide plot of land that stretched for several acres from the back of the temple. Rows of headstones marked the places where the deceased lay, and I trod lightly over the grass, careful not to step on any flowers or other offerings left for the dead. It didn't take me long to find Roanas's grave – it was heaped with offerings from his many Shiftertown admirers, and beneath them lay freshly-turned dirt upon which grass had not yet grown.

I clenched my fist around my own meager offering, a bouquet of dandelions, which I thought a fitting tribute since Roanas had been a lion shifter. I should have been there at the funeral, to say a proper goodbye, to ensure the clerics laid him to rest respectfully and placed a gold coin atop each of his eyelids to pay the Ferryman who would lead him to the afterlife. I should have been there to grieve with his sister, who must have taken a dirigible all the way out from the southwest to see her brother buried. I should have been there to glare holes into my aunt Mafiela and demand that she and the rest of the Council fill Roanas's shoes with a competent Inspector immediately, one who would pick up where Roanas left off and catch the bastard who was doing all this.

But I hadn't, because I'd been imprisoned in Solantha Palace due to my own stupidity.

I squeezed my eyelids shut as I dropped to my knees, pressing my forehead to the gravestone. Cool granite rasped against my skin, a stark contrast to the hot tears running down my cheeks. For a long moment I could do nothing except kneel there, my tears dripping on the freshly-tilled earth, a salty offering lost on the body buried six feet beneath. After all, Roanas was no longer in that body to receive them – the tears were more for me, an opportunity to unleash the grief I'd shoved deep into the recesses of my mind since this whole ordeal had started. Tears that I'd not dared show while in the palace, not only because no one would care, but because in enemy territory grief was a luxury I couldn't afford.

Roanas, I thought silently, praying my thoughts would reach him in the afterlife. *I'm sorry I couldn't be there for you. I'm sorry I wasn't there to help you while you were investigating in the first place. Maybe if I had been, I could have helped you solve these murders before the killer caught on to you. Maybe if I hadn't been so wrapped up in my own problems, you wouldn't be dead now.*

A soft breeze stirred the hair on the nape of my neck and whispered gently in my ear. *There is little point in wishing upon what could have been. Your time is far better spent focusing on what could be, or better yet, what will be.*

I chuckled through my tears at the oft-quoted line. I couldn't say whether or not Roanas had actually spoken to me from beyond the grave, but the words soothed me nonetheless.

"Come to pay your respects?"

My head snapped up at the sound of an unfamiliar male voice. To my right stood a tall man dressed in a long brown leather coat, tight-fitting pants and a pair of boots that looked as though they'd seen a few hundred miles. The breeze tousled his short blond hair, drawing my attention to his raw-boned face. His hawk nose and slightly too-wide mouth pushed him out of the classically handsome category, but he was pleasant enough to look at. There was a certain charm to the way the left corner of his mouth turned up, and his sharp, reddish-yellow shifter eyes commanded attention.

I slowly got to my feet, nose twitching. My hackles rose as I caught his scent – he was a jaguar shifter. Around these parts that could only mean one thing.

"You must be my aunt Mafiela's latest messenger boy." I tossed my head, and a sudden gust of wind caught at my hair, streaming the thick black curls out from behind me like a banner. "Did she send you here to taunt me in her stead? Is she so busy she can't make the time herself?"

The shifter arched a brow. "I am a recent addition to the

Baine clan... but no, I'm not the Chieftain's 'messenger boy'. I'm Shiftertown Inspector Boon Lakin."

I froze. The new Shiftertown Inspector? I eyed him up and down again, noting the knives cleverly concealed in his boots. That long coat of his could have many pockets in which to store more weapons and other useful tools...

"Let's see some I.D. then, Inspector." I closed the distance between us and held out a hand.

He reached beneath the collar of his coat and pulled out a golden medallion. My heart constricted as I caught sight of the fang symbol stamped into the center, as well as the runes that danced around the edges of the circle – it was the same one Roanas had worn.

"Convinced?"

I stared deep into his eyes. Unlike the other members of my former clan, Inspector Lakin's eyes held no contempt when he looked at me, and they should have. I was an outsider, an abomination by my aunt Mafiela's standards, and whatever she said, the rest of the clan followed.

"You're not from around here, are you?"

Inspector Lakin shook his head. "I'm a transplant from the Jaguar clan in Pardas," he admitted, referring to a capital city in one of the northwestern states. "I used to be the Inspector up there, but I felt like a change of scenery, and I had a deputy who was more than willing to fill my shoes."

"Must be nice," I muttered, shoving my hands into my jacket pockets. If I hadn't been a hybrid, I would have been the one to fill Roanas's shoes – I was more than capable between the training that I'd received from him and my experience as an Enforcer. "Fresh start, new life."

I'd thought about that myself once or twice – just packing up and moving somewhere else where nobody knew who I was. Sure, any shifter with a good nose could still tell I was a hybrid, but not that I was a mage if I didn't use my magic, and there were states, or at least cities, in the Northia Federation where half-human shifters were welcome. But any chance of that happening was gone now that my magic was public knowledge – my case was unique enough that news of my apprentice status would eventually spread across the country, at least amongst mage circles.

"Yeah." Inspector Lakin stared at me for a long moment. "I'm sorry for your loss. From what I hear, you two were close."

I snorted. "You're not sorry for my loss. You're just exchanging pleasantries while beating around the bush. Why don't you tell me the real reason you came here to intrude on me while I'm paying my respects?"

Inspector Lakin's eyes gleamed. "I see the rumors about you having a smart mouth are true."

I jutted my chin out. "Yeah? You got a problem with that?"

Lakin only shrugged. "The reason I approached you is because I was going through Roanas's case files and I noticed that he didn't seem to have a file regarding these silver poisonings." His eyes narrowed. "From everything I've heard of him, he was good at what he did. I don't see how he would have forgotten to put a file together."

"Not really sure what this has to do with me."

"You were the last one to see Roanas alive."

"I don't have his case file." Not a lie. I sent a mental thank-you to Comenius; I'd left the file at his shop before responding to the emergency call that had gotten me into so much trouble.

"But you know where it is."

I said nothing.

"You know that I could have you brought before the Council for willfully hiding evidence." His voice lowered into a dangerous growl. "This isn't just about Roanas, Miss Baine. This is about getting justice for all the shifters who have died at the hands of this monster, and stopping him from hurting anyone else."

I laughed bitterly. "I belong to no clan, and I'm a quasi-member of the Mage's Guild now. I don't think you actually *can* drag me before the Council."

Lakin opened his mouth to answer, but the medallion around his neck lit up, bathing his throat in a golden glow. *Emergency reported at 1922 Third Street,* a metallic voice said. *Doctor on scene. Please respond.*

Lakin's face whitened at the same time the blood drained from mine. That was my Aunt Mafiela's house.

He sprinted for the street, where a sleek silver steambike was parked in front of mine. I hesitated for only a second before racing after him. He peeled out into the road with a shrill whistle from the engine, and I followed right after. If this was connected in any way to the silver poisonings, I had to know.

THIRD STREET WAS ALL the way on the other side of Shiftertown, near the bay where the more affluent shifters lived. Lakin parked in front of my aunt's residence, a three-story house with grey siding, dark purple roof tiling, and matching purple shutters. A horse-drawn carriage was already parked at the curb in front of the steps. The front door was wide open, and the sound of a woman wailing was clearly audible from the street.

"Stay out here," Lakin snapped as he ripped off his helmet. He raced up the steps and into the house. I followed after him, knowing he didn't have the time to stand around and argue with me.

We found the source of the wailing in the parlor, where a veritable party of shifters were gathered, dressed in dinner finery. I recognized them all – this was the shifter Council and their respective families, likely all here at my aunt's house for some kind of social event. They were gathered in a circle around a low couch, where a man lay with marble skin that looked like death. He had rich, dark brown hair and was wearing a gold waistcoat, white linen shirt and white slacks. I recognized him instantly as Corin Finehorn – the head of the Deer Clan, and one of the five council members.

"No!" Larana, Finehorn's wife wailed, clutching her mate's hand. She wore a dark green dress, gold jewelry dripping from her ears and throat. "It can't be. He can't be gone!"

"I'm sorry," the doctor said. He placed a gentle hand on the woman's slim shoulder. "There's nothing more I can do for him."

"By Magorah." My Aunt Mafiela spoke in a clipped voice. She wore a white dress that highlighted her slim figure, and her wealth of golden hair was piled atop her head in a matronly up-do. Pearls gleamed softly at her ears, throat and wrists, and if not for her yellow shifter eyes, I would have thought her a human socialite. "This is outrageous. Corin was perfectly healthy when he arrived at dinner tonight. How could this happen?"

"He was poisoned, wasn't he?"

Lakin winced as every single person in the room turned to look at me. Mafiela's eyes widened in outrage. "What are you doing in my home!" she demanded, her cheeks coloring.

"My apologies, Chieftain Baine." Lakin took a step forward to deflect attention onto him. "I was questioning your niece when I got the alert, and she followed me here."

"Well it's about time," Mafiela snapped. "We've been waiting for ten minutes."

"Is... is it true that poison is what killed my mate?" Larana rose to her feet from her position beside the couch. Her doe eyes were filled with tears.

"The reaction does seem alarmingly similar to that of someone afflicted with silver poisoning," the doctor hedged.

Larana's eyes flashed. "You!" she pointed a trembling finger at my aunt. "You killed my mate!"

"That's absurd!" Mafiela snapped. "Why would I do such a thing? Corin and I were good friends, fellow council members!"

"He was eating your food." Larana's voice wobbled. "Drinking from your glasses." Her face crumpled as she dissolved into tears again. "He's gone, and it's all your fault!"

The woman lunged at my aunt, her eyes wild with grief and rage. Mafiela sidestepped, her own face mottled with fury. She raised her hand to strike Larana, and I darted forward, catching the blow before it could land.

"Don't you think this poor woman's gone through enough?" I snarled. "You couldn't even take a moment to offer her some consolation, and now you're going to beat her up too?"

Silence froze the room. Mafiela's yellow eyes glittered at me with pure malice, and for a moment I wondered whether or not she would try to strike me too. I had no illusions about her – she might be dressed up like a lady, but beneath the façade she was all beast, one of the most ruthless people I knew. Part of me wished that she would lash out – I longed for provocation of any kind to take my years of pent-up anger out on her. But my more rational side knew that I could never get away with such behavior in front of the Council, even if I was the Chief Mage's apprentice.

"Mafiela." The deep voice of Toras, the Tiger Clan Chieftain, rumbled through the air. "The half-breed is right."

"Fine." Sneering, Mafiela wrenched her hand from mine. "I apologize for my behavior. Now get out of my house."

Trembling with anger, I took a step toward her, intending to give her a piece of my mind.

"Don't." Lakin's hand clamped around my wrist. I whirled on him, a fiery retort on my lips, but the silent plea in his yellow-orange eyes gave me pause. "This isn't the time."

Larana's sobs started up again, and I glanced to where she sat on the floor, her shoulders shaking, her face buried in her hands. The weighty gazes of the crowd standing behind me settled onto my back, and I knew that I was only holding things up.

"Alright." I pulled my wrist from Lakin's grasp. "Ask for Comenius over at Witches End," I muttered as I brushed past him. "He has what you're looking for."

Lakin started, but I didn't wait around – my four hours were up and it was time I got back to the palace before the Chief Mage decided to fry my ass.

15

I threw open the doors to the Chief Mage's study and stormed over to his desk, where he sat reading a thick, leather-bound book.

He barely looked up as I slapped down a newspaper on his desk, simply flicking his eyes up from the tome he was studying before returning to it. "You're late."

I balled my hands into fists, then unclenched them before I did something I would regret. "Sorry. I was a little busy dealing with the aftermath of another murder."

The Chief Mage lowered the book onto his desk.

Taking that as an invitation to speak, I plowed on. "I was visiting Roanas's grave when I got the news. Councilman Finehorn was murdered."

Iannis listened as I recounted the story, his expression unreadable. When I was done, he simply gave me a look. "While alarming, there is no proof of interracial involvement here, or that silver was involved either. In fact, from what I'm hearing, Chieftain Baine sounds like the prime suspect."

"She didn't do this." I ground my teeth. "Believe me, if I thought she did I would be the first to step aside and let the authorities nail her. But I heard the doctor – he said it looked a lot like silver poisoning. You *can't* tell me it doesn't sound like there's a connection. And if that's not enough, there's also this." I slapped my hand on the desk, drawing his attention back to the newspaper.

A frown creased the Chief Mage's alabaster face as his eyes flicked down toward the paper, and then back up again. "I saw this headline this morning. Why are you bringing it to me now?"

I grabbed the paper – a copy of the latest issue from the Herald – and shook it in front of his face. "'Strung-Out Shifters – The Newest Danger in Solantha,'" I recited, the headline burned into my retinas. I'd seen a copy of it fluttering from a newsstand on my way back, and had grabbed it. "Are you seriously saying that this piece of bullshit propaganda means nothing to you?"

Sighing, the Chief Mage picked up the paper, his violet eyes scanning the article. They narrowed as the seconds ticked by. "The Herald is reporting high incidence of drug use among shifters."

I folded my arms. "Yeah, and you don't see a problem with that?" I decided not to mention that the Herald had basically painted shifters as irresponsible druggies who were a danger to society and practically outright demanded that the mages anni-hilate them. The Chief Mage probably wouldn't care.

"Of course there's a problem." The Chief Mage slowly set the paper down. "Shifters aren't affected by narcotics. We bred you that way specifically so that as soldiers you wouldn't be suscep-tible to the drugs and poisons normal humans would die from."

I decided to pretend he didn't say that last part – the last thing I needed was to get into another argument with him over the cruelty mages had inflicted upon shifters through the centuries. "Right. And all the shifter deaths in the papers that appear to be poison-related... those shouldn't be possible either, right?"

The Chief Mage scowled. "This is not the appropriate time for this conversation, Miss Baine. My time is limited, and has been set aside so that we can work on your magical education, not on solving murders."

"Oh yeah?" I scowled, wanting very much to plow my fist into that superior expression.

And that's when an idea came to me.

"Why can't we combine both?" I asked, dropping my scowl in favor of a sly grin.

Iannis looked taken aback. "What exactly are you proposing?"

I propped my hands on my hips. "I'm proposing that you teach me some kind of spell that I can use to drag your stiff ass around the city and show you what's really going on in this town."

I expected him to snap at me for the comment about his ass, but instead he simply pressed his lips together in thought, saying nothing as a calculating gleam shone in his violet eyes.

"You're proposing some kind of... reconnaissance?" he finally asked. "Where we can observe without being observed ourselves?"

I arched a brow. Did he have to make everything sound so academic?

"Yeah, I guess."

"Very well." His lips curved into a small smile. Electricity skipped through my veins. "I will play your game. This spell is a bit beyond your current skill level, but if you master it, I will do as you ask."

We spent the next two hours struggling through an illusion spell - or rather, I struggled while Iannis stood in front of me and showed off. He made it look easy, the way he flickered from the form of a young girl to a hulking dog to a hunched old man, while I had trouble maintaining the singular form I was trying to recreate. By the time I'd mastered it, I was sweaty, hungry, and had a hell of a headache.

"Well done," the Chief Mage said as I stood there in my new form. I wasn't sure if the admiration in his eyes was due to my magical prowess or because I looked like a curvy redhead. Either way, though, it was gratifying. If I could distract someone as rigid and logical as Iannis with an illusion, then I could do it to lesser-willed people too, which would come in handy as an Enforcer.

"Am I ever going to get my Enforcer's bracelet back?" I asked grumpily, now that I'd been reminded of it.

The Chief Mage arched a brow. "In due time." He flickered from his own form to that of a muscular human with shaggy blond hair, tight red pants and an electric blue shirt that stretched across his broad chest. "For now, I suggest we go and embark upon this adventure of yours... and perhaps get some sustenance for you as well."

I snorted, trying not to stare. For a stuffy old mage he seemed to have a good grip on human fashion sense. "You're going to have to lose the 'holier than thou' dialect if you want to blend in," I told him. "No human looking like you is going to talk like that."

"Alright," he said easily. "Let's go have some fun on the town, huh?"

I blinked. That was a lot easier for him than I'd thought it would be. "Let's," I agreed uncertainly, no longer sure this 'adventure' was going to go quite the way I thought it would.

My steambike would only make us stand out, so we took a cab to the Sycamore, a popular gastro pub in Maintown that served as the local watering hole for humans. The cab let us off on Argent Street, across from the restaurant, and I took a moment to eye the place nervously as Iannis paid the fare. The black-and-red corner building had a line snaking out the door, and every single one of those trendy men and women were one hundred percent human, not a single shifter in sight.

"Alright," Iannis said as the cab drove off. "Let's go."

"Wait."

He paused, his foot already halfway off the curb.

"What names are we going by? We can't exactly go in there using our own." My name was unusual enough as it was, and now it was being printed all over the papers. And I doubted there was a human named after the Chief Mage.

Iannis shrugged. "You can call me Ian for the occasion," he decided. "And you'll be Nadia."

"Nadia?" I grumbled, but then he hooked his arm through mine and I forgot all about complaining about the name, which wouldn't have been my first choice. A warm current flowed through me as he tucked my body against his and escorted me across the street.

"Umm, what are you doing?" I muttered as we headed for the back of the line.

Iannis didn't even look down at me. "We're getting in line. It would be suspicious if I used my rank or my magic to try and bypass all these people to gain entrance."

I would have rolled my eyes if I hadn't been so damned uncomfortable. "No, I meant what are you doing *here*?" I hissed, tugging a little on my arm through his to draw attention to it.

He arched his brow as he looked down at me with pale blue eyes like Comenius's, and suddenly I wished they were their normal violet hue. I tugged at the collar of my jacket nervously, uncomfortably warm beneath his gaze.

"We're undercover, aren't we?" he murmured, knowing that my sensitive ears would catch his words despite the buzz of conversation from the line. "If we're coming here as a couple we should look the part."

I gritted my teeth as heat continued to spread throughout my body, and glanced up at the moon as we settled in at the back of the line. It hung bright and round in the inky, star-splattered sky, perilously close to being full, and my hormones surged in response to its magical pull. Shifters were always strongest at the height of the lunar cycle – for some reason it gave us a boost, allowing us to shift more frequently and faster than usual.

"Are you alright?"

I glanced up to see Iannis watching me, once again disconcerted by the fact that I was looking up at a tanned blond rather than a pale redhead. His illusion was so good that even I couldn't see through it – which boded well for us, as it meant none of the humans in the bar would be able to either.

Unfortunately that thought didn't do anything to calm my nerves.

"I'm fine," I told him, giving him a sweet smile I didn't feel, in case anyone was looking. "Why do you ask?"

He dropped my hand and slipped his arm around my waist, drawing me in against his body. "I sense a lot of tension coming from you," he murmured into my hair as his big hand rubbed up and down the curve where my hip met my torso. "I've seen males do this with their females to offer them comfort in social situations. Is it helping?"

"No," I hissed, keeping my voice down so the other humans in line wouldn't hear. I shivered as white-hot sparks skipped up and down my nerve endings. "Probably because you're not my male and I'm not your female."

"You are for the purposes of this outing," he pointed out, but he stopped rubbing his hand up and down my side. "Though perhaps your overly emotional mind can't make that distinction."

"That. Is. Not. The. Point." I sucked in a deep breath through my nostrils to keep from decking him, annoyed by his jab at my race. Shifters *were* more emotional than the average human as a general rule, but he didn't have to keep rubbing it in. Unfortunately, taking a breath didn't help calm my nerves as it only caused me to inhale his musky sandalwood scent. The sparks raced through my body double-time, and I bit my lip.

"You're right, of course." He had the grace to look apologetic. "I suppose I'm going off topic."

Ya think? I turned my attention to the conversations around us and did my best to ignore my unlikely date.

To my annoyance, no one was talking about anything interesting, and we spent the next twenty minutes crawling at a snail's pace toward the entrance, Iannis's hard body pressed against mine. My traitorous mind wondered if the muscles moving beneath his t-shirt were his, or if they were just part of the illusion. After all, he'd changed his coloring, outfit and facial features, but his weight-height proportions seemed to be the same...

This is so *not helping.*

I was saved from my raging hormones by the doorman, who gave us a cursory inspection before allowing us into the bar. The color scheme on the inside was exactly the same as the outside, with burgundy drapes covering the walls and black, glossy countertops and tables everywhere. Light music blended with the buzz of chatter as patrons sat and talked, and the aroma of fried foods made my stomach growl.

Iannis led me to the crowded bar, and we somehow managed to find two burgundy and black barstools near the middle. We ordered drinks from the bartender, who served them up along with two menus for us to look at.

I arched a brow as Iannis raised a beer bottle to his lips, tickled by the incongruity of the sight. "Know what you want?" I asked, noticing that he hadn't touched the menu.

He nodded. "I'm partial to the pork belly donuts and the beer-battered tilapia."

My jaw dropped. "You've *been* here before?"

He grinned at me, and my stomach flip-flopped. "You don't really think I've never ventured out into the city, do you?" he asked, leaning in so he could murmur in my ear. I shivered as his warm, beer-scented breath tickled my earlobe. "Perhaps it's been a while since I've been out, but I'm not as stuffy as you might think, *Miss Baine*."

He sat back to enjoy his beer, and I snatched up the menu and began perusing the selection to cover my amazement. Sure enough, both the donuts and the tilapia were listed on the menu, along with a slew of other things. I decided on the lamb burger and an order of donuts for myself, and set the menu down so I could focus on the conversations going on around the bar.

"Hey," Iannis said casually to a pair of young male humans wearing band t-shirts and shredded pants sitting next to us. "You two studying at the Academy?"

"Yeah." The human closest to us lifted his can of beer in greeting. He was lean as a whip, and sported a bright blue mohawk, a septum piercing, and a days-old shiner on his right eye. "Going for an engineering degree, and my buddy here's doing music." He nudged his friend, a muscular guy with shaggy black hair and sunglasses. "How about you?"

Iannis leaned casually against the counter. "I'm majoring in chemistry, and my girlfriend Nadia's going to culinary school." He snagged me by the waist, and I swallowed a yelp as he drew me onto his lap. My heart rate skyrocketed as he looped his long, lanky arms around my hips, resting his clasped hands on the tops of my thighs, and my cheeks burned as his lips brushed my cheek before he grinned at the two humans. "She makes a killer lasagna."

"That's pretty sweet," Shaggy Black Hair said, looking me up and down, and I knew he wasn't just talking about my imagined culinary skills. "My band makes the rounds at a lot of restaurants around here. I could put in a good word if you need one."

"Thanks." I smiled sweetly, burying the urge to slam my heel into Iannis's shin. I had no idea Mr. Ice King would throw himself into his role with such enthusiasm, or I might've thought twice about going out with him tonight. "So, how are things going for you two at the Academy?"

"Ugh." Blue Mohawk rolled his eyes. "Don't get me started. You'd think that the Mage's Guild would stick to their own schools and apprenticeships, but a few of 'em have been dropping in on the humanities classes at the Academy. They thumb their noses at science or engineering, take the best seats and most of them refuse to work with any of us humans." He curled his lip. "They think that magic is the only viable way to accomplish things."

"Well that's just stupid," Iannis chimed in, surprising me. His muscular thighs shifted beneath me, sending the butterflies in my stomach into a frenzy. "We have an electrical plant in Solantha that powers most areas of the city, including this building." He waved an arm to indicate the bulbs hanging down from the ceiling.

I twisted in his lap to look down at him, and he simply stared up at me quizzically as if he couldn't comprehend the skepticism on my face. It threw me off balance that he could understand the argument for technology so well, yet not permit much of it in the castle. Since I couldn't call him on it, I turned back to the two humans.

"... yeah, and it doesn't help things that those feckless shifters are always causing trouble, too," Shaggy Black Hair was saying.

"Excuse me?" I said, a little too sharply, and the humans blinked.

Shaggy scowled at me. "There've been a lot of shifter-human

fights breaking out on campus recently," he said. "Some kinda drug's been going around makin' em crazy. Now that they've finally got a way to get high, they just can't keep a lid on themselves."

Blue Mohawk nodded, pointing to the shiner on his face. "Yeah, I got this from a rabbit shifter because I bumped into him in the hallway last week."

My jaw dropped. "That's crazy!" Rabbit shifters weren't known for being particularly aggressive. I couldn't imagine one getting into a fistfight over a simple accident.

Shaggy gave me the stink eye. "Seems like you're defending the shifters, pretty lady. Don't know if that'll make you very popular around here."

Iannis tightened his arms around my waist and straightened in his stool. "You'll have to forgive her – she grew up in Rowanville, and as you know things are different over there."

The two humans nodded. "I guess so," Shaggy said suspiciously. "But still, you'd have to be blind not to see what's been happening these last few days. These violent outbreaks are getting worse."

Worry began to brew in my gut, and I stiffened. We were going to have to track down the source of these drugs, and soon, or the reputation of shifters as a race would be ruined. I squirmed in Iannis's lap, suddenly tired of sitting here and making small talk, but he gave my hip a warning squeeze.

"Yeah, and worse, the mages aren't doing anything about it," Blue Mohawk added. Despite his shiner, he seemed more blasé about the whole thing, and simply sighed before taking a long drink from his beer bottle. "By the time they get around to it, there'll probably be a civil war or something between humans and shifters. Lazy bastards are too busy up in their ivory towers, practicing their sacred magic spells, to think about anything else."

"I'll drink to that," I said, raising my glass. I tossed Iannis the stink eye before downing my drink, happy that the hatred had been redirected back to mages again, who were clearly the root of the problem, and *not* shifters.

"Well, it was nice to meet you guys, but we're catching a play later tonight with some friends and we'd better get going." Blue Mohawk slid off his barstool, and Shaggy Black Hair followed suit. "See you around sometime, huh?"

"Yeah, see you." Iannis lifted his beer to them in salute and took another long pull from it as they walked off.

A mixture of relief and triumph filled my chest as I leaned in to whisper in his ear. "See? I told you things are bad out here. I'm not the only one who hates mages."

"Yes, and it seems that, at least in Maintown, mages aren't the only ones who are hated." He grinned at me.

Heat scalded the tips of my ears. "That's not fair," I said hotly.

He held up a long-fingered hand. "I know, I know," he said. "All of this talk about drugs and shifters is alarming. It will be looked into."

The gravity of his voice and expression settled me – this was the Iannis I knew. But before I could open my mouth, the bartender finally returned with our food.

"Thank Magorah," I groaned, hopping back onto my own stool so I could grab my lamb burger. I bit into it, and closed my eyes as the rich flavors burst across my tongue. I'd forgotten how hungry I was.

We ate in silence, Iannis calmly eating his tilapia as I wolfed down my burger. I finished the thing in less than five minutes, and was about to start in on my donuts when a brunette in a slinky black dress inserted herself between us. She leaned her bare shoulders against the counter, smelling of perfume and stale sweat, and I wrinkled my nose.

"Hey sugar," she said in a high, breathy voice, batting her long lashes at Iannis. "Care to have a drink with me?"

Iannis arched his blond brows, his pale eyes running up and down her body in a way that made my blood boil. "I –"

"We've got a play to catch," I snapped, sliding off my barstool. The girl glared at me, and I gave her a smile that was both sweet and deadly as I snatched Iannis's hand and pulled him off his own barstool. "Sorry, sweetheart, but go and pick on someone else's guy."

"'Someone else's guy'?" Iannis murmured as I dragged him out of the club, his voice tinged with amusement. "I thought we'd established that I wasn't your male and you weren't my female."

"You are for the purposes of this outing," I retorted, tossing his words right back into his face as I hailed a cab. My fingers tightened around his, and for reasons best not examined, I didn't let go until we were safely headed back to the palace. Maybe I hated it there, but within those walls at least I understood the territory and rules between us.

16

T he next morning, a servant knocked on my door and told me that the Chief Mage required my presence in the audience chamber for an important meeting. Groaning, I dragged myself out of bed and made myself as presentable as I could – I'd spent most of the night tossing and turning, my mind replaying my outing with Iannis over and over.

As soon as we'd gotten into the cab, Iannis had dropped the illusion, and along with it the lax, easygoing manner he'd adopted in his human guise. I'd plied him with questions about how he'd blended in with the humans so easily and why, even though he seemed to acknowledge the importance and validity of technology, he didn't really use it in his palace, but he blew me off and told me to be quiet. He'd spent most of the time staring pensively out the window, and I'd left him alone.

Hopefully, whatever had been going through his mind last night would result in positive action this morning.

When I arrived at the audience chamber, I was surprised to see Captain Galling of the Enforcer's Guild there, along with three other people I didn't know. Iannis was standing behind his desk, and I caught a glimpse of Fenris standing next to him in wolf form, his bushy brown tail sticking out from behind the stone desk.

"Miss Baine." The Chief Mage nodded at me in greeting. "I'd like to introduce you to Lalia Chen, the future Director of the Mage's Guild, and her apprentice, Benalin Liu." He gestured to the two mages on his right.

"Pleased to meet you, Miss Baine." Director Chen nodded at me, and I automatically returned the gesture. She was a beautiful woman, with ivory skin and a head full of fine, glossy dark hair that was pulled back from her oval face into a ponytail. Her willowy form was clothed in deep red robes embroidered in gold and tied with a sash at her trim waist. The apprentice, a slender man with close-cropped dark hair, bowed, though hesitantly. The look in his glittering eyes told me he wasn't at all happy about having to show deference to someone like me.

"And you as well," I told the Director, too surprised to remember to be snarky. I didn't recognize either of these mages from the party, which meant they had to be from somewhere outside of Solantha. Their accents placed them as Northian, though they clearly were both of Garaian ancestry. Had Iannis actually intended on picking a replacement from any of the mages who'd been to the banquet? Or was there some other reason he'd called them all together that night that I wasn't aware of? "I hadn't realized a replacement had been found so quickly."

Director Chen smiled slightly. "My appointment is not yet official," she said in a quiet voice that was like river water flowing over smooth pebbles – deceptively calm with a hidden strength behind it. "Lord Iannis wishes to test me first, before officially instating me."

"Well, that makes sense." I turned to the third man, who wore the same blue uniform as all the other Privacy Guard employees, except that he had gold epaulets on his shoulders and the sword swinging from his hip was more fancy than others I'd seen.

"I'm guessing you're Privacy Guard's Regional Director for Solantha?" Privacy Guard was a worldwide company, and each branch had a Director that oversaw the operations for that particular location.

"I am." The Regional Director inclined his shining head of black hair, a little stiffly. His dark blue eyes were as hard as his face, his thin lips showing no emotion. He turned to Iannis. "Are we ready to proceed with this meeting now that the girl is here, my Lord?"

The Chief Mage's violet eyes flashed. "The 'girl', as you so daringly put it, is my apprentice, Mr. Channing," he said, and the Regional Director's cheeks flushed. "I expect you to treat her with the respect befitting her station."

I opened my mouth to protest, not at all sure I liked where this was going – sure, I wanted to be respected just as much as anyone else, but on my own terms and not because of my association with the Chief Mage. But the Regional Director apologized before I could say anything, and Iannis took that as a sign the meeting could get underway.

"It has come to my attention these past few days that the people I depend upon have not all been doing their jobs," the Chief Mage said. He pinned each person in the room with a penetrating stare, and though not one moved a muscle, the air thickened with tension. "Amongst other things, the last Director was not passing on crucial reports to me, instead choosing to handle things as he saw fit, which is why he is being replaced." He gestured to Chen, who inclined her head fractionally.

"However," the Chief Mage continued. "I have been going through the reports myself, and there are still important issues that are not being passed through the correct channels. For example," he turned his hawk-like gaze on Captain Galling, "I should have found out about this drug issue from you, not the Herald." He picked up a copy of the paper I'd slapped on his desk yesterday, and something inside me warmed. Finally, someone was taking this seriously!

Captain Galling's cheeks reddened as his eyes flickered over the headline. "The papers are just speculating," he argued. "My main crew has been investigating the rumors, and I planned on sending a full report as soon as I had more concrete information –"

"Which would be never," I interrupted, folding my arms. Captain Galling slashed a glare my way, and I pushed away the tremor of fear in my belly – he might be my boss as an Enforcer, but Iannis outranked him. "The Main Crew only put their attention on jobs that result in bounties, and usually go after the easiest ones. Since investigating rumors pays exactly zilch, I think it's safe to say I'll be cold in my grave by the time they get around to it."

"How dare you –"

"Captain Galling," the Chief Mage interrupted. "Is this true?"

The Captain snapped his mouth shut and turned his frigid gaze back to Iannis. "It is true that the Main Crew isn't getting paid for the task," he said finally. "That isn't how our reward structure works – we pay per head."

"Well, it sounds like you need to come up with some better incentives, and perhaps a better Crew," the Chief Mage said firmly. "I'll give you one week to sort it out, and I'll be coming by to inspect things at the Enforcer's Guild myself. If I don't like what I see, I'm afraid I'll have to replace you."

"Yes, sir." Captain Galling clenched his jaw. My insides squirmed as he shot me a hateful glare out of the corner of his eye, but I stiffened my shoulders and lifted my chin. I knew well enough that sometimes you had to make enemies in order to get anything done around here – it seemed that was all I was doing these days. Though Captain Galling wasn't the worst of the lot, things had still fallen down under his watch, and he needed to be held accountable for it.

"Good." The Chief Mage turned to Director Chen. "I want you and your apprentice to spend the next week gathering intelligence in the city, incognito. I went out myself last night and there is a significant amount of discontent. I want you to adopt different guises to suit whichever communities you are in, and report everything you hear back to me."

Director Chen blinked, but otherwise managed to cover her surprise. "As you wish," she said, bowing, and her apprentice followed suit. I was impressed at how graciously she accepted the assignment, which would normally be delegated far below her on the chain of command – but then, she did have to prove herself. "We will leave right away."

The others filed out of the room, leaving Iannis, Fenris, and myself behind. As the double doors closed, Fenris changed from wolf to human form. He leaned his hip against the desk casually, as if we were in the study or in the Chief Mage's private chambers rather than the more formal audience room.

Iannis arched a brow. "I assume you have something to say?"

Fenris nodded. "I would like to conduct a parallel investigation myself, with Sunaya's help."

The Chief Mage's eyes narrowed. "I'm not certain that is an appropriate use of my apprentice's time," he said. "We already spent a significant amount of time investigating last night." His eyes flickered as he slanted his gaze toward me. Heat curled in my belly as I remembered how casual he'd been, and the way his body had felt against mine. I broke contact before the warmth spread to my cheeks, not wanting him to know I was still affected by the memory.

"Perhaps, but we both know this situation has been

weighing on her mind since before she got here, and her knowledge and connections could be useful," Fenris insisted. "I will be with her the whole time, so it is not as if she'll be without protection."

The Chief Mage pondered this for a long moment before he finally spoke, looking at me. "Give me your hands."

My pulse spiked. "Why?"

He didn't answer, just held his hands out, palms up, in a gesture that was becoming familiar. Sighing, I placed my hands in his, wondering what kind of magical diagnostic he was going to run on me this time.

A bolt of energy lanced through me, and I gasped as a current of magic passed through us, like an electrical circuit being completed. Iannis's eyes glowed as he looked down at me, and I imagined that I was glowing too – the amount of magical energy emanating from my center was so great I could probably power an entire grid block.

Eventually the magical surge died off, but the circle within my chest seemed to burn a little brighter. "Did... did you just increase my power level?" I asked, my voice more breathless than I would have liked.

"I did." He held my gaze for a long moment, then seemed to remember himself and dropped my hands. "You're ready, and I want you to be able to defend yourself with your magic if need be." He hesitated. "Come back safely."

For once, I actually smiled at him. "Don't worry," I said as I followed Fenris out the door. "I'll make sure to come back in one piece. Someone needs to be around to keep you on your toes."

As I closed the door behind me, I could swear I caught a glimpse of a smile on his lips.

∾

"I AM *NOT* GETTING on that thing."

I stared in amazement as Fenris folded his arms across his broad chest and tucked his chin in. There was no other word for it – the man was pouting.

"Yes, you are," I said calmly, offering him my spare helmet for the third time. "It'll be faster if we take the steambike."

His boxy jaw tightened as he glared at my steambike, his yellow eyes scouring every surface of the gleaming black and steel frame as if hoping to find some grave flaw. "Those things are dangerous," he snapped. "I don't have any problem taking a few extra minutes between destinations if it means my life."

I rolled my eyes. "Quit being such a baby." I shoved my spare helmet into his chest, and he grabbed it instinctively before it fell to the ground. "I'm an excellent rider, so you'll be fine. If it makes you feel better I'll make like I'm a little old lady, okay?"

"You're not a little old lady," he muttered, but he put on the helmet, which did a lot to cover his scowl. Shaking my head, I put my own helmet on and straddled the bike. I waited until he was in position behind me before I started it up and peeled off into the street.

"Fenris," I snapped mentally as Fenris's arms tightened with bruising force around my waist. *"You're crushing my ribs here!"*

"You said you were going to drive like an old granny!" Fenris whined as I careened around a corner where a stately villa perched. A female mage in long, pink robes snatched her toddler up from the dirt at the sight of me, her beautiful face pinched in a disapproving scowl. I grinned at her through my visor even though I doubted she could see, and waved at the little girl.

"Clearly you and I have different ideas about what old-granny-driving is like," I retorted, more to be petty than anything else. But I slowed down a little now that we were approaching traffic and unwieldy steamcars began to clog up the streets.

Ten minutes later, we pulled up outside the Enforcer's Guild building in Rowanville. I parked the bike outside the tall, stained grey building with its cracked windows, and waited for Fenris to regain his footing before we went inside.

"I'm taking a cab home," he snapped as we walked through the thick steel double doors. His tanned complexion had gone a little pale. "That was horrific."

I slapped him on the back. "Aww, c'mon," I said cheerfully. "You'll get used to it." Truthfully, though, I found his reaction a bit strange – we shifters, as a species, don't fear much, and even though we don't all ride steambikes, it isn't because we're afraid of them. I wasn't sure what his deal was.

The Enforcer trainees who'd been stuck on front desk duty glanced up as we entered, their eyes widening as they caught sight of me. I ignored their gaping stares, and led Fenris past them and into the waiting room. Our footsteps rang against the cracked tile as we traversed the wide space, past visitors sitting on ratty couches drinking cups of bad coffee and munching on stale sandwiches. Most of these people were here to see an Enforcer about a case regarding a loved one – others, like the tattooed, emaciated human slouched in an armchair, were here to be questioned.

"We're going to see the Main Crew?" Fenris asked as I strode up to the bank of elevators and punched the call button.

I nodded. "I'm hoping Nila and Brin will be there, at least." I wanted to knock them around a bit for not working harder on solving Roanas's murder, and I also wanted to find out what they'd done with my weapons.

We took the rickety elevator up to the third floor, where the Main Crew's offices were – and by offices, I meant a huge open space with drab grey walls and carpet scattered with cheap plywood desks and chairs that would turn your ass to stone if you sat in them too long.

Since Enforcers hated paperwork, there were few people at their desks, but the ones that were here lifted their heads to stare at me. Some of the stares were curious, some disdainful, and others downright green with jealousy. The jealous gazes were mostly from the few low-level mage Enforcers – they would all kill to be the Chief Mage's apprentice, I knew, and it wouldn't matter to them that I hadn't asked for the position.

I scanned the desks for Brin and Nila, but there was no sign of them. Bastards were probably avoiding me on purpose.

"Hey Baine," a blond Enforcer in the back sneered. "Nice of you to join us again. You finally tired of living it up in Solantha Place?"

"Fuck off, Widler." I paused to glare at him. "I've been out like, a day and a half now. Sorry if I bruised your tender little heart by not coming to visit right away."

"Oh I don't know that my heart's the one that's bruised." Widler rose from his beat up metal chair and leaned his hip on his desk, a snide grin on his handsome face. He stroked the five o'clock shadow dusting his jaw as he regarded me with sharp green eyes that weren't at all friendly – but then, he *was* part of the Main Crew. "It's the Foreman you've really stuck it to. You should've known better than to go tattling to the Chief Mage about us. He's gonna make your life a living hell."

"Now that's where you're wrong, Widler." I stepped right up into his space, shoving my face into his, and his green eyes widened a little. "I'm here to make his life a living hell – in fact, *all* of your lives a living hell, for sitting here on your lazy asses instead of getting out there on the streets and finding out who's behind the drug trafficking and the silver murders." I held up a hand and let a trickle of magic flow into my palm, which burst into crackling blue-green flame. "Wanna know what your flesh smells like when it's on fire?"

Widler's nostrils flared in outrage, his green eyes narrowing on me. "You wouldn't dare," he hissed as I gave him a fang-toothed grin, but I could smell the beads of sweat trickling from his pores. "Not in front of witnesses."

I shrugged. "How do you know I can't do some kind of magic spell to make them all forget?" I reached out with my flaming hand until it was close enough to singe his sideburns. "After all, I'm apprenticed to one of the most powerful mages in the country."

"F-fuck off." Widler stumbled back until his hips hit the desk.

"Sunaya." Fenris's hand was on my shoulder, a combination of amusement and alarm in his deep voice. "I think you've made your point."

"I dunno. I think he's still being a dick." I shrugged, but extinguished the flame. "Truth is, though, I don't have time to stand around here and shoot the shit with you, Widler. I'm here to see the Foreman... and you're coming with me," I decided on the spur of the moment.

I grabbed his ear and dragged him across the room, ignoring his yelps as I made my way to the Crew Foreman's office – the only real office on this floor, a corner room encased in concrete walls that were newer than the actual building and featured a long, glass door. The blinds were open, so I could see the Foreman was in there, his dark head ducked down as he hunched over his desk, poring over some report. I kicked open the door, and he jerked up, splashing coffee from the mug in his hands all over his desk.

"Baine!" he barked, his swarthy features contorting with fury as he grabbed for a tissue to mop up the spill. His eyes narrowed as he caught sight of Widler, whose ear was still firmly in my grasp. "How dare you show up in my office like this!"

"Oww, oww, oww, oww, oww!" Widler finally yanked his ear

from my grip, and scurried to hide behind his Lord and Master. He glared daggers at me from behind the Foreman's black leather chair, which was a hell of a lot nicer than any of the other chairs outside his office. His desk was solid wood, too, and he had some nice-looking weapons displayed on the walls, along with several paintings of half-naked women in provocative poses. I twisted my mouth at the sight – each time a new crew foreman took the office, they got to redecorate it however they liked, but this definitely crossed a line.

"Foreman Vance." I propped my hip up on the corner of his desk – something I would have never had the balls to do before. I jerked my thumb to the largest painting on the wall, of a dark-skinned Sandian lying on a bed of rose petals. Her sari was half undone, exposing her nipples, and she stared provocatively out of the painting through long-lashed, half-lidded eyes rimmed with kohl. "This what you jerk off to on your lunch break every afternoon?"

The Foreman's face turned bright red, and his jaw flexed. He rose slowly to his feet, all six foot two inches of him, and I had to remind myself I had nothing to fear as his imposing bulk filled the space. His position as the Crew Foreman didn't endanger me anymore, and even though he was huge, he was still a human and I could kick his ass.

"You put my job on the line," he growled, his meaty hands clenching into fists. "And now you come strolling in here like you own the place, hauling my crew mates around and criticizing my decorations?"

I snorted. "Decorations? Seriously?" The painting hanging to his left was of two half-naked Garaian women kissing each other, draped in nothing but the ivory sheets of the bed they were sprawling on. "I think the term you're looking for is *soft-core porn*."

"Perhaps we're getting a little off track here." Fenris, who'd been standing just beyond the door, stepped into the room, drawing all eyes to him.

Foreman Vance raked his black gaze over Fenris's simple brown tunic. "And just who the hell are you? If you're looking to get an Enforcer's license, this sure isn't the way to do it."

"My name is Fenris, and I am a close friend of the Chief Mage." Fenris folded his arms over his broad chest, pinning Vance with a stern gaze. "One of my primary occupations is to serve as eyes and ears to Lord Iannis. I am acting in that capacity today." His gaze flickered to the paintings on the walls.

Foreman Vance's ruddy cheeks blanched. "I'll get rid of those right away –" he began.

"Save it." I slapped my palm against the desk to get his attention. "I didn't actually come here to harass you about these paintings – although if you want to keep your job I *really* suggest you get rid of them." I smirked, already envisioning the look on Iannis's face if he ever saw this place. I half hoped Foreman Vance wouldn't take my warning seriously, just so I could have the pleasure of watching him piss his pants when the Chief Mage came to visit. "We came to question you and your crew about the murders and the drug trafficking."

Vance sat down in his chair again, lifting his square chin. "Aside from myself and Widler, everyone involved in that is out on assignment. I can't pull them back in just because you decide to waltz in here unannounced with questions."

I leaned in and bared my fangs at him. "You all have bracelets, the last time I checked. *Call them back.*"

"I won't!" Foreman Vance slammed his fist against the desk, rattling the half-empty coffee cup and the typewriter that sat there. "Captain Galling ordered us to scour the city for information. If he finds out I've brought them all in without anything decent to report, he'll have my hide."

"Hmph." I sat back, part of me wanting to push him on it

more, but my nose didn't lie – he was telling the truth about this. "Fine. Then you two need to tell me what *you* know."

Vance pressed his fingers to his left temple, his eyes briefly fluttering closed. "Tell her, Widler."

Widler's face flushed, and his eyes shifted around the room, looking everywhere but me. "Tell her what?"

I grabbed a fistful of Widler's shirt and yanked him forward. "I have a pretty good nose," I snarled, "and it's especially good at sniffing out rats."

"I'm not a rat!" Widler growled, yanking himself from my grip. "It's just... I don't want to share the gold on this bounty with anyone else."

I rolled my eyes. "I don't care about the money, Widler. Just tell me what you know."

He scowled, shoving his hands into the pockets of his vest. "We caught a deer shifter chewing on the remains of a raven shifter in an alleyway," he admitted. "She was pretty fucked in the head."

"What?" Cold horror curled in my gut, and I stared at Widler in disbelief.

"A deer shifter?" Fenris echoed, shock and disgust evident in his tone as well. "Are you certain?"

Widler snorted. "I've been on this job for a long time. I know my shifters, and I know how crazy it sounds, but it's true." He shrugged. "Whatever shit she's on must've really fucked with her head. Guess drugs affect shifters differently than humans. I never heard of drugs turning us into cannibals or anything like that."

I decided not to point out that a deer shifter eating a raven wasn't cannibalism, mostly because there wasn't any point – this was just as awful in its way.

"You found drugs on her?" I demanded.

"Yes."

"I want a sample."

"This is our investigation –"

"A sample, and I want to question the suspect." I pinned Foreman Vance with a glare. "Or I take all your porno paintings down and burn them to ashes, so you can't even enjoy them from the comfort of your home."

The Crew Foreman blanched again. *"Fine."* He shoved up from his chair, and Fenris and I followed him out of the room. Looked like I was calling the shots around here after all.

17

"Well shit," I muttered as we trotted down the steps of Enforcer's Guild HQ. "That was a total bust."

"Not a total bust," Fenris argued, holding up a little silk bag of powder between his thumb and forefinger – the sample we'd threatened out of Widler and Vance. "We got this, didn't we?"

I sighed. "True... but I was hoping the suspect would have been more helpful." She wasn't, not even remotely. When the guards had brought her into the interrogation room, she'd been limp and glassy-eyed, her body trembling from withdrawal. Hearing about it from Widler and Crew Foreman Vance had been one thing, but seeing it was another, and it shocked the questions right out of me at first. Not that it had mattered – she couldn't seem to remember much of anything except that she'd gotten the drug from human dealers hanging around the border where Shiftertown and Downtown met.

Part of me itched to go downtown – the slums and the Black Market were located there, and if ever there was a likely place to find drug dealers that was it. But the other part of me wanted to get this drug to Com and Noria, so they could get it analyzed along with the cerebust I'd given them earlier.

"Oh well. At least we managed to get one of these." I held my wrist up to the light and grinned as my Enforcer bracelet gleamed. I was happy to have that little bronze shield back on my arm again, even if half the Guild did hate me right now. It meant my life was one step closer to normal.

Fenris grinned. "True. Guess it pays to be the Chief Mage's apprentice." The grin faded as he noticed we were approaching my steambike. "No. Not happening. I'm calling a cab."

"Not yet you aren't. We've got one more place to visit."

Fenris groaned.

By the time I parked the bike outside Comenius's shop, Fenris's tan was tinged with green. "Don't worry," I said, gingerly patting him on the shoulder – I didn't want him to hurl all over Com's storefront. "Comenius'll fix you right up."

The shop was crowded, Comenius working double-time by himself to service the customers, so Fenris and I hung off to the side while we waited for the rush to subside. Nearly half an hour passed before everyone finally filed out of the store. By that time Fenris's nausea had passed, and he was across the room rifling through a basket of handmade bath salts.

"Hmm." He sniffed it. "Very interesting. You've infused these crystals with basil, chamomile, and cloud wort. I imagine the user would feel relaxed, their mind free of clutter, after bathing with these."

Comenius smiled at Fenris as he came around the counter. "That's why that particular blend is called 'Calming Focus'." He embraced me, and I inhaled his woodsy, herbal scent as his strong arms wrapped around me. "Naya." He beamed down at me. "I'm still getting used to the fact that you're a free woman again."

I grinned. "Business seems to be good," I remarked, looking

around the shop. The shelves normally filled with amulets and charms were practically empty. "There a new trend going around?"

"People have been buying protection amulets and warding charms," he said, looking suddenly uncomfortable. "In response to all the panic being spread by the Herald regarding shifters."

"Comenius!" Noria burst into the shop, her red curls flying wild around her wide-eyed, freckled face. Her left cheek was smudged with grease, and she wore a pair of coveralls and black gloves on her hands, indicating that she'd been working on something mechanical. "You'll never believe what happened in Shiftertown this morning! Some humans –" She stopped short at the sight of me, hesitation crossing her face. "Oh, hey, Naya and, umm, Wolf-guy –"

"Fenris," Fenris corrected her mildly. She continued to stare at him, uncertainty warring with the excitement and fear in her eyes.

"Go on," I encouraged, my voice casual despite the cold pit of dread hollowing out my stomach. "What happened in Shiftertown?"

Guilt flashed across Noria's face. "Some humans decided to go and riot in the Shiftertown Square," she said. "They came with bats and swords and stuff, and started bashing in windows and looting stores."

"Fuck." I collapsed into one of the chairs in the sitting area, overwhelmed. Humans buying magic protection and looting shifter stores... "We're looking at civil war if something isn't done."

Comenius sighed. "That doesn't necessarily surprise me."

I glanced up at him. "Why?"

Noria flopped down into the chair across from me. "Com did some divination magic last night, and as usual it gave us a lot more questions than answers." She rolled her eyes. "But according to him, the tea leaves point to a shit-stirrer in the works."

"I believe the term I used was 'provocateur'," Comenius corrected mildly. "But nonetheless, I'm afraid it's true. Someone behind the scenes is stirring up this trouble, and it seems their objective is to create strife between humans and shifters."

I frowned. "Who would want to do that?"

We all turned to look at Fenris at the same time, our brows arched. He took a step back, palms up. "What?"

"I don't mean to state the obvious here, but –" Noria started.

"The Mage's Guild would definitely have motive," I finished for her. "Or at least someone in it. If humans and shifters are united against them, they'd have a harder time controlling us, and we might even be able to overthrow them."

"That's outrageous." Fenris drew himself up, and in that moment he looked a lot like the Chief Mage. "The Mage's Guild would have much less harmful ways of ensuring obedience. We need the residents of the city to co-exist peacefully in order for everything to continue running smoothly."

"*We?*" Noria's eyes narrowed, and she slowly stood up. "You know, I've never heard a shifter refer to himself as 'we' in conjunction with mages. Most shifters hate mages."

Fenris's yellow gaze hardened. "I am not most shifters."

Normally I would have told Noria to back off, since Fenris was a friend, but something about her words struck a chord with me. "Still," I interjected, "you have to admit it's a little strange that your loyalties seem to lie more with the mages, than with your own people. Don't you have a clan, or at the very least a family, who deserves your loyalty more?"

Fenris glared imperiously down at me, and my heart shrank a little – he'd never looked at me like that before. "Lord Iannis is the only family I have," he said stiffly. "I don't have anyone else, not that my past is any business of yours."

By Magorah, I felt like the biggest fool in the world. "Fenris, I
–"

"It doesn't seem as though you have any more need of me."
Fenris bowed to us all. "I'm going to catch a cab back to the
palace, where I can be more useful. Good day to you all."

The bell on the door jangled as Fenris left the shop, and my
heart sank straight into my shoes.

"I think I just won the award for biggest asshole of the year,"
I muttered.

Noria frowned. "I don't know, Naya," she said. "He's clearly
hiding something."

"And who are we to judge him for his secrets?" Comenius
laid a hand on Noria's shoulder, and she looked up at him with a
startled expression on her face. His voice was gentle, but his
clear blue eyes were stern, filled with that ageless wisdom that
tended to grace magic users. "We all have them buried in our
past, and Fenris is entitled not to share his secrets if he doesn't
want to, just as the rest of us are." His gaze swept over me as
well. I wondered if there was a spell that would enable me to
sink through the cracks in the wooden floor, and if so, why I
hadn't learned it by now.

I ran a hand through my hair, and pain jabbed at my scalp as
my fingers caught on some of the more unruly curls. "You're
right, Com. I shouldn't have pried."

Noria's scowl returned. "I don't think it's wrong to be suspicious, especially since he's allied with the enemy."

I sighed. "It's not as black-and-white as that, Noria. Actions
speak louder than words, and Fenris has been nothing but
helpful to me."

Noria bit her bottom lip. "Maybe now, but when the
time comes –"

I held up a hand, suddenly weary of all the "us against them"
talk for the first time in my life. Couldn't we all get along, instead

of constantly going at each other's throats? "Look, this isn't really why we came here," I told her, pulling out the little bag of drugs. "The Enforcer's Guild took in a deer shifter who was super high off something that smells a lot like anticium – a hallucinogenic if I remember correctly." I handed it to Noria, deciding not to mention the more gruesome details – there was no need for them to know. "I was thinking maybe your mage friend could compare it to the other sample and see if it was tampered with in the same way."

"Oh, that's right!" Noria's eyes lit up as she took the bag. "Elnos says he's totally cracked the code on how these dealers are sneaking silver into their drugs."

"Really?" I sat up straight. "How?"

Noria frowned. "I don't totally understand how it works, but he basically said he isolated some really rare derivative from a plant that only grows in certain countries in Faricia. Tribal warriors use it to cover up poisons, so they can't be detected by the shifter slaves who have to taste and drink everything before their masters will touch it."

"Kalois!" Comenius exclaimed, clapping his hands together. "I remember reading about it before – it's a tropical flower. Brilliant! I don't know why I didn't think of it myself."

My grin widened. "Aww, c'mon, Com, you can't fit everything you've learned in that head of yours." I jumped to my feet. "So, what are we waiting for? Let's go get your mage friend so he can present his findings to the Chief Mage!"

"Umm, yeah, about that." Noria shrank back in her seat. "He doesn't exactly want to."

I scowled. "Why not?"

"Well, to be honest he doesn't really want to draw the Chief Mage's attention toward our magitech experiments, and I have to agree with him." Noria folded her arms.

I arched an eyebrow. "Magitech?"

"Yeah. You know, magic plus technology equals magitech." Excitement lit her eyes again. "Speaking of magitech, the Herald and the Academy have partnered to sponsor a contest for magitech inventions. Whoever comes up with the best new technology will win a hundred gold coins!" She rubbed her hands together. "I've already come up with that jammer, so it shouldn't be too hard to create something that'll do the job. Elnos and I are *so* going to win."

"I would be careful who you tell that to," Comenius warned. "If you come up with something the Mage's Guild doesn't approve of, they wouldn't hesitate to come down on you and Elnos, especially if you started making a profit off it."

Noria shrugged. "Eh, I'm not worried. We're just gonna make a prototype so we can earn the prize money. I'm more than happy to let the bigwigs worry about bringing it to mass market."

The gleam in her eye suggested that she hadn't completely discounted the idea of capitalizing on the invention herself, but I decided not to press, and instead brought the conversation back on topic. "Noria, if I get the Chief Mage to agree to grant Elnos amnesty in exchange for the information, do you think he would come?"

Noria blinked. "I don't see why not. But do you really think you can do it?"

I stood up and shrugged my jacket back on. "I dunno. But I'm definitely gonna give it a shot."

18

I told Comenius to keep an eye out for Inspector Lakin and give him the case file, and then hustled back to Solantha Palace as fast as I could. The plan was to browbeat the Chief Mage with my findings and demand he grant Noria's friend amnesty, so that we could get our hands on that evidence. Unfortunately, traffic turned out to be horrendous, so I gave up trying to maneuver my steambike through all the cars and parked in Nob Hill, a hoity-toity area of Rowanville where people strolled the sidewalks wearing fancy togs while oohing and aahing over the objects displayed in boutique windows. I looked out of place in my black pants and leather jacket, stepping around two female humans in brightly colored dresses and wide brimmed hats dripping in jewelry, but since I wasn't here to see and be seen I ducked into a café and ordered some food.

The place was a lot more cutesy than I liked, done in pastel blue and white with owl decorations scattered everywhere, but the bacon cheeseburger with onion rings sounded good enough, so I ordered, forking over some of the few measly coppers I'd found amongst my delivered belongings. As I sat down at the bar to wait for my grub, I noticed someone had left a copy of the

Herald on the counter. It looked like the owner had ditched it, so I slid the paper over to my side of the bar and started flipping through the pages.

SHOULD SHIFTERS BE BANNED FROM MAINTOWN? COUNCIL DEBATES.

I FROZE as the headline on page three caught my eye. Next to it was a black-and-white photograph of a snarling wolf shifter in human form, his fangs and claws extended. Anger bubbled up inside me as I stared at the photograph – likely it was just some shifter teen who'd been asked to pose for a couple of bucks. Fucking sell-outs. My burger arrived on the counter, and I snatched it up and munched on it, bacon grease coating my fingers as I read.

WITH THE RECENT slew of shifter-human fighting, the Maintown Council is seriously debating whether or not shifters should continue to be allowed to work and interact with our community. Only yesterday, a raven shifter attacked his boss, hardware shop owner Antano Lopkin, simply for asking him to put a broom away. The crazed shifter, who was later discovered to be under the influence of narcotics, reportedly took the broom and proceeded to shove...

I SKIMMED over the next couple of paragraphs detailing all the recent drug-fueled crimes committed by shifters, knowing that I was liable to start shredding the paper with my claws if I started reading them.

Some have suggested that new shifter drugs hitting the black market are responsible for these outbreaks, rather than the shifters themselves. However, experts suggest that these drugs are merely exposing the inherent weakness of the shifter psyche. It has long been known that shifters are emotionally unstable, hardly surprising when one considers that they originated as a hybrid species several thousand years ago. If this weren't the case, human crime would be skyrocketing in relation to the amount of drug trafficking as well.

I raked my claws through the paper, furious beyond belief at the writer's audacity. Human drug addicts committed plenty of crimes while under the influence! I'd dealt with dozens of strung-out addicts during my time as an Enforcer, and knew from experience that these bastards would do anything, and I mean *anything*, for a hit when they were hard up for drugs. This wasn't reporting at all, but a hit piece. Whoever had written this article was intentionally trying to paint shifters in a negative light.

I scanned the shredded article for the byline, which had miraculously survived my claws. A tick started in my jaw as I recognized the name – Hanley Fintz. The same reporter who had tried to interview me in my cell the night before my hearing. The man who'd told me he was sympathetic to shifters and would try to paint me in a positive light.

Apparently he'd lied.

Two human guards jerked to attention as I strode through the revolving door of the Herald's offices – a large circular white building in the heart of Maintown. Ignoring them, I made a beeline for the white reception desk that stood in the middle of the gleaming white lobby, and slapped my hand down on the counter to get the attention of the curly-haired brunette manning the desk.

Not that I really needed to get her attention – her wide-eyed gaze had been on me the moment I walked through the door.

"C-can I help you?" she stuttered, her oval face pale. Clearly she wasn't used to seeing shifters in the office much – that, or she was worried that we were all going to come and riot right here in the Herald because of all the shitty propaganda they'd been writing against us.

"You sure can." I gave her a gamine grin, resisting the urge to show some fang – the guards' hands were already too close to their swords, and I didn't need some reporter snapping a picture of me brawling right here in the Herald's office. "I'm here to see Hanley Fintz."

"I see." The receptionist's plump lips thinned, as if I'd confirmed her suspicions. "I'm afraid he's not taking any visitors right now –"

"He'll see me." I held up my wrist so the woman could see my Enforcer bracelet. "This is regarding an investigation."

The woman's face whitened even more as she leaned closer to inspect the bronze shield on my wrist. As she did, my nerves began to itch – I didn't know how smart it was for me to barge in here by myself, with no backup. As soon as I'd realized that Fintz must be connected to all this bullshit, I'd rushed over right away, wanting to catch the bastard before he left his office.

"Very well," the receptionist finally said in a clipped voice. She settled back into her chair and pointed to a hallway on my right. "His office is upstairs, five doors down from the elevator. Gerod will escort you." She nodded to one of the guards, who stepped forward, pinning me with an intimidating glare.

I shrugged, refusing to let a mere human guard bother me. "Fine. Lead the way."

The elevators, like everything else in this building, were white, with white flooring and walls, and the black call buttons stood out. I rode up to the second floor, then strode down a white-carpeted hallway to the sixth office door, my new pet guard in tow.

I didn't knock or ask for entry. I just kicked the door open and strode in, ignoring the protesting voice of the guard behind me.

Hanley Fintz was hunched over the typewriter on his desk, no doubt clacking out another slanderous article. He jumped as the door banged against a metal filing cabinet. "What is the meaning of this!" he shouted, his eyes rounding behind his spectacles. Without his large slicker draped over his spindly frame, he looked distinctly unimpressive in his shirtsleeves and slacks.

"I'm here to interrogate you, you slime." I bared my fangs, fury taking hold as I grabbed him by his flimsy collar.

"Guards!" Fintz squeaked, and the guard who'd accompanied me grabbed my arm.

"Ma'am," he said sternly, hauling me back. "I'm afraid you're going to have to leave –"

I whirled around, using the momentum from his own grip, and slammed my knee into his midsection, hard. The guard crumpled against me with a painful gasp and I let him fall to the floor, then shoved him aside so that anybody passing by wouldn't be able to see him.

Sure, that might've been a little harsher than warranted, but I wasn't feeling too chummy toward Privacy Guard employees these days.

"There." I turned back to the reporter, who was quivering in the corner, his back pressed up between two metal bookshelves. "Now, Fintz, you're going to be a good boy and tell me the truth. Who's been bribing you?"

"W-what?" His cheeks colored, his eyes narrowing despite

his quivering fear. "Nobody! I'm employed by the Herald, just doing my job. Did you really barge into my office and injure a guard just to ask me that?"

"You're going to have to do a lot better than that." I snagged him by the collar again and drew him close until we were nose to nose, and bit back a grimace at the acrid stench of fear. "I want to know who's paying you to write these nasty propaganda articles about shifters."

"It isn't propaganda!" Fintz protested, sweat rolling down the sides of his narrow face. His clammy hands pawed ineffectually at my grasp. "What I reported in that article is completely true! You shifters are an emotional and unstable lot! Just look at you! Manhandling me like some kind of wild animal –"

I slammed him into the bookshelf, knocking down several volumes. One of them bounced off the top of his head, and he yelped. "Cut the crap, Fintz." I kept my voice even. "I've been looking at the papers, and the Herald has been using its influence to pit humans and shifters against each other. Tell me, right now, who's been paying you off for that, and you might not have to spend the rest of the night lounging in the same jail cell that I did."

"I-I don't know what you're talking about!" Fintz's lower lip wobbled. "Mr. Yantz tells me what to write! He's my boss!"

"I'm afraid he's correct, Miss Baine." The door opened, and Petros Yantz, the Editor-in-Chief of the Herald, strolled in. A tall man with glossy chestnut hair dressed in a sleek, three-piece suit, he was slicker than a puddle of grease, and flashed me a charming smile, ignoring the guard on the floor. "I am the one who ordered those articles. We have to make a living here, and this kind of stuff is pretty sensational."

"Sensational!" I let go of Fintz and spun toward Yantz. My nose told me that both men were telling the truth... but my gut told me there was still something terribly wrong about all of this. "Your articles are doing more than creating a sensation, Mr. Yantz."

He arched his brows. "Perhaps instead of terrorizing my poor reporter, you can come with me to my office," he suggested. "You're more than welcome to interrogate me all you like."

I crossed my arms. "Just like that?"

Yantz shrugged. "I'm not aware that printing news is considered a crime."

Oh, I'll bet I can dig up something connected to you that is *a crime,* I thought, but I just gave him a gimlet stare.

"Well? Are you coming?"

I hesitated, feeling this was all way too easy. But I had questions, and he was my best shot at answers. "Fine," I said, stepping forward. "But no bullshit. I'll know if you're lying."

"Of course not," he said smoothly. "I assure you I know better than to lie to you."

"Wait, Miss Baine."

I turned at the sound of Fintz's voice. "What is it?" I asked, and that's when Yantz grabbed my wrist.

I gasped as a needle plunged into my wrist and pain spiked through my arm. I whirled back to face Yantz, yanking my arm away as fast as I could, but not before he'd hit the plunger and sent whatever murky liquid was in there shooting into my veins. A strange, giddy sensation washed over me, and I sank to my knees as the room began to rock. I barely felt the pair of strong, meaty hands that hooked beneath my upper arms, and simply stared at the colors of the room swirling together, until all I could see was blackness.

19

When I came to, the first thing I was aware of was a terrible burning pain, as if someone had pulled irons directly from a forge and clamped them on my wrists. My head throbbed, and my mouth tasted like someone had tried to pour a concoction of vomit and bile down my throat.

What made me open my eyes, however, was the scent of two humans, one of whom I fully expected to be there; the other one, not so much.

I expected to find myself in some dingy basement with a light bulb hovering over my head. Instead, I was sitting in a circle of sofas and chairs in a well-appointed parlor room. Seated across from me, in two separate chairs, were Yantz and Deputy Talcon. The former sat upright, looking grave as if I were a naughty student, and the latter sprawled in his chair, grinning smugly like a schoolyard bully.

"Miss Baine," Yantz said, leaning forward. He'd draped his suit jacket across the back of his chair, and his cufflinks glinted beneath the chandelier's light as he rested his hands on his knees. "How nice of you to rejoin us. For a moment I thought I'd given you too much of the drug."

I gritted my teeth. "What the fuck did you pump into my veins?"

Yantz sat back and waved his hand airily. "Oh, just a hefty dose of liquamine," he said, referring to an anesthetic that human veterinarians used on their pets. "Nothing your system can't handle."

"Yeah, except that you laced it with kalois and silver, didn't you?" I snarled, leaning forward so I could shove my face into his. But the manacles clamped around my wrists bit into my skin, nearly blinding me with burning pain. I drew back hastily, trying to relieve the agony.

"Ah, yes, those silver manacles do hurt, don't they?" Yantz arched a dark brow, completely unsympathetic to my plight. "You know, if you didn't know so much this wouldn't be necessary. But that you've already figured out the compound we're lacing the drugs with proves you're far too dangerous to be allowed to run free. Tell me, how *did* you figure it out?"

"Fuck you." With no other form of retaliation, I spat in his face.

Yantz recoiled, as I expected, but I didn't have time to gloat because Talcon rose from his chair and punched me straight in the mouth. Pain exploded through my face as I rocked back, and I cried out as the silver manacles bit into my skin again. The smell of burning flesh laced the air, along with the coppery scent of the blood gushing out of my split lip and down my chin.

"Oh, I knew I was going to have fun when Yantz invited me to *this* party." Talcon grinned down at me, and for the first time ever, the sight of his hulking form sent a tremor of fear through me. "I'd suggest you answer his questions, Baine. Or else things are gonna get real painful for you, real fast."

"Oh yeah, like things are going swell right now." I glared up at him. "I always knew you were scum, Talcon, but I never expected you to sink this low. You're an Enforcer, for Magorah's sake."

Talcon shrugged. "Yeah, well our boss's pockets are a lot deeper than the Guild's," he said. "The Benefactor pays us well to turn a blind eye."

"The Benefactor?" I echoed, disbelief flooding through me. "Who the fuck is that?"

"Ah, so you haven't gotten that far," Yantz said. His dark eyes glittered coldly as he regarded me.

I bared my fangs at him, trying my best to ignore the pain and sickness ravaging my senses. "I would have, in time."

Yantz nodded. "I'm well aware of that. Which is why you're in chains. The Benefactor has big plans for the future of this country, and we can't allow you to get in the way."

This country? That sounded a lot bigger than just Solantha. "What kind of plan involves drugging and killing shifters?"

Yantz nodded to Talcon, who delivered another blow to my face. This one I expected, so only my head snapped back. Pain radiated from my cheekbone, and I hoped to Magorah the crack I'd heard was just my neck popping and not a broken bone.

"I ask the questions around here, not you," Yantz said, his voice soft. "Now tell me, how did you find out about the compound?"

"I paid some Academy student to analyze it," I half-lied, and spat out a mouthful of blood. Flecks of dark red spattered across Yantz's shiny black shoes and the thick carpet. "Hope that doesn't stain."

Talcon reared back to hit me again, but Yantz held up a hand. "You'll kill her if you keep hitting her in the head, Garius."

Talcon's eyes glittered maliciously down at me, his fist still poised to strike. "I've known this bitch for a long time, Petros. She's pretty hard headed."

"Nevertheless, stand down for now." Yantz waited until Talcon reluctantly lowered his arm before turning his gaze back to me. "An Academy student, you say? Which one?"

I lifted my bloody chin. "I'll answer your questions if you answer mine."

Yantz's eyes narrowed. "And why would I want to do that?"

I shrugged, and immediately regretted it as more pain lanced through my wrists. "I'm pretty good at putting up with pain, and since you guys are going to kill me anyway, torture isn't much of an incentive to get me to talk. If you want answers, you're going to have to give me some first."

"Let's just kill her," Talcon growled, but Yantz leaned back in his chair, stroking his clean-shaven chin with his manicured fingers.

"I can't imagine any information I'd give you will be much use to you beyond the grave."

Maybe not, but this conversation was buying me time – time that I was using to heat the shackles around my wrists with tiny flames. I couldn't use larger flames or they would notice, but if I did this a little bit at a time the silver would eventually melt and fall off.

"Let's just say it'll give me closure." My gaze flickered back and forth between the two of them. "Why don't you start by telling me why you killed Roanas Tillmore." I couldn't die without at least learning *that*.

Yantz laughed. "Of all the questions you might pick, you ask the most obvious one?" He regarded me with a mixture of amusement and disdain. "I had Tillmore killed for the same reason I'm having you killed now. He was asking too many questions, following the trail of the shifter deaths."

Rage boiled in my gut at the way he dismissed my mentor's life so casually. I channeled the fury into my magic, knowing it would do no good to direct it toward Yantz just now.

"Why were you going after those shifters?" I challenged.

"Ah, ah, ah." Yantz wagged a finger. "It's my turn to ask the next question. Who is the Academy student who helped you figure out the compound?"

I opened my mouth to answer, but just then the silver around my wrists softened, coming into contact with my skin. I clamped my jaw shut on a shriek as the white-hot metal seared my skin, and blinked my watering eyes.

Yantz's eyes narrowed. "Why do I smell burning flesh?"

"It's the silver –" Talcon began, but the cuffs had softened enough to break free, and I wasn't going to waste time. A surge of adrenaline whipped through me, and I kicked my legs wide. The chair legs snapped from the seat, not quite clearing it, but enough for me to launch myself at Yantz, my claws extended.

"Stop her!" Yantz shrieked, throwing himself back in his chair. He skidded across the room as I landed on my stomach, but before I could scramble to my feet Talcon tackled me. I grunted as the weight of his heavy body crushed me into the carpet.

"I've got you now, bitch." He panted heavily in my ear as I squirmed beneath him. Something hard pressed against my ass, and I gasped. "You're mine."

"You sick fuck!" I bucked beneath him, disgust rippling through me. The motion created just enough space for me to bring my knee up and wedge it beneath my torso. He grunted as he tried to squash me back into the ground, but the new position had thrown him off balance, and I was able to twist around beneath him so that my back was on the ground.

"Oh, so you like missionary?" He drew back his arm to punch me again, but I whipped my head to the side and his fist sank into the carpet instead. "Hold still, you bitch, so I can give it to you the way you like it!"

"I'm a feline, not a bitch," I hissed, and then I reared up and sank my fangs into his neck. A roar echoed from Talcon's throat, and his fist slammed into my head, over and over, trying to get me to let go. But I held on, my jaws clamped around his neck as firmly as a bulldog's. He would weaken eventually; he had to, or I was done.

"Sunaya!" A door crashed open, and the sound of running footsteps followed. The Enforcer's Guild must've hired someone new, because whoever it was sounded a hell of a lot like Iannis. Whoever it was though, I would never know, because Talcon's fist smashed into my head again. The blow was weaker than the last, but it was one hit too many, and I fell into the darkness.

20

T he next time I opened my eyes, a pair of shimmering violet irises hovered over me. It took me a moment to remember who they belonged to, and when I did, I shot upright.

"Oww!" Iannis snapped as our skulls collided. He slapped a long-fingered hand over his forehead and glared down at me, the concern and relief I'd glimpsed eclipsed by annoyance. "Miss Baine, do you give no thought toward your actions before making them?"

"Sorry," I grumbled, rubbing my own forehead. "But you shouldn't have been hovering over me like that." I looked around to see that I was back in my room at the palace, sitting up in my green-canopied bed. Heat rose to my cheeks as I realized I wore nothing but a thin tank top and underwear, and that Iannis was alone in the room with me. "Where's Fenris?"

"Dealing with this disaster, along with Director Chen." The Chief Mage sat down in a chair that had been pulled up next to my bed, and I wondered just how long he'd been sitting in it, watching me sleep. "He wanted to be here instead, and I don't blame him. You were quite a mess when we found you."

The memory of Talcon's body crushing mine, of his hard-on grinding into me, and of my fangs sunk deep into his neck, made me shudder. "Yeah, I'm not exactly surprised," I said, quietly.

The Chief Mage's lips curled downward. "Did he... *do* anything to you?" he asked, the barest hesitation in his voice.

I arched a brow. "You mean aside from binding my wrists with silver and beating the shit out of me?"

"I..." Iannis's expression didn't change, but spots of color appeared high on his cheekbones. "All your clothes were on when we found you, but Captain Galling has reported to me that his Deputy had an interest in you that went beyond professional."

Yeah, no kidding. I swallowed back the bile rising in my throat. "I'm fine," I said, not wanting to dwell on it. "What happened to Talcon, though? And Yantz?"

The Chief Mage scowled. "Deputy Talcon bled out before I could heal him, and Petros Yantz was already gone. Fenris found a secret passage that allows escape from his mansion, and from the scent could tell that Yantz used it recently. He's leading a search party to find him now."

Hearing that Yantz was missing, and the answers to the questions bouncing around in my head gone with him, galvanized me into action. I swung my legs off the bed. "I need to get out there."

"You're not going anywhere." Iannis was suddenly right in front of me, his hands braced on either side of my hips. My bare legs brushed against his blue robes, and I sucked in a sharp breath as heat raced through my limbs and lit a fire in my core. Once again, I was acutely aware of how little clothing I wore.

"I just finished healing you again, and I'm not going to let you run out this door so soon." His voice was rough now, his violet eyes blazing down at me.

I should have been outraged that he was pushing me

around, but my pulse was pounding too hard for me to think straight. "And just how the hell do you think you're going to stop me?"

A sharp knock at the door interrupted us. Iannis straightened as I hastily shoved myself backwards, annoyance flashing across his sharp features.

"Who is it?" he demanded.

"Garen, sir. I'm one of the guards."

I let out a sigh of relief as Iannis answered the door. Saved by the guard. I had no idea what would have happened if he hadn't knocked on the door... but I had a feeling it was something we both would have regretted later.

"Well? What is it?" he demanded of the guard as I belted a robe around my waist.

"I'm sorry to bother you, sir." The guard bowed hastily. "An important visitor is here to see you."

"At this time of night? Who is it?"

Garen's eyes slanted towards me as I joined Iannis at the door, and then back to the Chief Mage.

"It's Thorgana Mills, the owner of Mills Media and Entertainment. She's here to see you, and Miss Baine."

I HAD TO ADMIT, for once it was nice to be standing next to the Chief Mage on his side of the desk instead of traveling towards him down the never-ending blue carpet. But as I watched Thorgana Mills walk through the doors, I reminded myself she was hardly in the situation I'd been when I was first dragged in here. For one, the two huge men who flanked her were her personal bodyguards, and for two, she was here of her own accord. She looked pretty damn good too, with her shoulder-length ice blonde hair curled, her makeup perfectly applied, and her white skirt suit wrinkle and smudge free – something I myself would never be able to accomplish, given my knack for attracting dirt. And blood.

Neither of which a woman like her knew anything about.

"Lord Iannis," she greeted, bowing, and her bodyguards bowed briefly as well. Her silvery voice was as cultured as the rest of her, and she used it to great effect while hosting her many garden parties. Though Thorgana was the owner of one of the largest news and entertainment companies in the country – of which the Herald was a mere branch – she'd inherited the company from her father and left most of the management to CEOs and assistants. I had reason to know she was much more comfortable in her role as a socialite, hosting and attending parties and functions and working with charities – she'd hired me as a bodyguard once or twice. While she'd paid well, it had been one of the most boring jobs I'd ever done.

"Lovely to see you again."

"Mrs. Mills." The Chief Mage inclined his head. "Welcome back to Solantha." Thorgana had a summer home here, but she hadn't been in residence to my knowledge. That, and the fact that she almost never had any dealings with her own paper, made this visit a little strange. "What brings you to my doorstep this late at night?"

Thorgana's smiling face took on a grave expression. "My husband and I arrived in town this evening, when we heard the news about Petros." Her lush red mouth curved downwards in a brief expression of regret. "I decided to come here myself, to offer an apology in person. The fact that a serial killer had been hired to run my paper is very embarrassing."

The Chief Mage arched a brow. "Your embarrassment is the least of our issues, Mrs. Mills. Yantz killed over twenty shifters in the last month, and when we searched his mansion we found a host of illegal bombs and weapons in his basement. We have reason to think that he was allied with a terrorist organization, most likely the Resistance."

I jolted at this piece of information. Hot anger rushed through me, at the fact that Iannis hadn't told me, and because he was pointing the finger at the Resistance. But I couldn't argue with him now, not with Thorgana standing right there, her pretty silver-blue eyes wide with shock.

"Bombs?" Thorgana echoed, placing a dainty hand to her mouth. "Oh my. That is not at all acceptable. And that Petros was going to continue murdering all these shifters…" Tears filled her eyes, and she looked away for a moment. "All this anti-shifter bigotry is very upsetting." She turned those huge, tear-filled eyes onto me. "That's the other reason I came here tonight, so that I could apologize to you, Miss Baine. I have heard that you lost your mentor, and nearly lost your own life tonight because of Petros."

I shifted, uncomfortable beneath her teary gaze. "I appreciate your kind words, Mrs. Mills, but it wasn't your fault."

Thorgana lifted her chin. "Nevertheless, I am the owner of the paper, so I do feel responsible." She turned her gaze back to Iannis. "I will ensure an unexceptionable replacement is found for Petros."

"That is very well," the Chief Mage acknowledged. "Just so long as you understand that I shall be vetting this replacement, and that until he is found and approved, your paper is placed under the temporary control of Director Chen."

Thorgana's eyes flickered, but whatever emotion I'd glimpsed was gone too quickly for me to get a read. "That sounds like an excellent idea, Lord Iannis. I'm afraid perhaps my lack of experience has caused me to make poor choices in my staff, so I could use the insight." She bowed again, and I scowled as her scent changed subtly. It didn't smell like she was lying… and yet, I felt she was holding something back.

She's probably just irritated that the Mage's Guild is getting involved with her business, I thought. Just because she didn't actually run her company, didn't mean she wanted an outsider doing it. I would feel the same in her place.

"Well, I'm afraid I must be going now." Thorgana rose smoothly, her practiced smile back in place. "Do have a good evening, and again, I extend my heartfelt apologies to both of you."

The door to my left opened as Thorgana left the hall, and Fenris walked through the door, looking sweaty and slightly disheveled. "Iannis –" he began, and then stopped when he saw me.

"Fenris." Guilt bit into my chest as I remembered how we'd parted, and I stepped forward, wanting to apologize. "I –"

He engulfed me in a tight embrace. "I'm so glad you're alright." His muscular arms squished my face against his broad chest, but I was so happy he didn't hate me that I didn't care. "When Iannis and I found you crushed beneath that disgusting lout, I thought we'd arrived too late."

"No, you guys were right on time." I extricated myself from his embrace, and as I looked up into his dark, handsome face, I lamented that I wasn't attracted to him. We'd developed respect and liking for each other, and I could see us working well together. But instead, my body wanted the most unsuitable man in the universe. "I'm sorry I was such an ass earlier."

"It's fine." Fenris smiled sadly. "I should probably tell you the truth of it sometime –"

"I hate to interrupt," the Chief Mage said, his voice mild. "But I would really like to know whether or not you've apprehended our serial killer."

Fenris sighed. "We tracked him to the docks and his scent disappeared from there. He probably managed to stow away last minute on some ship."

The Chief Mage's face darkened. "You've sent word to all appropriate ports telling them to keep a lookout for a man matching Yantz's description?"

"Of course." Fenris folded his arms. "We'll find him yet. With all the eyes and ears we have, he's bound to turn up in our sights somewhere soon. We should have him apprehended within a week."

21

"So they still haven't found Yantz?" Comenius asked, forking up a mouthful of noodles. "I would have thought he'd be apprehended by now."

I sighed, pushing bits of lasagna around my plate. "Yeah, he's been pretty elusive so far." It had been ten days since the night he'd escaped, and though the Chief Mage's contacts were on full alert, there was no sign of the former editor.

"Maybe, but that's no reason to look so bummed." Noria twirled a bunch of spaghetti around her fork and gestured towards Comenius and Annia, who were seated around the large glass patio table with us. I'd invited them all out to dinner at *Pomodoro*, an Elanian restaurant in Rowanville, so that we could catch up after this whole ordeal. "We're all here together, alive and well, aren't we?"

"Yeah, and considering that *you're* here with us too, that's a damned miracle." Annia lifted her glass of wine to me, her dark eyes sparkling. She was a more sophisticated version of Noria, with wavy, dark red hair, flawless ivory skin and a slender figure. "When Noria sent me that telegram telling me that you'd been arrested for killing with magic, I thought you were a goner for sure. Instead, here you are sitting at this table, and not only do you have your Enforcer's bracelet back, but you're a freaking apprentice to the most powerful mage in this city."

"Hear, hear," Comenius agreed, and we all lifted our glasses and drank.

"Thanks guys." I gave them a grin that I didn't really feel. "I really appreciate you all being here."

Noria shrugged. "Hey, you're paying, right? Why wouldn't we come?"

I plucked a piece of bread from the basket in the center of the table and threw it at her, and she caught it, grinning. "Yeah, yeah, laugh it up," I said as everyone else snickered. "Just because the Enforcer's Guild rewarded me with a small fortune for solving the case doesn't mean I'm filthy rich."

Noria snorted. "It practically does. Now that you're the Chief Mage's apprentice, I'm sure you'll get the choicest cases. If you play your cards right, you might end up being like all the other hoity-toity mages and never have to work again."

Annia elbowed Noria in the side, who yelped. "Don't say nasty things like that," she scolded her sister. "Naya's not the kind of person who'd sit back and rest on her laurels." She grinned at me. "I'm sure we can expect her to continue getting into all kinds of trouble."

"What *are* you going to do now though?" Comenius asked. He tapped the Enforcer's bracelet on my wrist. "Are you going to chase bounties again, or pursue your magical studies full time?"

I sighed, leaning back in my chair. "I'd like to do both in combination," I said. "But it depends on whether or not the Chief Mage is going to stop giving me the silent treatment."

Iannis and I hadn't spoken for four days now, ever since I'd announced to him that I was moving out of the palace. He'd been utterly furious, claiming that I wasn't ready to be without his protection because I'd barely been able to defend myself against Yantz and Talcon, and that he had a responsibility to look out for me as his apprentice, and he couldn't do that if I was living outside the palace. I'd told him that I wasn't a child, that I could take care of myself, and that if I wanted to continue doing work as an Enforcer I needed to put some distance between us so that people would stop treating me so differently.

He'd threatened to take my Enforcer bracelet away, and I'd threatened to publicly refuse his apprenticeship and humiliate him. We'd nearly come to blows, but in the end he'd just given me one of his frigid looks and swept from the room.

I hadn't heard from him since.

"Do you really need to continue your apprenticeship after all this?" Noria wrinkled her nose. "I mean, it seems like you've learned enough to be able to control your magic. If I were you, I'd ditch town and join up with the Resistance."

I shook my head. "I'm not so sure that my morals align with the Resistance after all." I told them about the bombs and weapons Fenris found in Yantz's mansion, as well as his possible ties to the Resistance, and brought up the terrorist attack I'd heard about at the banquet again. "Their methods are starting to sound pretty questionable to me."

"I don't know that any of that stuff is true." Noria scowled. "So far all the data you've gotten has been passed down by mages or people allied with mages. You're just falling for enemy propaganda."

"I don't know about that." I felt guilty raising my doubts, but I couldn't back down. Something didn't feel right about this. "I'm going to have to look into it more before I make a decision."

Noria tossed her fiery mane of curls. "Do what you want, but I'm definitely joining up once I finish my studies."

"Noria!" Annia punched her in the arm. "Don't say things like that in public."

Noria shrugged, pulling a device that looked like a cross

between an amulet and a gadget out of her pocket. It reminded me of the jammer she'd given me earlier. "This thing's been muffling our conversations," she said. "So I wouldn't worry about it."

Comenius's eyes widened as he leaned forward to get a better look. "Did your friend Elnos help you with that?"

Noria grinned. "Pretty impressive, right?"

"Yes, actually." He slumped back in his chair. "It makes me wish that I could work with technology."

Noria patted Comenius's hand. "Hey, maybe sometime I can bring something by the shop for you to help me with."

Comenius pursed his lips thoughtfully. "That would be interesting."

I couldn't believe what I was hearing. "Com, you're a hedge-witch! You and technology don't go together."

Comenius frowned. "Maybe, but if any of Noria's inventions do end up helping the Resistance, I would like to contribute. You know I support the idea of equality amongst the races just as much as you do."

"Exactly," Noria chimed in. "Which is why you should ditch the mages, and join the Resistance."

"Maybe Naya's got a different plan in mind," Annia suggested, arching a brow at her little sister. "There's more than one way to skin a cat, as the saying goes."

I wrinkled my nose at the uncouth metaphor, and Anna grinned at me.

"Hmph." Noria jutted out her bottom lip, but she didn't argue. "I guess so."

"Besides," I said, spearing a broccoli floret with my fork, "I want to find out what exactly Yantz was really up to, before anything else, and I'm more useful on my own than in the Resistance. Yantz mentioned that someone called the Benefactor was giving him orders, and I mean to find out who that is."

"That's true," Comenius said. "From what you've told us, we still don't understand why all the shifters who were targeted had to die, or exactly how the poison was delivered to them. I hope the new Shiftertown Inspector finds the answers. There could be other players involved who are still in town."

That thought nagged at me as I walked the six blocks back to my new apartment in the Heights – a middle-class complex in Rowanville that was a few steps shy of luxury, but still pretty nice. It was on the other side of the artsy district, so the buildings I passed by were covered in New Age murals, and the sidewalks were humming with artists and street performers. I paused briefly as I watched a human caricature artist draw a portrait of a lion shifter child, and felt a pang as I wondered if someone close to this child would be the next victim. It was too soon to tell whether or not Yantz had someone in place to continue the poisonings without him. Then again, according to Yantz the poisonings were part of a grander plan, so maybe they'd already moved on to its next phase. The idea that there *was* a next phase made my stomach turn – I needed to find out what was going on before things got worse.

I turned the key in the lock on my apartment door, then flopped down on the purple corduroy couch just inside the living room and stretched out. I'd only moved in four days ago, so the walls were still bare of decorations and boxes still needed to be unpacked, but the place was mine and I was happy with it.

I'd briefly considered moving into Roanas's house, as I'd found out that he'd left it to me in his will. In fact, I'd spent my first two days of real freedom roaming the place, packing up things in boxes, smiling and crying as I looked through photo albums. But in the end I hadn't been able to do it – the ghost of his presence would have haunted me forever if I'd stayed there, and I'd never be able to move on. I needed my own space, my own life.

"Delivery service!" an unfamiliar voice called, jolting me out of my morose thoughts. I sat up, apprehension and curiosity warring within me. I wasn't expecting a package from anyone, but the freckled face of a young boy wearing a green and white uniform peered up at me as I peeked through the peephole, confirming that he was from Solantha's main courier service.

"Hello," I said as I opened the door. As I moved to take the package, the courier's scent hit me, and I stiffened.

It was Rylan.

"Hey, cousin." He tapped a gold pin on the collar of his polo shirt, murmuring a Word, and the illusion faded away, revealing a man with long, black hair, yellow eyes and a square jaw. He was still dressed in the courier uniform, which looked pretty silly with his swarthy complexion, but it was definitely Rylan. "How's it going?"

"By Magorah," I hissed, grabbing his arm and pulling him inside the apartment before someone saw him. "What the fuck are you doing here, Rylan?" I didn't ask him where he'd gotten the illusion charm – they were rare, and unless you found a mage to custom make one for you, only sold on the black market.

He arched a black brow as I slid the deadbolt home, and set the package he was holding on the counter. "I'm just checking up on my baby cousin. Is that a crime now?"

"No," I muttered, leaning against the door. "But you've committed plenty of others you could be arrested for." Having a wanted fugitive in my home after I'd just been cleared myself was just what I needed – *not*.

"Yeah, including breaking into Solantha Palace to try and rescue you." Rylan's tone was mild, but his yellow eyes blazed, and I resisted the urge to squirm guiltily. "I don't remember receiving a thank you card."

"Yeah, well I don't remember ever getting an address from

you to send one to," I snapped. He was *not* going to make me feel guilty, especially since his half-baked plan had nearly fucked us all. "Or giving mine out, for that matter."

Rylan gave me a lopsided grin. "I guess I've only got myself to blame for that," he admitted. "And you know I have my ways of getting information."

I sighed. I loved my cousin, really, I did, but his recklessness made me feel old and matronly in comparison, even though I was the younger one. I'd always assumed my half-mage heritage was the reason I was more sensible than him.

"Since you've decided to risk getting your ass arrested, you must be here for a reason. Mind telling me what it is?"

"Other than delivering this package?" His lopsided smile didn't change, but his yellow eyes narrowed. "My superiors sent me to offer you a position in the Resistance. They've seen what you're capable of, and having a shifter who can use magic against the enemy would be very valuable."

My heart sank. It was one thing to tell my friends that I wasn't interested in joining the Resistance, but another thing entirely to tell my cousin, who'd devoted his life to it.

"Tell your superiors that I appreciate the offer, but I'm not ready to make that leap yet." I pushed off the door I was leaning on, and walked around the counter to grab some glasses from the kitchen cupboards. "You want anything to drink?"

"Cranberry juice would be great." Rylan frowned, confusion and hurt on his face. "Why wouldn't you want to join the Resistance and take down the mages once and for all, after everything the system has put you through, Naya? Don't you see that things have to change?"

I grabbed the bottle of cranberry juice from the cherry red icebox and poured glasses for both of us. "I see that more than ever," I told him. "But I've realized that I might be of more help effecting change by sticking close to the Chief Mage's side." *That is, if he ever decides to talk to me again.* "I've already managed to open his eyes a bit to what's really going on in this town."

Rylan took his cranberry juice from me with a scoff. "Please, Naya. Do you really think that the Chief Mage has been blind to everything that's been happening around here, and he just now woke up because you shoved his nose into it?" He downed his cranberry juice in one go. "He's just as complicit as the rest of these power-hungry mages, and he's using his centuries of experience to get you on his side. He knows that with hybrids like you on our side, the Resistance would be too powerful for the mages to control."

Rylan's words slapped me in the face. All the mistrust and doubt I'd ever had about mages, which had been pushed to the back of my mind during my time at the palace, came rising up all over again. Dread curdled in my gut, and I felt suddenly ill. Had the Chief Mage been playing me the whole time? Was I really such a fool?

But then other memories flooded into my brain – the way he looked at me sometimes, with concern and admiration in his eyes lurking just behind the annoyance, the way his hands felt against mine as he unlocked the magic inside me, and the way his lips sometimes curled up at the corners when he thought I wasn't looking. There was more to him than the icy exterior he presented to the world.

"By Magorah." Rylan's expression twisted in disgust as he noticed the rising heat in my cheeks. "You've slept with him, haven't you?"

"No!" My cheeks burned. "Why would you say that?"

Rylan's eyes narrowed. "You're telling the truth... but I recognize that faraway look in your eye, Naya. Don't tell me you haven't at least thought about spending the night in his bed."

"It's just hormones." I gritted my teeth, ready to rip into Rylan if he pushed the matter... and then an idea came to me.

"And besides, I can't deny there is a certain... camaraderie between us. As his apprentice, I can get close to him and learn things that could be of use to the Resistance."

Rylan arched a brow. "There is merit to what you say," he said slowly. "But you should know that it's not going to look good to the Resistance if you stay so close to the Chief Mage. They may mark you as an enemy."

Anger sparked within me, and I leaned across the counter to pin Rylan with a glare. "Oh yeah? And then what? Should I expect to walk out of a store and have a bomb thrown in my face? Maybe I should stay in my apartment then, so that when you guys come after me, at least no innocent bystanders get killed."

Rylan stiffened. "Those were accidents," he growled, his fangs sliding out. "Careless actions by new members. They've been reprimanded since."

"I'm sure the families of those who were killed find that real comforting," I snarled.

Rylan's features contorted in fury. "Don't tell me you're condemning us for a few small missteps. They're nothing compared to the damage the mages have wrought on our world."

"That's pretty fanatical, even for you." Sadness dragged at my heart, and I realized that somewhere in the back of my mind, I'd been hoping he would refute my accusations instead of just defending them. "I can't believe that you'd choose to sacrifice family for the Resistance."

"The Cause is greater than any single individual," Rylan said, but guilt flickered in his eyes, and he looked away. "I'll tell my superiors that you're gathering intel during your magical training and that you intend to turn it over as an initiation gift when you've joined. That should keep them off your backs."

I narrowed my eyes. "Sounds a hell of a lot like a promise that I'm not sure I plan to keep."

Rylan shrugged. "It's the best I can do under these circumstances. I can't protect you if you decide to throw in your lot with the enemy, Naya. You know that."

I scowled. Things were so much better when I was neutral... now that I was so closely associated with the Chief Mage, I knew the Resistance couldn't categorize me as a non-issue anymore. But if they were going to be a thorn in my side, perhaps I could use that.

"Maybe you can do me one better."

Rylan's brows flicked up to his hairline. "How so?"

"I'm sure you've been following the shifter killings," I said, "and when I was alone with Yantz and Talcon, they told me they were working for someone called the Benefactor. Any chance you can find out who that is?"

Rylan's brow furrowed. "The Benefactor... the name sounds familiar. I've heard it mentioned amongst Resistance members before."

Dread pooled in my stomach again. "That doesn't sound good."

Rylan gave me a sharp look. "Just because the name was mentioned doesn't mean it's connected to us. But if this person is responsible for killing shifters, I'd like to know who he is too. I'll look into it."

Relief flooded through me, and I flung my arms around him. "Thanks, cousin," I murmured into his hair. We might not be standing quite on the same side, but our mutual loyalty towards shifters was something we had in common. I couldn't trust Rylan to protect me from the Resistance completely, but I could count on him to do this.

"You're welcome." He pressed his lips to my forehead, then stepped out of my embrace. "I've got to go now." He tapped the charm on his collar and muttered that Word again, and his freckle-faced illusion slid back into place. "Enjoy whatever's in that package." He winked at me before letting himself out of the apartment.

The package. I'd completely forgotten about it. Frowning, I lifted the brown cardboard box and checked the address. My heart rate sped up a little bit as I saw the return address was from the palace, with my name and address written across it in flowing, bold, script. And when I leaned closer to sniff the box, an amalgam of sandalwood, musk and magic tickled my nostrils.

I ripped open the box.

Inside, to my amazement, were my crescent knives and my chakram pouch. It had been so long since I'd seen them that at first I thought I was imagining things, but as I wrapped my hands around the handles of the knives and lifted them up to the afternoon light filtering in through my kitchen window, a burst of joy filled me. Rushing to my room, I found the strap and pouch that I used to hold them and fastened my weapons to my legs. Having them back was like welcoming home two old friends.

I then lifted the note that sat at the bottom of the box, and held it up to the light so I could read it. It was written in the same flowing, bold script that was on the outside of the box.

MISS BAINE,

AFTER MUCH SEARCHING, I have recovered your weapons from an unsavory pawnshop in Downtown, and enchanted them so that you will not lose them again. Though I am still not convinced letting you live outside the palace walls is the best decision for your wellbeing, I *recognize the futility of arguing with you and only ask that you remain armed and aware when you are not under my protection.*

I fully expect to see you tomorrow at 1 o'clock sharp for your lessons.

IANNIS *ar'Sannin*

Chief Mage

I GRINNED as I pocketed the note. Maybe I still had problems, but I had my weapons and my magic and the most powerful mage in the state on my side – who apparently was willing to venture into the slums of the city to ensure I was armed and dangerous. If that wasn't enough to put a smile on a girl's face, I don't know what was.

To be continued...

SUNAYA BAINE'S adventure continues in **Bound by Magic**, Book 2 of the Baine Chronicles. Make sure to join her mailing list so you can be notified of future release dates, and to receive special updates, freebies and giveaways!

Join at www.jasminewalt.com/newsletter-signup

If you want to keep up with Jasmine Walt in the meantime,

you can like her Facebook page, and follow her on Twitter, Goodreads, and Amazon.

DID YOU ENJOY THIS BOOK? Please consider leaving a review. Reviews help us authors sell books so we can afford to write more of them. Writing a review is the best way to ensure that the author writes the next one as it lets them know readers are enjoying their work and want more. Thank you very much for taking the time to read, and we hope you enjoyed the book!

ACKNOWLEDGMENTS

Thank you very much to my awesome beta readers Amanda Miller, Jo Walsh, Carmen Lund, Jason Stanley, Rob Brown, Rachel Berquist, Angel Ray, John Hamilton, Nicole, and Jett. This book would not be what it is without your invaluable feedback and insight.

I'd also like to give a big thank you to my editor and writing partner-in-crime, Mary Burnett. This book would not have been possible without her.

Lastly, I would like to thank Judah Dobin, my biggest supporter in writing and everything else in life. Despite not being a much of reader, you've somehow managed to make me a better person *and* a better writer. One day I'll figure out what kind of sorcery you've used on me, but for now, I'd just like to say that I love you very, very much.

ABOUT THE AUTHOR

Jasmine Walt is a devourer of books, chocolate, and all things martial arts. Somehow, those three things melded together in her head and transformed into a desire to write, usually fantastical stuff with a healthy dose of action and romance. Her characters are a little (okay, a lot) on the snarky side, and they swear, but they mean well. Even the villains sometimes.

When Jasmine isn't chained to her keyboard, you can find her working on her dao sword form, spending time with her family, or binge-watching superhero shows on Netflix.

Want to connect with Jasmine? You can find her on Twitter at @jasmine_writes, on Instagram at @jasmine.walt, on Facebook, or at www.jasminewalt.com.

ALSO BY JASMINE WALT

The Baine Chronicles Series:

Burned by Magic

Bound by Magic

Hunted by Magic

Marked by Magic

Betrayed by Magic

Deceived by Magic

Scorched by Magic

Tested by Magic (Novella)

Forsaken by Magic (Novella)

The Nia Rivers Adventures

Dragon Bones

Demeter's Tablet

Templar Scrolls

Serpent Mound

Eden's Garden

The Gatekeeper Chronicles

Marked by Sin

Hunted by Sin

Claimed by Sin

The Dragon's Gift Trilogy